Part I
THE PAWN STORM

AUTHOR'S NOTE: *The name "Dr. Paul Hansen" (see pp. 98, 175 ff, 211, 213 ff) is a fictionalized name for Dr. Paul Farmer, who has indeed been central to reviving medical care in Haiti, and who, as part of Partners in Health, built the hospital at Mirebalais.*

Chapter One

The old general gazed at the dignified officer sitting across from him and laughed, in spite of himself.

Cold, dark eyes looked up from the chess board, at his older opponent. "Something is funny?"

"A little," said Toussaint. "You are without doubt the most powerful man in the world, Monsieur First Consul, and you brought me to this cold, wet dungeon to kill me. But here you are playing chess with me, like it mattered. I find that a little humorous." Saying so many words in his delicate condition sent him into a coughing fit, which is why his opponent delayed in responding.

"It amuses me, and that is what is important. Power means I can do whatever amuses me," said the First Consul. "Besides, chess is a very serious game. What happens in the game, is a miniature of what happens in this world. Take where our game is now, for instance. Your king is alone, with none of your most powerful pieces to protect him. They have all either been taken, or fled in some futile effort to change the inevitable. Is that not you, Toussaint? Do you not feel alone and abandoned in this dungeon? Where are your generals who pledged their allegiance to you?" The French commander glanced around the little dungeon, which barely measured seven meters by four meters, and appeared truly surprised at the absence of Toussaint's military. The only other person connected to the one who had once commanded the armies of Saint-Domingue, was his valet, Mars Plaisir, who sat on the floor in his tattered coat, about two meters away, shivering. Then the commander sneered and leaned forward toward Toussaint. "Even your sons – where are they, O great general some were calling 'The Black Napoleon'? Do your own sons not stand by you?"

Toussaint felt as if his spirit had been ripped from his body. There was a time when both Isaac and Placide had tried to convince him to work with the French, but he knew both would be by his side now if they could. The man who sat across from him now prevented them, and it tore his heart apart. He did indeed feel alone.

"It is your move, First Consul," said Toussaint.

"Always the way I like it!" said the diminutive general. "And I have so many moves I can make, as you see. My king is free to move where he wants, and his entourage goes with him, to protect him. While your king is alone, as I said, and restricted in movement. By the way, how do you like these fine accommodations here at Fort de Joux? Not as warm, I guess, as what you are used to on Saint-Domingue?"

Fort de Joux was the farthest-flung military outpost in France, at the top of a dauntingly steep hill of rocks in the Jura Mountains. At the height of nearly a thousand meters, the fort was frigid in winter, which it now was. The icy wind penetrated the cracks and crevices in the stone structure. Toussaint knew this was why the place had been chosen for him. Too high and isolated to escape, and too cold to survive without adequate warm clothing.

He looked at his opponent. A black felt bicorn warmed his head. He wore a blue coat, red- piped white collar and cuffs, white-piped red lapels, blue-piped red cuff flaps and shoulder straps, white turnbacks piped red, with brass buttons. An additional blanket, draped over his shoulders, was positioned so as not to entirely hide his epaulets. Toussaint's own hat had been taken. He had been allowed to wear his military uniform, but only because it had been ripped and soiled, with large, gaping holes. It was his crown of thorns – granted as a mockery of his claim to glory.

Toussaint broke into a fit of coughing, which he thought would not end. All inside of him heaved, and it was as if his guts were being torn apart. He felt light-headed, and he wondered if the tiny dungeon were truly rotating. When the coughing fit finally did subside, he saw his opponent smiling at him, with his arms crossed.

"It's your move," Toussaint said again, though this time just above a whisper.

Both players focused on the board. Although Toussaint's vision had become hazy from his illness, he could see what the First Consul had said earlier was true: his own king was indeed alone on his back rank, protected only by three pawns on the next rank. Of his initial force, only a bishop, a knight and four pawns remained. On the other side, his opponent's king sat on the edge of the board, to Toussaint's right, at king's rook 4. He was indeed surrounded by protectors, with his bishops on king's knight 3 and king's bishop 3, respectively. In addition, his king's knight sat on king's rook 5. He also had his queen, another rook and knight, and a pawn on the queen side.

The First Consul smiled and moved his queen to queen's rook 4. From that position, Toussaint could see he had a clear shot to Toussaint's own back rank, where the First Consul could checkmate his king.

But something about the number of pieces surrounding the First Consul's king had grabbed hold of Toussaint's admittedly blurry mind. From the right edge position, his opponent's king touched on five other squares. Three of them were occupied by the First Consul's own pieces, leaving but two places for that king to move, his king's knight 4 and his king's knight 5. Toussaint's lone bishop covered the First Consul's king's knight 4 position. Toussaint smiled. This new leader of France had left himself but one place to move his king. He had smothered himself with protectors.

Toussaint slowly moved a pawn ahead two spaces to his opponent's king's knight 5, at a diagonal from where the First Consul's king sat. He cocked his head slightly to the right. "Checkmate!"

The First Consul gave a nervous laugh. "Impossible!" Then as he leaned forward to take a closer look, his whole body began to shake, and his eyes filled with rage. He swept his right hand across the board, scattering pieces to every corner of the room. "That did not happen!' he shouted. He jumped up. "You do not checkmate Napoleon Bonaparte with a mere pawn!"

Toussaint's smile only broadened. "I already have, Monsieur First Consul. I already have.

You may have swept me from the board, but I have thousands of pawns who remain in Saint-Domingue, and they move forward as we speak to take your forces down!"

Napoleon stormed toward the door, and motioned his three body guards, as well as Mars Plaisir, to follow. At the door he turned and glared back at Toussaint. "You smirk now, you dirty black brigand! But in a year you will be dead, and I will be proclaimed Emperor – not only throughout Europe, but on your little island as well. A pity you won't be alive to see that! Now pick up and clean those chess pieces. I will not have my chess set polluted by this grunge you live in!"

And he left. The door slammed shut, and Toussaint heard it being bolted from the outside. Toussaint Louverture, once commander of the armies of Saint-Domingue, was alone with his memories.

Near Cap-Français, Saint-Domingue, 1801

Toussaint had seen it far too often. The whippings. The burning of slaves alive. Even crucifixions. The so-called Code Noir had sought to limit such atrocities against the slaves of his country, but to little effect. No wonder. How could people think a human code could regulate what the Catholicism he had grown up with had been so impotent in suppressing?

The one who was himself a former slave had come to believe God had called him personally to stop what all else before had not been able to stop. Surely God had him born into this world on All Saints Day for such a purpose. Surely

15

it was with such in mind that God even had his parents name him Toussaint, after this day on which he was born. Living with evil would not be an option.

He had personally written a new constitution for Saint-Domingue, one that declared, "there can be no slaves in this territory, servitude is abolished forever," and further that "all men whatever their color are eligible for all positions." The last phrase affirmed this country would be one where black, white and those of mixed race could live together in peace. He knew he faced opposition on that from some of his black rivals who were so angry at their former white masters they wanted Saint-Domingue to wipe out or drive out all white people, whether French, Spanish or British. General Dessalines and General Moise were among these. He had only recently gone to battle with General Moise to enforce his own vision of an inclusive society.

Today, however, he would have to enforce the former part of his declaration. He rode his horse to the crest of the hill and looked down on the plantation below. As far as he could see lay fields of sugar cane, with black men and women harvesting them in the sweltering heat. But Toussaint focused on what lay in a clearing immediately below. In front of a palatial mansion a black woman had been nailed to a post through her hands and feet. Her screams sent a chill through Toussaint's body. Around the post gathered four whites and around fifteen to twenty black men and women, their heads lowered. Three of the whites, two men and a woman, shuffled back and forth and looked around nervously. The fourth, a large middle-aged man, was in a rage as he lashed the crucified woman with a whip, heightening her misery.

Toussaint motioned for his men to follow, as he charged down the embankment on his steed. Those below noticed their coming. The blacks became animated and rushed his way to prostrate themselves before him. With the exception of the man with the whip, the whites pulled away and cowered beside a colonnade of the house. Although the men carried muskets, seeing the numbers with Toussaint, they let them drop to their side.

When Toussaint's horse came to an abrupt stop beside the man with the whip, the man looked up at him, eyes wide and a sneer on his lips. "Ah, yes! You would be the Head Nigger, Toussaint Louverture. Pardon me if I do not bow to His Highness, but I have a little rheumatism in my back at present."

Toussaint could smell the liquor on his breath, even from where he sat.

"Besides," the man continued, "perhaps you have not heard that one Napoleon Bonaparte has taken over in France, and he does not take kindly to so-called 'reformers' who disrupt the natural order, who would steal a respectable French man's property, and set ignorant niggers against their master!"

The man was bleary-eyed and so most probably barely had time to notice when Toussaint swept his sword from its scabbard. Numbed by liquor, he no doubt didn't even feel it when that sword first met the left side of his neck, before it sliced its way through, severing his head.

The black general looked at the other white people still huddled on the porch. "Would there be others among you who would wish to speak for the policies of Napoleon

Bonaparte, and against the French Declaration of the Rights of Man?"

They looked back and forth at each other, and then they all shook their heads, and the men kicked their weapons off the porch.

"I assume this man was the owner of the plantation. Do any of you know how to run it?"

One of the white men stepped forward and bowed to the ground. "I…uh…I am the foreman, Monsieur. At your pleasure…"

"I want this plantation to keep on producing as before," said Toussaint. "Saint-Domingue cannot afford to languish in the midst of the transition to a nation of free people. Can you assure me that it will not?"

"Yes, Monsieur! Most certainly, Monsieur! Well, that is if the slaves…er…the workers continue to work."

Toussaint nodded. "Let me take care of that. But there is a condition I would impose on you." He pointed toward the woman nailed to the pole. "Get that woman down from this pole immediately, and get her all the medical care she needs. Because if I find that she has died, I will be back and hold you responsible. Am I clear?"

"Yes, Monsieur. Right away, Monsieur." The three whites were joined by a couple of black men, as they began careful work to get her down from the pole.

Hundreds of other black men and women had now gathered. Some were jumping and celebrating, while others showed a quiet anxiety for the injured woman, and still others bowed to the ground before Toussaint. An additional ten to fifteen white men who had been supervising the field workers threw down their weapons and huddled together near a tree.

"Workers of this plantation, hear me!" said Toussaint in Creole. 'You are all now free men and women--"

Cheers resounded across the hills. Toussaint held his sword high in his right hand. For a while this made people cheer even louder, but then people perceived Toussaint wanted to say more and the cheers died down.

"The future of Saint-Domingue depends on you! If this country is to prosper – and it must, or many will starve -- you need to use your freedom wisely. Saint Paul told us, 'you were called to freedom, brothers and sisters; only do not use your freedom as an opportunity for self-indulgence, but through love become slaves to one another.' So, although you are free, Saint-Domingue needs you to not become self-indulgent, but rather to go back to your hard work, not out of fear of a master, but out of love for each other and your country!"

Suddenly the crowd was silent. Many began to mutter. A tall thin black man stepped forward, and spoke in Creole. "You said we are to be free! What if we do not want to work for these white men, and what if we don't want to do this hard work in the hot sun?"

"You do have a choice."

The crowd once again buzzed with excitement.

"Your choice is, you can come join my army and fight, or you can work in these fields."

"That is no freedom at all!" said the man. "We expected you to deliver us!"

"This is the only freedom that matters!" shouted Toussaint to all those gathered. "Do you think it a great privilege to wander wherever you want while your children and your fellow countrymen starve?" He perused the crowd with a sharp eye, but none would look him in the face. "These white people are the ones who know how to run a plantation. They must keep you clothed and fed, they must pay you, give you two days off, including Sunday, and must not abuse you. You are equal to them before God and man, but you must discipline yourselves to do the work they tell you. There will be time later to learn and use other skills, but this is how your country needs you right now. Black, white and mulatto – we are all brothers and sisters and we need each other."

Some in the crowd shouted their loyalty, but the man who had stepped forward took one more defiant step and raised his fist. "I will die before I work one more day for these white bastards!"

Toussaint's sword descended in a flash, but stopped just short of the man's neck. "That can be arranged, if you wish. It is indeed your choice."

The man shivered, pulled back and bowed his head.

Toussaint shifted his attention to the white men who had been supervising the field work. "Get these people some food and water and let them rest from the sun. Then back to work!" He looked again at the man who had challenged him. "And one more thing – train this man and a few others to help with field supervision."

As the workers dispersed, a white French general who traveled with Toussaint, Pamphile De la Croix, rode up beside him. "I admire your efforts, General Louverture, but I fear you are fighting a losing battle."

Toussaint turned abruptly toward his white colleague. "Against Napoleon?"

"No, Monsieur. Against your own people."

Toussaint nodded. "I only pray they will understand before it is too late."

"And the violence of your sword," asked the white general, "will they understand that too?"

"Do you think if I make war *politely*, I could defeat a general like Napoleon?"

"I think not, *Monsieur*. I think not. It is the curse of our profession, but it hangs heavy on my heart."

Toussaint turned his horse back up the hill, and motioned for his troops to follow. "Mine, too, General. Mine too. God will just have to forgive."

And they rode to the next plantation.

Chapter Two

Cap Haitien, Haiti, January 1, 2016

Henri moved his king's pawn two spaces ahead to the position known as e4.

"Such a surprise opening," said Isaac, leaning back and touching his hand to his chest. "Oh, let me catch my breath! I am taken so off-guard. Whatever will be my strategy now?"

Henri scowled. "Cut the drama. You are just trying to distract me. Your move!"

Isaac laughed. He gingerly plucked his own king's pawn and placed it firmly on e5.

"Oh, and notice how I don't mimic your mockery as you have mimicked my opening move!" said Henri. "Well, we both know that pawns, whether black or white, are just nuisances to get out of the way of more important pieces. So, one should not mock logic." He slid his queen across to h5.

Isaac smiled. "If that is your idea of the worth of pawns, then I will most certainly win." He took his queen-side knight and placed it on c6.

Henri did not lift his eyes from the board, as he moved his queen-side bishop to c4. "It's a matter of historical fact, my boy. For hundreds of years we Haitian pawns have been whisked aside by the world's power pieces, and not a one of us has made a difference."

Isaac turned his head to the left and looked out the window of his Cap Haitian apartment at the street two floors below. Although his family had money by Haiti's standards, he had chosen to live here to be closer to the lives of the many who did not. He saw them down below, lined up four deep on motorcycles, hanging on to a load of grain with ten others in the back of a rickety old truck, or walking past with baskets and sacks loaded high on their heads. Garbage was piled two meters deep near the corner, and children were battling the goats for their pick of the prime refuse.

He returned his attention to the chess board, but his conversation went elsewhere. "You forget, do you not, Toussaint Louverture? The former slave who led our country to freedom? Was he not a 'pawn' who fought those in power on behalf of liberty and equality?"

Henri shrugged. "Napoleon swept him off the board a long time ago. Besides, you just looked out the window, did you not? Where did it get us?"

Isaac's eyes turned inward, before returning to his opponent-friend. "I believe that remains to be seen." He moved his pawn to g6, simultaneously blocking and threatening Henri's queen. "You didn't really expect to pull 'Scholar's Mate' on me, did you?"

"You aren't out of the woods yet, my friend." He withdrew his queen to f3. "I should say, 'You aren't out of the woods in this game – or in life, for that matter.' You are a smart guy, with a lot going for you. But if you stay here in this hell-hole of a country, you will be 'swept off the board' along with all the other pawns down there." Henri had motioned toward the window as he spoke. "Me, I have that scholarship to Rutgers in the United States. I'm going there, and never coming back. You should join me."

Isaac moved his king-side knight to f6, and he smiled again at Henri. "You see, I do not allow you an opening to attack where you are seeking to attack. And so, here might be a good time to remind you I am descended from Toussaint Louverture."

His opponent scowled at both the move and Isaac's comment. "The last name he chose had nothing to do with how he dealt with openings in military lines. He had a gap between his front teeth. That's it – pure and simple. And his first name? Toussaint was no saint, let me tell you."

"Didn't say he was."

"He waxed righteous and all about his Catholicism and how he made the people be so sexually pure and such. But guess what? He had a whole bevy of women on the side -- black, white and mixed. You wouldn't be descended from one of those, would you?"

Isaac froze with his eyes fixed on his opponent, pupils dilated.

Henri flinched. "Okay, too much -- I see that now."

Isaac shook his head. His voice came out just above a whisper. "I am descended from Toussaint's legal union with Suzanne Simon-Baptiste, a slave he freed."

"All right. Sorry!" Henri squirmed. "He did some good, or at least tried, I'll give you that. But look out the window and tell me what difference it really made. Do you want to stay here and be part of that?"

Isaac gazed out the window once more. As far as he could see there were poor black Haitians struggling through the congested traffic, but believing, it seemed, they were going somewhere. The only nice car he saw had the initials "U.N." in large letters on the side.

He returned his attention to Henri. "Toussaint wanted a country where black people are truly free and equal with the whites and people of other races around them. That's what I want to be part of building. The United States says they have that, but they are trying to kick out the Hispanics, and people like us their police arrest or shoot."

"My cousins in America say that is an exaggeration."

"Perhaps. Haiti is my country. I let the people in the United States deal with their issues. But if we don't fix Haiti, it won't get done – and by the way, Haiti is also America. Where did Christopher Columbus land, you tell me that?"

Henri refocused on the chess board. "Yeah, a lost and confused Italian. What did he know about where to go?" He moved a pawn to d3.

The door to Isaac's little apartment swung open and in strode Marie-Noëlle.

"Hey, little sister," said Henri, "you come into a guy's apartment and you don't knock?"

"I am younger than you by five minutes, my twin." She smiled sexily at Isaac. "And I have yet to meet a guy who would object to my entering his bedroom."

Isaac blushed deeply. Marie-Noëlle was the most beautiful girl he had ever met. The sister of his best friend had caught his eye even four years before, when she was 13 - - her large, wide eyes like circles of dark chocolate on vanilla ice cream, her skin a flawless cinnamon, and her body already blossoming into womanhood. Now he looked at her and thought of Haitian supermodel Sophia Clerius.

"Hey, Marie-Noëlle," he said in his best attempt at nonchalance. He sought to refocus on the chess board, but he could now see it only as a meaningless pattern of distractions.

Henri rolled his eyes at Isaac, and then pointed emphatically at his last move. "Sister, you are interrupting our male-bonding ritual, so tell us what it is you want, and be gone."

The young beauty slinked over next to Isaac and looked down at the chess board. "So, Isaac, who would you rather bond with, my brother...or me?"

The chess board was now a total blur.

Henri glared at his sister. "You are just 17 years old – don't be such a slut!"

It was Marie-Noëlle's turn to roll her eyes. "A slut, huh? You chase after any girl who wiggles her ass on the street, but if I show an aggressive interest in a nice guy who I know to be kind of shy, I am a slut? Right!"

Henri held onto his glare, but could give no verbal response.

His sister returned her focus to the chess board. "It appears to me you made a fine defense, Isaac. But now I am sure you are wanting to go on the offensive and turn the tables on little Napoleon over there. Am I right?"

Isaac remembered his strategy, and his vision of the board cleared. "Yes. You are right." He moved his queen-side knight to d4, threatening Henri's queen.

"You aren't taking my queen so easily!" Henri said testily, and he moved his queen to e3, making a diagonal threat on Isaac's knight.

Isaac immediately moved his knight to c2, incidentally taking a pawn. "Check."

Marie-Noëlle folded her arms and smiled. "Ah, yes – nice! I believe he has both your queen and your rook in a bit of trouble as well – a royal fork, with your rook as an optional side dish!"

Henri scowled, first at the board and then at his sister. "We were having such a nice game until you came along. Well, it's over now." He upended his king, resigning. "I am a busy person, and I don't have time for this. Have him to yourself!"

"Your sister did not take you down, dear friend," said Isaac, "your lack of respect for my rank-and-file did."

Henri grumbled something to himself, as he headed for the door, but then he stopped and turned before exiting. "Remember what I said about going to the United States. You can do better than Haiti."

He left. Isaac was alone with Marie-Noëlle.

Marie-Noëlle knew she was beautiful. She had long taken delight in the power of her eyes when she opened them wide, smiled and tilted her head just so at some defenseless male -- whether the male be 13 or 93, lying on his death bed, he would be ready to spend his last ounce of energy just to see that smile again. Then as she matured into womanhood, she learned to delight in the other weapons of her developing arsenal: her legs, slender and smooth, flowing from underneath a short dress, drew the eyes of every passer-by, male or female; her breasts, soft and firm, even with their partial veiling, were emblems of her goddess authority to command the world of men.

Her brother, Henri, was good-looking, but not even close to being in her league when it came to attracting the opposite sex. When US tourists came to Cap Haitian, he always looked for young women he could come on to, even propose marriage to, with the hope of getting into the United States. In contrast, when male US tourists came to their city, if they got one look at Marie-Noëlle, they were the ones begging for a chance to whisk her away to a better life.

Yes, Marie-Noëlle knew she was a stunning beauty. What she didn't yet know was what else she was, and what to do about it. At first it was a lot of fun having all the young men make fools of themselves over her, but the fun was now ebbing. She wanted more.

Marie-Noëlle came to Isaac's room looking for more. After her brother left, she sat down in the chair opposite Isaac, cocked her head to the right, looked at him and smiled. It was his move.

Isaac shifted in his chair. "Uh…did you want to play some chess, or…?"

"No."

"Talk about your brother?"

"No."

Isaac shifted again in his chair, and looked out the window, but with seemingly nothing to focus on, returned his gaze to his visitor. He laughed nervously. "Look, I've got to be honest here. I've no idea what to say, and your being here is scaring me to death. What do you want from me?"

Marie-Noëlle crossed her arms on the table, and put her chin down on those arms, looking up still with a smile. "Honest is good. I like honest."

"Okay…I honestly don't know what you are doing here with me," Isaac said, his voice cracking. "You can pretty much be with any guy you want."

Marie-Noëlle sat up again and shrugged. "You and my brother – you were talking about going to the United States?"

Isaac nodded.

"So, are you going?"

"Why? Are you?"

Marie-Noëlle had thought about that question a lot, but when Isaac asked it, it hit her as an entirely new possibility. "I don't know," she said. "There isn't much of a future here, so, maybe."

Isaac was staring out the window again.

Marie-Noëlle put two fingers in her mouth and gave a shrill whistle, and he turned back her way. "Yo, Isaac! I answered the question. Now it's your turn. Are you going to the U.S.?"

As Isaac gazed at her, Marie-Noëlle looked back in amazement. She had never seen that look in a guy's eyes before. It was neither the nervous, unsure appearance of moments ago, nor the lust she had seen so many times before. He looked contemplative.

"Would you go with me for a walk?" he asked.

"A walk?"

"Yes." He stood up. "I think maybe it would help me answer your question."

The Haitian beauty rose abruptly. "Okay, then. As much as I am not normally in the habit of following guys, instead of them following me, since you are answering MY question – show me the way!"

Leaving the apartment, Marie-Noëlle felt amused by this new experience of following a male. The stairway down to the ground floor was narrow and rickety, and yet Isaac kept turning and looking back at her. Once it made him nearly stumble. She felt as though she were a private detective, stalking her prey. It came as no surprise, then, that as they reached the street, Isaac turned quickly and motioned her to come up beside him. She complied.

"Do you know much about the history of Cap-Haïtien, the city in which we live?" he asked.

"Not really," she replied. "History bores me."

As they walked down the street, they looked around at the dilapidated concrete structures, the overcrowded street, and the gaunt, hard-working people piled onto the back of old trucks.

"Cap-Haïtien was once known as the Paris of the Antilles," said Isaac, launching into a mini-lecture. "That was, of course, during pre-revolutionary times, when our city was called Cap-Français. Haiti was called Saint-Domingue. Did you know it was the most prosperous and treasured colony of the New World?"

Marie-Noëlle rolled her eyes. "Really?"

"We were Europe's prime source for sugar and coffee. Those products made a lot of white plantation owner's rich. Our land was called, the Pearl of the Antilles, because of its value to France. But it was all built on the backs of slaves – our ancestors, yours and mine."

"Is this depressing little narration actually going somewhere?"

"Yes. Be patient." Isaac took Marie-Noëlle's arm and pulled her close to an old building to let pass an old woman riding a donkey. "The point is, we weren't always the place everyone wanted to leave. But the ones who made the prosperity possible didn't benefit from it. Our ancestors were terribly mistreated. Then along came Toussaint--"

"Yes...your ancestor, as I understand."

"That's right. Of course, it was not only him. Jean-Jacques Dessalines and Henry Christophe also played important roles..."

He was caught short in his narration because there was now a totally naked man standing in front of them on the sidewalk. The man had a smile on his face, as if he didn't have a care in the world. Isaac turned to Marie-Noëlle. "My father would say, 'Now there stands a totally free man!'"

Marie-Noëlle threw her right fist into the air. *"Vive la révolution!"*

Isaac took her arm, and slipped past the naked man, and down the sidewalk. Then he continued. "Actually, that sets up my point. Today is our Independence Day, when we supposedly won our freedom—"

Marie-Noëlle nodded. "Yeah, a lot of my friends went down the Port-au-Prince for the festivities there."

"Sure, but freedom isn't just to be free from direct rule by a foreign power, or even to be able to stand around, doing whatever a destitute person wants to do, or can do without food or money. Freedom has to include opportunity, opportunity to realize your potential and to provide for yourself and your family. Haiti today doesn't have that. Haiti isn't free. We haven't realized Toussaint's vision. We are a naked country, standing clueless on a street corner of the world, thinking we are free just because we can be naked if we want."

Marie-Noëlle poked Isaac in the chest, becoming engaged in the argument. "Yes! And my brother would argue that is exactly why we must go to the United States, to have real opportunity. What do you say to that, Mister Freedom Fighter?"

Isaac stopped walking, and turned and looked directly into the young girl's eyes. "I would say, we have better choices. When the Haitian Revolution happened, we were being leaders, not followers. We were the first country in the New World to free slaves and to have black people lead their own country. The United States followed us! But Napoleon betrayed us and killed our best leader. And then France and the United States stole our economy, ravaged our resources and left us with nothing."

Marie-Noëlle smiled and tossed her hair back. She was thinking about what Isaac had just said, and how it was nice to be with a guy with such a passion. But, unwittingly, her action seemed to derail Isaac's thoughts. His mouth had frozen and his eyes seemed lost in hers.

"I'm sorry," he said after a long pause, "You are so beautiful…"

Marie-Noëlle shrugged.

"I mean, you probably hear that all of the time, and I should not have said it, but it was like one moment I was totally into what I was saying, and the next moment I saw you – I really saw you, and my mind went numb. Those words came out before I had a chance to think."

Marie-Noëlle smiled. "God, for a history nerd, that was actually kind of romantic."

Isaac blushed. He looked down at the ground and mumbled something indiscernible. He quickly recovered, however, and looked up. "I suppose your brother is trying to convince you to go to the U.S. and make some money off your appearance – like modeling or something."

"He has made that point."

"So, what do you think about that?" Isaac was noticeably avoiding looking into her eyes.

"I'm not sure," she said. "It makes sense, I guess. My mother has always said, 'Take advantage of your assets.' And I guess my appearance is my greatest asset." She shrugged again.

"It's not your only asset," said Isaac assertively.

Marie-Noëlle looked at him so quickly that she drew his eyes toward her. "What other assets do you think I have?"

Isaac's eyes had been re-captured, but still his words came. "A young woman's eyes are at their most beautiful when they reveal a beautiful spirit. An intense, insightful spirit. A giving spirit. All shining through."

"You see that in my eyes?"

"And in your actions. The way you correctly perceived the situation in our chess game. The way you stood up to your brother. The way you listened to me so carefully. You do not do justice to yourself, if you do not acknowledge these strengths in yourself."

Marie-Noëlle examined Isaac's face carefully and smiled. It was such an honest face. Still, she could see her gaze made him nervous. "Well, I have played a lot of chess myself. I've actually done rather well in that area." She added, "Let's continue to walk and talk."

They ambled down the street in the same direction they had been going before, but at first the talking was absent from their "walk and talk." After another block, she broke the silence. "You know, my father actually just calls me 'Mare.'"

"Really?"

"Yes. He likes my spirit, too. He says I remind him of a wild horse. So he calls me 'Mare.'"

Isaac nodded. "Anyone else call you that?"

"No, just Dad. My friends say my name goes with my beauty. Marie-Noëlle. Well, I guess there was one French-speaking American guy I met who thought the English translation of my name was 'Merry Christmas.'"

"Well, not exactly…"

"Yeah, but he was this real Romeo. He said that when we met, he took one look at me, and said to himself, 'Merry Christmas, Jack!' Okay, it was an ego boost, but I'm wary of guys like that."

Isaac smiled, but just a little. After another pause he looked at her again. "So, what should I call you?"

Marie-Noëlle did a little dance and twirl, and then spoke with a flirtatious lilt in her voice. "What do you want to call me, Mister Freedom Fighter?"

"Mare."

Marie-Noëlle coquettishly held out her hand. "Then, I grant you your wish. You may kiss my hand."

Isaac bowed and kissed her hand with such tenderness and warmth that the young woman simply stood still.

It was Isaac's turn to break a trance. "Well, Mare, I believe we are on a walk and talk – so let's walk!"

They had now made their way down to the waterfront. A river entered the bay from their right, and Isaac speculated that there had been a day when what lay before him was a scenic wonder. Now, however, used Styrofoam containers, broken bottles and garbage sacks filled the murky waters of the little river and flowed out into the already littered bay.

Marie-Noëlle stepped in a pile of human excrement, and threw her arms up in disgust, as she wiped off her shoe in a little patch of grass. "Wow, I've got to tell you, I'm losing the mood fast!"

Isaac laughed. He knelt down, pulled the sock off his right foot, took hold of the girl's desecrated shoe, and wiped off the remaining human waste.

"Ugh! Are you sure?" Mare screwed up her face. "You didn't really have to--"

"I've got other socks," said Isaac. Then he laughed. "And if you decide to join me, and stay in Haiti, I'm sure it's not the last pile of crap we will be stepping into."

The young Haitian girl laughed and shook her head. "Tell me again why you want to stay in this – literally – shitty country."

"It's my home, Mare. I have pride in it, and I want our people to have some pride, too." He quickly looked around and found what he was seeking. He pointed toward a group of children, wearing school uniforms. "You see those children? Those are all poor kids, and yet their parents take pride in them! Their hair is so neat, and their clothes are so clean. That's pride! That's what I want all Haitians to have in themselves. And if we have pride, then maybe we can all turn this thing around."

"I'm not sure I share your optimism, Isaac. But then maybe you don't need me to stay here and help--"

"I do! I need you a hell of a lot more than the United States needs another beautiful girl, turning heads, and selling overly-expensive clothes on a catwalk. I can't do this by myself!"

Mare saw nothing but earnestness in the eyes of the young man still cleaning the crap off of her shoe. But she could not yet see the future he saw.

"I'll think about it," she said. "That's all I'm promising. I'll think about it." She stared into his eyes for a moment longer. Then she looked at her shoe. "You understand, don't you, that you're just moving around those few bits of shit left, because your sock is now filthy?"

Isaac laughed. "I suppose that's true."

"Let's find some place to ditch that sock, and go back to your apartment and get you another pair. If I'm seen walking around with a guy with only one sock, I'll lose status."

"I think there is an actual container for trash around the corner. I'll toss the sock there."

After Isaac disposed of the sock, Mare pulled a sanitary wipe out of its container in her purse and handed it to him.

"Thanks," said Isaac.

"It's the least I can do, Sir Galahad."

They didn't talk on their way to Isaac's. For Marie-Noëlle, trying to un-jumble her thoughts occupied nearly all of her energy. She didn't know what she would possibly say, even if she did talk. Perhaps it was the same with Isaac. But the young man did find one subtle form of expression, nonetheless. About halfway there, he quietly reached over and curled the fingers of his right hand around her left.

She didn't want him to let go.

Chapter Three

Samana Bay, Saint-Domingue, February, 1802

Toussaint sat on his horse atop a hill overlooking Samana Bay. His spirit was as restless as his horse, as that animal snorted and pranced. Down below thousands of soldiers under the command of General Leclerk were disembarking from ships newly-arrived from France. It all seemed overwhelming.

When the ships had first come, Toussaint's officer Henry Christophe conveyed the message to Leclerk that he would not allow them to let the French troops ashore at Cap -Français without express permission from Toussaint Louverture himself. Such loyalty made Toussaint smile even now. The landings had been re-routed here to Samana Bay, on the Spanish side of the Island. Still, the man who had declared himself Governor-for-Life of Saint-Domingue had not anticipated these numbers. He now had 20,000 troops under his command, and 10,000 more ready to step in when needed. He had thought those forces to be substantial. The numbers he saw now before him could well dwarf those figures -- perhaps as many as 40,000 to 50,000. And these troops would be far better armed than the men under his command.

Henry Christophe rode up beside him once again. "Awaiting your orders" the general said.

Toussaint looked at him. "The whole of France has come to Saint-Domingue. She comes to avenge herself and force the blacks back into slavery. Shall we wait until he brings out the chains?"

"No, I suppose not."

Toussaint kept shaking his head, while watching the scene below unfold. "I had hoped they would see the improvements in our economy, and leave us alone. Coffee and sugar production are nearly up to our highest levels. I had to work hard for that to happen. Made a lot of enemies among our people doing it too, as you know."

"Yes, I know," said Christophe, meditatively. "But it is not, as you say, about our competence, but our skin color."

"Indeed," Toussaint whispered to himself.

A cool breeze caressed Toussaint's hot skin as he continued to gaze at the scene below, hoping desperately for some sign that would lift his spirit. He saw none.

"I understand your sons are on one of those ships," said Christophe.

Toussaint nodded. "I sent them to France to educate them – educate them to one day lead this country to better things. But I wonder now if it was a mistake. Some of their communications have shown more understanding of what France wants, than of the needs of Saint-Domingue. And I miss them so." He looked at Christophe once again. "You don't have sons, do you, Henry?"

His commander shook his head. "Only daughters."

"I would give my life for my sons," Toussaint said. "But what causes me the most agony is I do not know how to pass along to them what is important, what is worth living and

38

dying for. They have been in France and they have learned the ways of Napoleon. But have they learned what 'The Declaration of the Rights of Man' means for France and Saint-Domingue? That's what keeps me up at night."

General Pierre Age, the highest ranking white officer in Toussaint's army, rode up beside them. "A message has come from Leclerc. He says your sons are here, and they want to speak to you about France, and what is happening in Saint-Domingue. He suggests meeting with them and their tutor back in Cap-Français."

"General Leclerc wants me to meet with my sons?"

"Yes, Sir," said General Age.

"That can only mean he is using them as pawns in some gambit," said Toussaint. He gazed once more at the scene below. Then he turned his horse's head. "Well, then, I must go to see my sons. Love and the guidance of God will show me my next move."

He urged his horse into a gallop down the back of the hill.

Cap-Français, Saint Domingue, February, 1802

The only time Toussaint had been more nervous was when he had proposed marriage to Suzanne. No, he took it back. There had been no time as nerve-wrecking as this. With Suzanne, he at least had felt secure in the relationship, and he had a moderate degree of confidence she would accept. Even if she hadn't, he knew there were others with an interest. Though not strikingly handsome, he knew women were attracted to his competence and swagger. His accumulation of wealth and property was unrivaled by other black men, and hence there was no black man in Saint-Domingue more sought after by the women than he. Had he said that aloud, it would not have been seen as bragging. It would have been a mere statement of fact.

But in coming to meet his sons for the first time in six years, he had no such confidence. He knew the love had been strong when they were children. Both Placide and Isaac had at one time ridden proudly on his shoulders, heads held as high as if they were heirs to one of the thrones of Europe. When his younger son Saint-Jean was born, the birth seemed to cement them together even more as a family.

Placide was now 21 and Isaac 16, and their childhoods seemed a lifetime ago. They were meeting in a second-story room in a building owned by the Masonic lodge of Saint-Domingue. Toussaint sat at a table in the middle of a large gathering room. There was a knock at the door. Toussaint's personal valet, Mars Plaisir, walked to the door and opened it. In walked three men, one white and two black. The white man he guessed to be the young men's tutor, M. Coisnon. He recognized the two youths right away, in spite of six years of growth from children to young men. Tears welled up in his eyes.

Both young men seemed nervous. Placide, the older, stepped forward and bowed. "Father, we have come to express our affection for you, and to appeal to you on behalf of our beloved France. We--"

Toussaint waved off the rest of the speech. "Not yet, my son. Not yet. Let me look at you first." He walked to where the young men stood and looked over each one carefully with loving eyes. Then he gave each one a hug and kiss on the cheek. "You both look well!"

"We miss you, Father," said Placide.

Isaac looked down at the floor, and shuffled back and forth.

"You have not sent enough letters to your father," said Toussaint. "I have read each one hungrily." He turned to the tutor. "Are they learning their lessons well?"

"Remarkably well, Monsieur. They seem to have inherited the intelligence of their highly-esteemed father."

Toussaint smiled and nodded.

"We have become loyal, well-educated Frenchmen," said Isaac, his head still lowered. Then he looked up at his father. "I assume that is what you were wanting when you sent us away."

Toussaint flinched. "I wanted what was best for you."

"Perhaps that is what happened, then. Being in France was better for us than being with our father."

"That is not what I meant!" said Toussaint.

"And not what I think, either!" interjected Placide. "I'm afraid my brother lets his anger cloud the truth, and I apologize on his behalf. But, Father, we have been asked to speak to you on behalf of the France we have been taught to revere."

"I also revere France," said Toussaint. "And that means loving and revering what France stands for: *The Declaration of the Rights of Man,* as formulated by the likes of General Lafayette, influenced by the American President, Thomas Jefferson, and Honore Mirabeau. It was adopted by the National Constituent Assembly in 1789, was it not? This great document calls for freedom and equal rights for all men. That is what I especially revere. But I fear the First

Consul does not hold to this declaration, and hence he does not truly revere France. He wants Saint-Domingue to go back to slavery."

"That is a misconception, Sir," said Isaac. "Napoleon wants what is best for France and her colonies. He would not re-instate slavery. He merely wants stability and economic prosperity. He respects your leadership, Father, and wants your help in bringing good things to Saint-Domingue."

Toussaint nodded and shifted his gaze to his elder son. "Is this what you think as well, Placide?"

Placide glanced at his tutor. "This is the message we were asked to bring to you, Father."

"But do you believe it to be true?"

Placide looked his father in the eye. "I do not truly know."

"Nor do I, my son. Nor do I." Toussaint strolled to the nearest window and gazed at the scene. Close to a hundred of his best soldiers stood guard below. They were good men who fought hard and were loyal. They depended on his word and his discernment. He turned back toward his sons. "You must tell Leclerk and the First Consul I must decline their offer. But thank them for asking."

Isaac's brow furrowed deeply. "But, Father, surely you know such a refusal will not be received kindly by General Leclerk -- or by Napoleon certainly. Don't be stubborn, Father. This offer is a good thing -- for all of us."

"Not for this country. Not for people of our skin color."

"You will be at war with France!" said Isaac.

Toussaint nodded. "And you, my son. Whose side will you be on?"

"We will stand with our father, of course," said Placide.

Isaac shook his head. "Not having had a father since I was ten years old, I will stand with Father France."

Toussaint's body felt cold, and for a moment he thought his legs were going to collapse underneath him. Without even looking at Isaac, he nodded in the young man's general direction. "As you wish."

"Unless you are willing to reconsider," said the tutor, "I will report your response to General Leclerk. You will be at war."

Isaac looked at his brother. "I am also going to General Leclerk. Are you coming?"

Placide shook his head. "I am staying with father, and awaiting his direction."

Isaac's face fell. But as his tutor exited the room, Isaac immediately followed without even looking back.

Toussaint slowly returned to the window. Placide followed and stood next to him.

"He was only ten years old, Father. Leaving you and Mother was really difficult for him."

Toussaint swallowed hard, and even then spoke with a congested voice. "God gave me great skill as a warrior. I only wish he had given me similar skill as a father. Losing a son is more painful than losing a battle."

"Remember the story of the Prodigal, Father. Remember and wait."

"In this case, that might be a really long wait, my son."

"It always is, Father. It always is."

The Mountains of Saint-Domingue, 1802

Toussaint sat on his horse, perched on a mountaintop of Saint-Domingue. Even from that vantage point he could not see many of his troops, as they were hidden by the abundance of trees. He could, however, see his wife, Suzanne, seated on the ground nearby, along with their children and several other women. Although he looked at her for several minutes, she refused to even glance his way. Her furrowed brow and firm-set jaw reminded him of how she looked when she was disciplining one of their children, and yet he knew it was not the children she was angry at now.

Henri Christophe rode up beside him. "Cap-Français is burning, as you ordered, Sir. We called the populace to flee to the hills. Nothing will be left when Leclerk arrives there."

"'...Then let those who are in Judea flee to the mountains...For in those days there will be tribulation, since has not been since the beginning of the creation which God created until this time, nor ever shall be.'"

"Excuse me, Monsieur?"

"It's from the Gospel of Matthew, but never mind. What about the other coastal cities?"

"We have burned some. However, I'm afraid I must report some failures in that regard. Your brother Paul was deceived by the French and they are in Santo Domingo. A few others among our officers have believed the French promises of freedom."

"Naive idiots!" said Toussaint. "Napoleon will never let us retain our freedom. Why can't they see that, after all that has happened? We must defeat these French dogs! And with their power, the only way to do that is to attack them guerrilla-style, like the Americans did to the English in their revolution. Then we retreat to the mountains, and wait for yellow fever to do its job on them. But that won't work if we are not all together with the plan!"

"The plan is sound, General. Shall I read you a message we intercepted from General Leclerk, intended for Napoleon himself?"

Toussaint nodded his head.

Christophe pulled out a folded missive, and began perusing it. "Oh, yes, here it is. 'We are fighting an Arab-style war here. As soon as we have passed through, the blacks occupy the woods along the road and cut our communications.' He sounds frustrated, doesn't he? They think of you as one who could part the waters of the Caribbean, if need be, to win your battles. The soldiers are beginning to think of you as some Voodoo god."

"Pish! I am a good Catholic and have nothing to do with Voodoo--"

"Of course! Of course! But it shows their respect for you."

"If they truly respected me, they would negotiate peace. I have written several letters to Napoleon myself, proclaiming my loyalty to France, and calling only for iron-clad assurance that we will not return to slavery. But I get no response." ~

"Nor will you get one, I'm afraid -- except for Leclerk's cannon and muskets. Leclerk and the French soldiers respect you, but the First Consul thinks of himself as invincible, and fated to get what he wants. He is angry at you for writing a constitution without his express approval. He is determined to defeat you."

"It wasn't just me, you know. I appointed a constitutional assembly, and it included white planters. Dessalines didn't like that because he hates all whites, but I wanted it to express the will of all of Saint-Domingue."

"That constitution is from your hand, and they know it. Admit it and be proud."

Toussaint shrugged. "Speaking of General Dessalines, what do we hear from him? Is he for us or against us?"

Christophe scowled. "Can't he be both at once? He certainly would prefer to be. What good is having two faces if they both have to face the same direction?"

Toussaint laughed. "Well, we're going to need him -- *both* of him!"

Christophe returned his laugh. "But I should go now to check on the troops, especially those under Dessalines. We will stay on top of this, my Governor-General!"

Toussaint watched Christophe ride off down the mountain. Then his gaze shifted back to his wife. She was sitting on the ground with her back towards him. Toussaint slowly walked his horse next to her. He dismounted, and tied the stallion to a mango tree. As he sat down on the ground, his children flocked to him. The girls fought for a place on his lap, while Saint-Jean, who was twelve, sat down next to him.

"You will drive the French back into the ocean, won't you, Father!"

The certainty of Saint-Jean's proclamation touched Toussaint. "Yes, we will, son. But it might take some time. You will never be a slave, as your mother and father were."

"I am going to be a fearsome soldier -- like you, and Uncle Paul, and my brothers--"

"Children!" their mother shouted angrily, "leave your father alone. He is busy and I must talk to him without your chatter. Go play with your friends down the hill."

The children mumbled a few complaints, but nevertheless were obedient to their mother's directive. Toussaint knew when it came to their children, no general's wrath was more feared than that of Suzanne Simon-Baptiste Louverture.

No sooner were the children out of earshot than Suzanne glared in his direction. "So, my husband, if you meet our son Isaac in battle, are you planning on killing him? I just think that, as his mother, I should prepare."

Toussaint's mouth froze shut.

His wife, however, did not let up. "Certainly a clever general such as yourself, a man who sent his ten-year old son away for six years, would have no trouble with performing such a necessary strategic act?"

"I love that boy, too, Suzanne," said Toussaint. "Do you think this is easy?"

"Sometimes it seems to be so."

"My heart ached for those boys every day they were gone. You know that! His anger and his decision to fight with Leclerc crushed me."

"He would have stuck with you had he known you really wanted him to do so," Suzanne said more softly.

"I don't think so. You didn't see the anger in his eyes. You didn't hear it in his voice. Only the love and presence of Placide kept me from collapsing right there on the floor."

Suzanne put her hand on his.

"I have never been more frightened," said Toussaint.

"Then on this matter, we feel the same," she said. She stood and walked toward the children.

Chapter Four

Near Milot, Haiti, March 2016

Isaac had taken the steep hike up to the Citadelle Laferriere several times, but he had always been alone or in the company of strangers. Hiking it with Marie-Noëlle now made it seem easier and shorter, as they talked all along the route. And so it took him by surprise when he looked ahead and saw the stone wall looming a mere thirty meters away.

"Wow. Almost there."

"So, tell me again, why exactly did we come up here?" asked his beautiful companion.

"To touch our history!"

"Oh, yeah—you said that before. Except I kind of thought you were planning some—shall we say—more *intimate* kinds of touching along the way."

Isaac looked into her eyes. "What do you mean? I held your hand!"

Mare laughed. "God, you are such an innocent! Maybe that's why I like you."

"Oh! You were thinking I was planning to--"

Marie-Noëlle smiled coyly. "Incite a little heavy breathing, maybe? Heavy breathing not caused by ascending Mount Olympus -- or whatever this mountain is called."

"I'm not so innocent...I did think about it." Isaac looked back down the steep trail. Then he glanced at Mare. "So...would you have?"

"Oh, no. You're not getting out of the risky stuff that easily! Maybe I would have, and maybe I wouldn't. You'll never know because you didn't try."

They had reached the open courtyard around the front entryway to the old fortress called the Citadelle Laferriere. Isaac pointed to the top of the wall about forty meters above them. "You realize, of course, that tourists looking over the top of that wall can survey what is happening in the bay, as well as on this entire mountain. That is why Henri Christophe had it built. Even with all the trees and other vegetation on this mountain, I'm sure that someone with a camera and a close-up lens could get some really interesting pictures if, say, some couple strayed from the path and got all...involved with each other on the way up. Don't you think?"

Mare rolled her eyes.

"I really saved us a lot of embarrassment. You'll want to think of an appropriate way to thank me later."

The young beauty took his arm. "Hmpff! We'll see about that. Now to this 'touching history' thing. Show me what that is all about."

They walked through the entry, and through some corridors into a large courtyard. Stone stairs and passageways led off in different directions. "Henri Christophe had this fortress built in 1805 to protect against another French invasion. He knew, of course, that freedom was a tenuous thing and had to be protected. But the irony was that defending freedom cost them freedom. Nearly 20,000 men worked, many of them dying from the forced labor, constructing this fortress. You think it was hard making the

49

hike up this mountain? Men who thought their slave days were behind them had to haul the large stones you see in these walls up that same path. Then they had to haul 365 cannons, as well as cannon balls and other supplies to fight against an invasion that never came."

"Never came?"

"Never came!"

Isaac led Marie-Noëlle down a passageway and up some stairs to a long, narrow room. Cannons stood pointed out through square openings in the wall, and cannon balls were piled in pyramids nearby. He saw on the cannons the crests of several 18th Century monarchs, and recalled that various enemies of France had donated to the cause.

Mare went to the nearest cannon and eyed down its barrel, as if calculating where it aimed. "Boom! Boom!" She smiled at Isaac. "Wow! I feel like Keira Knightly in Pirates of the Caribbean—well, except this is a fortress and not a pirate ship."

Isaac smiled politely.

Mare blushed. "Sorry. You were being deep and all, and that was kind of shallow."

Isaac stepped closer to her, put his arms around her and kissed her at the corner of her mouth. Then he smiled more earnestly. "You weren't being shallow; you were just lightening things up a little. I need that. And these cannons are kind of cool."

Marie-Noëlle kissed him fully on the lips, and then turned quickly, and walked over to look out on the land below. "What do they call these windows where the cannons shoot from?"

Isaac followed her to the opening in the stone wall. "I'd say, 'windows where the cannons shoot from.'"

She swatted his arm with the back of her hand. "For that you have a homework assignment, history nerd: I want a definition by tomorrow!"

"As long as I can be 'teacher's pet', whatever you say."

Mare smiled and returned her attention to the scene below. After a minute or so, she looked back at him more reflectively. "So...do you think it was a mistake?"

"Do I think what was a mistake?"

"This fortress." Marie-Noëlle motioned toward the surrounding walls. "Henri Christophe's grand building project to defend Haiti. He never needed it, and people gave their lives to build it. So, was it a mistake?"

Isaac pulled her close and stroked her hair. "That is the question which begs to be asked, for sure. Is fighting for freedom worth it if you lose freedom in the process? And you said you were shallow!"

Mare frowned. "I was being serious about that, you know." She pushed away his hand. "There are serious questions inside me, but people don't want me to ask them -- men and women, both. It's just not what a beautiful girl is for. When life gets too serious, I'm there for the entertainment, the eye candy."

Isaac looked out the window with her. In the distance was the Atlantic Ocean, and Isaac could imagine French war ships gathering there even now. Closer by was the town of Milot, with its shanties and vendors of trinkets for tourists. "So, how would you answer your question?"

Mare leaned her head on her folded arms as she looked out the window. Her silence made Isaac think she was ignoring the question at first. But then she turned toward him. "I wish for every threat and every uncertainty I have in this life, I could aim a cannon at it and just blow the shit out of it."

"I hear you on that. But it doesn't exactly answer the question."

"No, but it kind of does. Maybe the men and women who gathered here back in 1805 felt the same way. Governing a country of ex-slaves who wanted to kill all their white former masters had to be tough. And you had to do it in such a way as to keep a strong economy and feed people. A couple of years of that and they were probably begging for someone to shoot cannons at. It would have been a much simpler task."

Isaac pointed out the window. "Look! Out the window! See that barren hill? That's Haiti's deforestation which destroys our agriculture! And over there, that pothole-filled road with the pile of garbage down in Milot? That's Haiti's terrible infrastructure! And out beyond it in the bay? That's our polluted waters which have destroyed fishing. Our enemies have invaded! Man the cannons! Hop to it, Wench! We cannot lose this battle!"

Mare mimed loading and firing the cannons. "Boom! Boom! Boom! Cannon fire away, Captain Nerd!"

"That's GENERAL Nerd to you, and keep loading those cannon balls. Poverty is at the gate!"

"Boom! Boom! Boom!"

"I think we have them on the run!" shouted Isaac.

"Then we must chase them down!" Mare jumped on Isaac's back, and threw her legs around his waist. She wrapped her left arm around his neck, and with her right she swatted his behind. "Come on, you old horse! They're getting away!"

Isaac laughed, reared back and pranced in a circle.

At that moment they both spotted the tourists at the

door to the gun room. Two men, three women and two teenagers. Americans with funny hats. They were standing there with their mouths open, looking at Isaac and Mare.

"Uh...I'm sorry," Isaac said in English, "I thought for sure we had reserved this room for our re-enactment. Did they not tell you at the gate?"

Mare suppressed a laugh. The women tourists looked back and forth at each other. The men stared, open-mouthed at Mare.

"Well, no matter," continued Isaac. "I believe we are done. Enjoy the view!"

Isaac and Mare edged past the newcomers, and when they reached the rooftop courtyard, Mare burst into laughter. "Quick thinking, General Nerd, and in a manner worthy of Toussaint, you squeezed us through that American tourist gap." She bowed towards him. "I commend your tactical wisdom."

Isaac put his arms around her. "Well, to tell the truth, my mind seems sharper when I am around you. So, that should settle it. You have to stay in Haiti and help me." He kissed her, and enfolded her in his arms.

Mare shared enthusiastically in the kiss, but then broke free and pranced away toward an historical sign. "You know," she said, pretending to read the sign, "I haven't really decided yet on whether I am going or staying."

Isaac's heart skipped a beat. "What do you mean?"

She looked at him with a furrowed brow. "Don't act so surprised. I told you before, I hadn't decided."

"Yes, but, I mean, we've been getting along so well, and—"

"I know! I know!" Marie-Noëlle walked back towards Issac, with her arms folded across her chest. "And I do like you -- more than I have liked any guy before you. And actually, to tell the truth, if I didn't like you so much, I would have already decided, decided to go to the United States. This is a decision about my whole future, Isaac!"

Isaac's stomach churned, and he felt light-headed. There were many ways he could respond that would make things worse, that would take away any chance he had with the girl. He would have to weigh each word carefully.

"Look...your future is important to me also. I am sure you could be a really successful model. Be on the cover of all the magazines. When that happens...I will be proud and happy for you."

"Thanks."

Isaac shrugged. "Yeah, well, don't thank me too quickly. I'm still trying to figure out how to say what else I feel about this, and it's not so positive."

"Then, just stop where you are, and let's go somewhere else and have fun! I don't like conflict, and this feels like it's going to end in conflict."

"Maybe -- but we should talk about it!"

Marie-Noëlle shrugged. "I got a letter a couple of days ago--"

"A letter?"

"Yes, a letter. Offering me an audition with a big New York modeling firm. It was from this...this guy...an American guy I met a couple of weeks ago. He's a talent scout for the agency."

"You're sure it wasn't just a come on?"

"The letter looked pretty official. And I checked them out on the Internet."

Isaac could think of nothing to say. He walked to the outside wall of the fortress, climbed up on it and sat down. Marie-Noëlle followed and sat beside him. For a few minutes they surveyed the countryside.

"Look," she finally said, "it's like what we said when we were back there playing. I don't know how to fight this battle you have been talking about -- helping to rebuild Haiti. But if I go to the United States and make a lot of money modeling, I can send back much of that money to you, and you can use it for the projects you think will help. Doesn't that make sense?"

"This is going to take more than money, Mare. It's going to take presence and dedication. It's going to take people like Toussaint and Suzanne Simon-Baptiste Louverture standing up together against those who only want to use Haiti for their greed and self-focus. That's what I want us to do together."

It was Mare's turn to be speechless.

Isaac knew there was another issue for him, one which was hard to talk about, but which had to be faced. He was not good at being vulnerable. In chess, he always castled his king, and sought to protect every little pawn. In life, he would prefer to fight his battles from behind fortress walls like the one on which they sat. But safe and protected often also meant "alone."

"What about...us?" he finally said. "What would your plan do to us? Or, is that even an issue?"

Mare's eyes flashed with anger, as she looked at him. "Of course it's an issue! I told you how I feel about you." She looked away, back at the horizon. "We'll...we'll keep in touch by phone, and Skype and Facebook. I'll come back for visits."

Isaac felt tied-up in knots, and so spoke just above a whisper. "That generally doesn't work, you know. Especially with...with working for a guy who gave you a big modeling break, and was impressed with how beautiful you are."

Mare curled her left hand around Isaac's right. "It will work, Isaac. I want us to make it work. Do you?"

Isaac nodded his head. "Of course, I had just hoped for a better choice."

"Ever done a 'queen sacrifice' in chess?"

He nodded again.

"So, now you might have to do it in life," Mare said as she jumped down from the wall back into the rooftop courtyard. "Let's stop talking about all of these 'what ifs and maybes'. We have today, for sure. Let's use it!" She held out her hand in his direction.

Isaac jumped the two meters down from the top of the wall, stopping abruptly as the soles of his shoes slammed into the rock surface. Somehow, though, as they walked toward the stairs leading to the front entry, he felt like his spirit was continuing to fall, and what might ever stop it he could not yet tell.

Chapter Five

Ravine-à-Couleuvres, Saint Domingue, February 1802

Toussaint rode up beside General Dessalines, as the latter sat on his horse, supervising troops digging trenches.

"Leclerc thinks he can surround us in this valley. Are we ready for him?"

"More ready than he will ever suspect," said Dessalines with a scowl.

"Your men better know they are in for a fight. Leclerc's men, accompanied by Rochambeau, are coming at us from all directions and they have us heavily outnumbered. We will need every bit of courage we can muster."

Dessalines looked at Toussaint with a steely-cold glare. "Are Leclerc's men white?"

"Certainly."

"They are white because all their blood and all their courage and all their spirit drains out of them when they are confronted with black men who can actually fight back!"

"I understand your hatred for the white man," said Toussaint. "But to win these battles, we must work with our white friends, while respecting the fighting prowess of our white enemies. I hope you can—"

Jean-Jacques Dessalines went into a rage, tearing his uniform off his chest while his horse circled and reared back, hooves flailing at the sky. He settled his horse looking away from Toussaint, Dessalines' now bare back clearly visible to his commander. Toussaint saw the deep scars snaking up and down the man's flesh, scars resembling an etching from Satan's claws.

"Do you see these scars?" screamed the general, flashing fiery eyes. "Vengeance for these is all I owe the white man! And I don't need the emblems and epaulets of a French uniform to lead my black men in exacting that vengeance, because they would follow my scarred back into the jaws of hell!"

Toussaint felt singed by the intensity of the man's anger. He knew the feeling. While his master had treated him rather well, Toussaint was certainly aware of what it was like to have black skin in a land where that color was treated like so much excrement. His next words were as much for himself as for the man to whom he spoke. He said them quietly and reverently. "'Love your enemies. Pray for those who persecute you.'"

Dessalines' whole body went rigid. For a moment Toussaint wondered if he himself might be the next object of the man's wrath. Then a wry smile spread across the other general's face. "Fine. Then when I next meet a white French soldier, I will kiss him on the forehead—right after I dissect his liver with my sword!"

Toussaint could say nothing else. This was no time to dilute the man's passion. He nodded in acquiescence. Dessalines calmed down, if only a little.

"And you need not worry about my understanding the practicalities of alliance. We have even captured a white

French doctor—one Michel Étienne Descourtilz—who treats our black soldiers. For free, I might add, since I make him."

"I know the man," said Toussaint. "But we have white friends on the island as well, people who support us without us having to point a sword at their head. We must work with them as well."

"They are your friends: you work with them."

"Enough discussion!" said Toussaint, "Leclerc's soldiers are coming, and we must have each other's back! May God be with you and your men!"

Toussaint turned his horse and rode down the valley, with his escort of thirty men following close behind. He had taken a risk to talk personally with Dessalines, a risk that he could be cut off by French forces. He had taken the risk in large part because he felt so strongly that Dessalines needed direction. But he also had confidence in the leadership of Henri Christophe directing the forces left behind, and he had confidence in his own mastery of the forests of Saint Domingue. He now took advantage of that mastery, as he and his men raced through the forest of the *Ravine-à-Couleuvres* as if directed by God himself. Toussaint smiled. The *Ravine-à-Couleuvres*. It was French for "snake gully." The forces of Leclerc and Rochambeau were about to be bitten.

When Toussaint arrived at the encampment, he had his officers quickly gather his men. He needed to re-invigorate the spirits of these men, and he had thought long and hard on exactly how he was going to do it. He looked over their expectant faces, and addressed them in Creole.

"Men, you are going to fight against enemies who have neither faith, law, nor religion. They promise you liberty, they intend your servitude. Why have so many ships traversed the ocean, if not to throw you again into chains? They disdain to recognize in you submissive children, and if you are not their slaves, you are rebels. The mother country, misled by the Consul, is no longer anything but a step-mother. Was there ever a defense more just than yours?"

Shouts of "No!" rang throughout the valley.

Toussaint's thoughts went to the cities of Saint-Domingue, burned to thwart the supply needs of Leclerc's army. "You have carried everywhere consuming fires, the flambeau of our liberty. The steps of our enemies have trodden only on ashes, their eyes have encountered nothing but smoking ruins, which you have watered with their blood. This is the road by which they have come to us. What do they hope for? Have we not all the presages of victory?"

Soldiers all around him thrust their muskets in the air, and shouted "Yes!" Many danced among the trees and chanted, "*Vive Toussaint!*"

Toussaint continued. "Not for their country, not for liberty do they fight, but to serve the hatred and the ambition of the Consul, my enemy, mine because he is yours..." He thought of Dessalines. "Their bodies are not mutilated by the punishments of servitude, their wives and their children are not near their camps, and the graves of their fathers are beyond the ocean." His eyes quickly surveyed the ravine, surrounded by steep mountains. "This sky, these mountains, these lands—all are strange to them! What do I say? As soon as they breathe the same air as we, their bravery sinks, their courage departs."

More cheers resounded throughout the valley.

"Fortune seems to have delivered them as victims into our hands. Those whom the sword spares, will be struck dead by an avenging climate. Their bones will be scattered among these mountains and rocks, and tossed about by the waves of our sea." He raised his sword high above them and his eyes flashed. "Never more will they behold their native land; never more will they receive the tender embraces of their wives, their sisters, and their mothers; and liberty will reign over their tomb!"

The soldiers roared their approval, and for a moment Toussaint feared he might have gone too far, as exuberant soldiers, most on foot, but some on horseback, seemed ready to rip out the very trees around them in celebration. He stood up in his stirrups and raised his sword as high as it would go, and his voice rose in a stirring crescendo.

"Ascend these mountains and prepare to swoop down like vultures on the living carrion even now trudging this way!"

Toussaint mostly believed what he told his troops that day. He firmly believed in the justice of their cause, their fight for liberty from those who would re-enslave them. He believed his strategy of slash and burn, then ambush and wait for yellow fever to do the rest, offered their best chance at victory. But he had also seen the numbers. He had seen the French weaponry and knew it was far superior to their own. Within his heart he wondered if the ones to be separated from embrace and left us carrion might be his own men and himself. That was a risk he had to take.

He also believed in his strategy for this day. Several thousand men ascended the flanks of the two adjacent mountains, while he and fighters on horseback hid in the thick forest of the ravine. They had also felled trees across the path down the ravine, thus blocking the path of the French forces. The enemy would be quickly surrounded in unfamiliar territory.

The strategy required waiting, and that was good and necessary, since Toussaint had confirmed the French were not close enough to be aware of the setting up of the trap. But Toussaint was not good at waiting. Waiting meant inaction, and inaction flew in the face of the nature God had given him. Still, waiting is what he did. He had to.

The first signs of the approach of General Leclerc's 5th French Light Infantry Regiment came from flashes of mirror light sent by lookouts on ridges further down the ravine. Then came the sounds: infantry marching through the crackling underbrush, the clomping of horses' hooves (he had muffled his own horses' hooves with cloth coverings), the rumbling of heavy cannon moving through the narrow pass.

When French officers saw the tree blockade ahead of them, their forces immediately prepared for attack, but not before Toussaint's infantry began streaming down from the mountains. Toussaint raised his sword and shouted, "For the liberty of Saint-Domingue!" His mounted troops quickly joined the fray.

Toussaint Louverture was not a general who supervised fighting from a distance. He had already been wounded over a dozen times in battle, including receiving a blow to the head by a cannon ball, which had knocked out a good number of his teeth. His men knew that he risked his own life right alongside them. This battle was no exception.

Many white French soldiers thought of blacks as animals, and he used this racial bias to his advantage. Let them fear the animal! He growled and snarled as he swung his sword, quickly disposing of one foe, then the next. Still, were he honest, his focus was jolted on those relatively rare occasions when he saw a black face in a French army uniform. A phrase from the lips of his wife flashed through his mind: If you meet our son Isaac in battle...? As quickly as this phrase cut into his psyche, an enemy sword from somewhere slashed into Toussaint's left arm. The black general roared in rage, and struck back, felling his assailant to the ground.

Toussaint could no longer afford to look at the color of faces, only the color of uniforms.

The rest of that day the blood flowed, although the black general had shut out the pain, and was completely unaware of whether the red stains on his uniform had come from the ones he had slain or his own neglected wound. Yet he was aware that the more soldiers he cut down, and the more he saw brought to their death by the fighting of brave former slaves around him, the more the soldiers kept coming. They seemed to emerge from the thick vegetation, and from behind every rock, as if a hundred ships had been dry-docked in that ravine, unloading wave after wave of fighting men. The sounds of musket-fire bludgeoned his eardrums and left his ears ringing. He and his officers had schemed to surround the enemy, and yet now it appeared that they and the French enemy were surrounding each other, every man desperate to survive and every man clinging to a hope they could not see.

In the few moments where Toussaint had vision beyond the battle in front of him, he saw none of his men fleeing the fight. Each one met their avowed enemy head-on, and deadly wounds came from thrusts into their chests and abdomens, not their already-scarred backs. The only entity seeming to be absent without leave was time itself. Had the fighting lasted minutes, or hours, or days? He simply did not know. Each moment was its own eternity.

Still, in the haze and confusion of battle there came a light. A gap was suddenly illuminated before him, not a gap allowing for the penetration of enemy defenses, as Toussaint was reputed to always find, but a gap for escape. A pathway to survival for his men, across the Petite-Rivière. Did no one else see how it had been lit? Perhaps it came from the lantern of one of God's angels going before them? In any case, he could not wait. He could already count the bodies of far more of his men splayed across the ground, than those who stood erect with open eyes. Toussaint raised his sword and shouted:

"This way to tomorrow!"

His horse charged toward the gap. Toussaint pulled on the reins, turned the stallion's head abruptly and looked back. Only then did his remaining men break from battle. He was joined by Henri Christophe, and those on foot ran past them up a narrow pass into the mountains. Many turned briefly to fire their muskets before running on. Toussaint and Henri astride their horses, guarded the retreat, slashing almost wildly with their swords. But in truth, the remaining French soldiers were not all that eager to pursue. They were glad to see it over. Toussaint left last, but quickly charged forward to lead his men on their way to Mount Cahos.

Somewhere in the Mountains of Saint-Domingue, April, 1802

Henri Christophe had never seen Toussaint so agitated. His superior and friend tried to sit down in a chair in the little mountain hideaway, but gave up on the idea after only a few seconds. He paced over to a small window, feigned to look out, but quickly turned back. He looked at Christophe.

"How many men did we lose in total?"

Henri Christophe groaned, and shook his head. "It's hard to get a good count. Probably easier to say how many men we have left, and that's not encouraging. We might have five or six thousand men. But several of our generals are defecting in hope of leniency and retaining their rank in French service."

"Which generals?"

Christophe shifted in his chair. "You know, we are all tired of the fighting, Toussaint. There are several generals, generals who have fought really hard, who are beginning to think we might have a better chance trusting the promises of Napoleon and Leclerc, than we have fighting the over-whelming odds."

Toussaint slammed his fist on the table in the middle of the room. "But don't they understand Leclerc's forces are decimated as well? We took more of their forces in *Ravine-à-Couleuvres* than they took of ours! And Dessalines men and the fort at *Crete-a-Pierrot*? They made us all proud!"

Christophe looked down at the floor and shifted again in his chair. *Toussaint just didn't understand.*

When Christophe raised his head to look at his commander, Toussaint was peering at him quizzically. "You aren't saying...Dessalines? He hates white people! Surely—"

"Defected. Maybe a thousand soldiers with him."

Toussaint threw his arms in the air. "Already Leclerc has five thousand men in the hospital with yellow fever--"

"But twenty thousand more are on their way from France."

Toussaint slumped into a chair and lay his head down on the table.

Christophe couldn't look in the man's direction any more. *He hasn't asked about me. Does he even suspect?*

Christophe stood and cleared his throat. When that did not draw his commander's attention, he took a few steps toward the door. "I must go. I fear I have urgent matters to which I must attend."

Toussaint nodded, almost imperceptibly.

Henri Christophe slowly opened the door, but before he could close it behind him, he heard from Toussaint one last phrase.

"What you must do, do quickly!"

Near Cap-Français, Saint-Domingue, April, 1802

Toussaint normally had great confidence in his own judgment—perhaps too much if you asked some. They had wondered aloud, *How could he always be so sure?* But only recently had he begun to question that judgment himself. Perhaps he had been wrong about Napoleon and Leclerc. Perhaps there really was no intent to re-enslave the blacks of Saint-Domingue. He had seen so many brave men die, trusting his own judgment about that. Now he faced the somber possibility that it might have been better to risk trusting Napoleon than to send former slaves into the jaws of his powerful army.

It was with such thoughts he occupied himself as he rode toward Cap-Français with around 300 of his remaining troops.

Toussaint galloped into the city popularly called *Le Cap,* and made his way to the local hospital. He had been told that Leclerc would be there reviewing the status of his sickened soldiers. He found the general out front, talking to a doctor. As Leclerc looked Toussaint's way, his eyes opened wide and his jaw dropped. Toussaint smiled. He had told no one of his plans. He always enjoyed the element of surprise. Leclerc's soldiers, however, did not, and they rapidly turned their muskets in the direction of the approaching black soldiers. But Leclerc, noting that none of Toussaint's soldiers had weapons raised, waved them off.

Toussaint stopped his horse directly in front the of the commander of the French soldiers who had attacked Saint-Domingue.

"General Leclerc, I have come here today to submit myself to your authority as commander of the French forces in Saint-Domingue. These hostilities have gone on too long, and the cost in deaths to both sides have been too great."

The French general continued to look at him open-mouthed, as did many of the soldiers with them. Many of LeClerk's soldiers saluted the black general, and many more of the local populace bowed in reverence. While Leclerc evidently wrestled with how to respond, Toussaint knew, at least for now, the man's response would have to be conciliatory.

When Leclerc's mouth finally did begin to function, he offered to keep Toussaint as governor of Saint-Domingue. In addition, he offered to keep all of Toussaint's officers at their present rank in the French army. "I swear," he said, "before the face of the Supreme Being to respect the liberty of the people of Saint-Domingue."

Toussaint very much wanted to accept the integrity of the general's words. Could he really afford not to? And yet the prospect of remaining entangled in French politics, even as governor, made his gut twist in knots.

"I accept everything which is favorable to the people and for the army," he said. "And for myself, I wish to live in retirement."

With a nod of dismissal from Leclerc, Toussaint turned his steed to leave that place, and to make the journey to his family home at Ennery. The journey home felt to Toussaint like a journey of triumph. Everywhere crowds pressed and prostrated themselves as if he had been a victorious general. They hailed him as their friend, they hailed him as their liberator; for in their acclaim they bore in mind that the liberty for which he had fought was sanctioned and secured by Captain-General Leclerc's solemn oath.

Ennery, Saint-Domingue, May, 1802

Toussaint had to admit it to himself: he was not made to live in retirement. Being physically away from the battlefields and the nerve center of Cap-Français did little to sooth his mind or salve his anxieties. Would General Leclerc really live up to his oath? What if Napoleon was of a different mind and overruled him? And even if these French leaders held true, there was the matter of bringing healing to the torn country of Saint-Domingue.

In an effort to keep his mind off such worries, Toussaint threw himself into the concerns of his more local world, the community of Ennery. Not only was there much to do to tend to his own beautiful property in this fertile valley, but he found himself assisting less-fortunate neighbors to repair and improve their dwellings, and he involved himself in other local challenges.

While he sought to forget the larger world, it both helped and hindered that the larger world did not forget him. Generals and sympathetic officers of the French army, as well as strangers from distant lands, came to visit him. They voiced their admiration and lauded his accomplishments, and this was in most ways reassuring. He was not forgotten. And yet each visitor brought with them, however unintended, the anxiety Toussaint had sought to leave behind.

His experience of one visitor was different from these, however. This one was a young man, also in a French army uniform. Toussaint first saw him walking up over a hill, while Toussaint was in front of his house, tending to some flowers. Something about this approaching figure was frightening and exciting at the same time. It was a face he had both been longing to see and fearful of confronting again.

"Hello, father."

"Hello, son."

Isaac Louverture took a few steps and fell to his knees. Then, apparently feeling that was not enough, he fell all the way forward, face pressed into the ground, and arms outstretched. He lifted his face just far enough off that ground to speak. "I am no longer worthy to be called your son."

Toussaint ran to his son, lifted him off the ground, and held him close. Tears streamed down Toussaint's cheeks. "You have never stopped being my son, and I will never stop loving you. Never!"

Isaac pulled away, if only slightly, from his father's embrace. "I was angry, father, and the anger blurred my judgment. I was wrong to trust the promises of Napoleon, instead of you. I was a fool."

"There are plenty of regrets to go around. I regret sending you and Placide away, when you needed me. You were right to be angry. But at the time, I thought it was best for you. I believed their promises. They would educate you for free, in the finest schools of Europe. How could that be bad? How could I know they would turn you against me?"

"But what about now, Father? You are believing French promises again. Are you not afraid these promises might fail both of us again?"

Toussaint nodded. "But this time there is a difference. This time we are on the same side. This time if the promises fail, we face that failure together, with your mother and your brothers. Together we will overcome."

Isaac nodded. "Yes, Father. God will show us the way."

And at that moment Toussaint smiled the fullest, richest smile he had smiled in as long as he could remember. His son had returned home.

Chapter Six

Isaac stared out the window of his father's 2008 Chevy van. Looking at the others traveling with them, Henri and Marie-Noëlle, would be far too uncomfortable. And looking in the back at their luggage would be absolutely unbearable. So he peered out the window and said nothing.

When Isaac had learned that the parents of his two friends would be unable to drive them to the airport, he had jumped at the opportunity to step in and volunteer his father. But now he wondered why he had been so eager. Did he think he might convince them at the last minute to stay? This arrangement was drawing out the agony.

As they passed through the plaza at the heart of Cap Haitien, he looked up at the statue, and could no longer keep silent. "Statue of Dessalines. That's Cap Haitien for you! It should be Toussaint."

"Well, there you have it," said Henri. "We were wondering what old Isaac could possibly do to rescue Haiti, and now we know. He can get them to replace the statues of Dessalines with statues of Toussaint! The country is saved!"

Isaac's jaw tightened.

"Shut up, Henri!" said Marie-Noëlle. Isaac glanced her way, but she was staring at the floor of the car, and so he returned his gaze to the safer territory of what appeared out his window. "We don't need your stupid jokes right now," she continued. "We need less tension in here, not more."

Isaac's father, Pierre, looked at them through his rearview mirror. "You guys probably aren't going to see each other for a while. Do you really want to waste this time being pissed off at each other? Friends need to do better than that."

Isaac knew his father was right, but friendly words refused to come from his mouth, and that appeared to be true of Henri and Marie-Noëlle as well. Everyone continued to avoid each other's eyes.

Pierre turned the van down the access road to the airport. There had been a time when Isaac had thought Cap Haitien had at least an adequate airport, but that was before his father had taken him on a business trip to Miami in the United States. There he had seen a different world. Now what he saw was the lack of automation, and the poor Haitians, fighting to carry baggage a few feet to get a tip, or playing Calypso on primitive instruments, hoping a few gourde or even dollars would be dropped in a basket. The ever-present begging culture. The blue and orange steel building which served as a terminal was miniscule by comparison to Miami, and the whole structure now appeared to Isaac as a warehouse for poverty.

Isaac's father turned the vehicle into the little parking lot, and each passenger quietly unbuckled his seatbelt, exited the van, and headed toward the back to help with luggage. Isaac wasn't sure why he immediately grabbed Marie-Noëlle's largest bag. Was he just wanting to help, or was he thinking of holding it as a bargaining chip? Marie-Noëlle didn't ask. She just picked up her carryon and stared at the ground.

In the terminal, Henri and Marie-Noëlle seemed relieved to have the opportunity to focus on concrete tasks: obtaining boarding passes, checking luggage, showing ID. But after that it was time to head through the security check where Isaac and his father could not enter. Both quickly turned to Pierre, gave him a quick embrace and thanked him for the ride. Then came a moment of silence.

Henri finally reached out his hand to Isaac. As he took it, a smile spread slowly across Isaac's face.

"When you give up on Haiti, you know where to find me," said Henri.

Isaac nodded. "Yeah – probably in some New Jersey bar, drinking with rich white guys."

Henri shrugged. "Maybe."

Now, the only ones left to say their good-byes were Isaac and Marie-Noëlle. Isaac looked at her until she raised her gaze off the floor and met his. Her eyes immediately teared over.

Isaac reached out with his right hand and gently took her left, and squeezed it. "Good-bye, Marie-Noëlle."

She sniffled. "Good-bye, General Nerd."

Isaac smiled. "Good-bye, Wench."

Marie-Noëlle returned the smile. "Good-bye, noble liberator of Haiti!"

"Good-bye, future Sports Illustrated cover girl!"

Marie-Noëlle threw her arms around Isaac's neck and kissed him all over his face. Then she held him close. "Good-bye, Isaac."

"Good-bye, Mare." Then he broke away, and without looking back, ran to his father's van.

When Isaac's father returned to the van, Isaac had his head buried in his arms, and he was crying. Pierre Breda climbed in the driver's side door, shut it behind him, and looked at his son. He put his hand softly on Isaac's head and stroked his hair.

"Dad, am I being an idiot?"

His father shook his head. "I don't think so."

Isaac leaned against the car seat back, slumped down and stared at the ceiling. "I have this passion to make Haiti better, but after talking to Henri, I don't know, maybe it's just a form of mental illness. A delusion of grandeur. A Haitian Don Quixote."

Pierre smiled. "I'm proud I have a son who knows Don Quixote. Do you know what my favorite quote is from that book by Miguel de Cervantes?"

Isaac shook his head.

"'The greatest sanity may be madness, and the maddest of all, to see life as it is, and not as it should be.' Yeah, well, at least that is how I remember it."

Isaac's gaze shifted to his father. "So, why is it, do you think, that they have that statue of Dessalines, and not Toussaint?"

"Jean Jacques Dessalines was a great military leader for Haiti. By the time our country gained its independence, Toussaint was dead, and Dessalines was in charge—well, him and Henri Christophe. On the 19th of November,

1803, the French signed the articles giving us independence, and within ten days the French were gone."

"But you've always taught me—"

"Yes, son, I've taught you that Toussaint won us our freedom. And there are two reasons I still say that is true. One is that even though he was dead, his spirit inspired those who remained. When the people of what was then called Saint-Domingue heard of Toussaint's deportation and later death they began to see the truth of all he had taught. Well, no prophet can be considered great until they are dead, as they say. His spirit drove them. The English poet William Wordsworth wrote of him,

'Though fallen thyself, never to rise again,

Live and take comfort. Thou has left behind

Powers that will work for thee: air, earth and skies,

There's not a breathing of the common wind

That will forget thee: thou hast great allies;

Thy friends are exultations, agonies,

And love, and man's unconquerable mind.'"

After Pierre Breda recited the poetic segment, he sat staring out the window in silence. He might have remained that way for some time had Isaac not broken in.

"Great memory for poetry, Dad."

"It's engraved into my soul," he whispered. Then he returned his attention to his son. "Dessalines took what Toussaint left behind and finished the work. He could never have inspired himself what Toussaint inspired. Jean-Jacques Dessalines was just a violent, angry man bent on revenge. He slaughtered thousands of French prisoners: men, women, even children and babies, all to satisfy his demand for blood.

"Toussaint had always taught against a spirit of vengeance. But the spirit of vengeance fanned into flame by Dessalines, ripped our country apart for many years. It made it difficult to establish good trade relations with other primarily-white countries, and that hobbled an economy which Toussaint as Governor had built up."

"So, once again," Isaac said, "why the statue of Dessalines, and not Toussaint?"

"Toussaint has statues in other places, and the airport in Port-au-Prince is named after him as well. Do you know where some of the best-known monuments to Toussaint are? France! There is one in La Rochelle, once a big slave trading post; there is a monument to him in Fort De Joux, and an inscription in his memory on the wall of the Pantheon in Paris. There are monuments and statues honoring Toussaint all over the world: the West African nation of Benin; Miami, Florida; Cuba, and at the Smithsonian in Washington, DC. You don't find monuments to Dessalines outside of Haiti."

Isaac's father started the van, and backed out of his parking space. Before proceeding further, he glanced back at his son. "But, you know, Henri was right in his own way. You can't change Haiti by changing statues. It has to be about changing attitudes."

Isaac smiled. "Yeah, but it would be a lot easier to change a statue."

The difficulty of change. That was on Isaac's mind from the time his father drove out of the airport parking lot until his father dropped him off at his apartment on Rue 15. It was on his mind as they passed a corner where unemployed young men and women sat, waiting for they knew not what.

Many of these had been his classmates. It was on his mind as they passed over a river that floated garbage from the city out to the sea. It was on his mind as he passed the market where old women, donning their most pathetic faces, sought to bargain with a paltry number of tourists over the price of some trinkets. To the tourist it was about bragging rights for getting a good bargain. To those selling those trinkets, it was about eating.

After Pierre Breda dropped off his son, Isaac looked back at him from the curbside with a wrinkled brow. "I'm not sure I can do it, Dad."

"If not you, then who?" his father asked. He reached out the car window and grabbed his son's hand firmly. "You remember, don't you, why I named you Isaac?"

Isaac nodded.

"I named you after Isaac Louverture, Toussaint's second oldest son. They had had a tumultuous relationship, but they loved each other dearly. After Toussaint died, Isaac dedicated his life to keeping alive not just his father's memory, but his legacy. He wrote an influential biography on Toussaint which remains important today. I figured we need a new Isaac for today, someone to keep alive the legacy. It was a lot to lay on you, I know. But would you rather I had raised you to sell Haitian coffee, as I do?"

Isaac shrugged. "Coffee is good."

"But you are capable of more, my son. I believe you compliment your children when you expect a lot of them. Would you agree?"

Isaac looked into his father's eyes as if he expected an answer to be written there on his retina. "I'm not sure, father."

"And it's not like you must do it on your own. You know the queen is the most powerful piece in chess, but one

77

who uses that piece alone, cannot win. They must utilize their rooks, their knights, their bishops, and especially their pawns. Each one lifted up. Each one having a role. The people are willing to hope if someone gives them a reason to hope. You can do that, son! There is a creole saying that my mother always used to say, and which I heard repeated after the 2010 earthquake: 'Ayiti p'ap peri'—"

"'Haiti will never be finished.'"

Pierre Breda smiled. "That's right, son. Haiti will never be finished. Remember that and you will do just fine."

After his father drove away, Isaac stood outside at the street's edge, simply watching those who passed by. What use was it to go into his apartment? He knew it held no answers to the questions which continually flooded his mind. What was he doing here? *Where was he needing to go? Had his vision of his life's purpose really only been his father's vision all along?*

He found himself wandering down the street. He hopped on a "tap-tap", a Haitian taxi, an old truck over-loaded with passengers. He stood on the bumper and held on, along with four other young men. Where was everyone else going? It was hard to say. Maybe they were all just wanting to be going *somewhere.*

After about an hour of riding and wandering, Isaac found himself walking down a road leading up a mountain overlooking Cap Haitien. As he ascended higher, he noted that this road, though as steep as the one going up to the Citadelle Laferriere, was not nearly as wooded. He spotted just three medium-sized trees, and the remains of a fourth was being enveloped in smoke. Isaac remembered that 70%

of Haiti's energy supply was from burning wood, primarily in the form of charcoal made from trees. Every year Haiti was losing more and more trees, and with it, more and more soil eroded.

Fewer people lived up here than down in the city, of course, and the ones Isaac saw beside the road, walking or riding emaciated donkeys, were thin and listless. While his own father made a good living, Haitians as whole made an average of around 120 gourdes, or two U.S. dollars, a day. Nearly 80% of the population was below the poverty line.

After walking longer than he could even say, Isaac came to a rock outcropping of the mountain overlooking the city. He sat down and surveyed the vista below. Cap Haitien was the second largest city in Haiti and was home to nearly 200,000 people. During the time of Toussaint it had been the largest city in the country and was referred to as "the Paris of the Antilles." Isaac shook his head. Paris. The comparison hardly fit today. There was very little elegance. With few exceptions, the city was a composite of barely-livable shacks, with broken-down cars and trucks lining the streets. Where was the hope?

Isaac became aware he was hungry. And then he thought about all the people who had looked down from that mountain, hungry. Nothing waiting for them down below. Nothing on the mountain but rocks that would never turn into bread. He considered his despair. Would it make one bit of difference in the world if he flung himself down from this rock? Then he considered those on this mountain who lived their whole lives assuming they would never make a difference beyond the one square foot of dust on which they stood. Perhaps it would lift them up if somewhere on the horizon they could see a Toussaint.

As the Boeing 747 banked to the right, Marie-Noëlle looked out the window at the city below, and became intensely aware of the new world she was about to enter. She had seen the edges of this world on television, but only now did its full scope hit her. Skyscrapers from horizon to horizon. Traffic flowing in a hundred different directions. Lights flashing at them from still thousands of feet below. New York City was preparing to swallow them like an ocean received a raindrop.

Instinctively, Marie-Noëlle grabbed her brother's arm as he sat in the seat next to her.

"Fingernails! Fingernails!" Henri sought to release her iron grip. "I'm losing circulation here!" He switched to a whisper. "Let go, or they might arrest you for using those nails as terrorist weapons!"

His sister looked at him. "I made a mistake. I don't belong here."

Henri succeeded in releasing her grip on his arm. "Well, then, you've got that big modeling agency fooled, because they're spending a lot of money bringing you here."

"They don't know me. They just know what I look like."

"For now, that's enough." Henri put his hand over his sister's and squeezed it gently. "Look, not only will you be able to talk to me anytime you want, but New Brunswick, New Jersey, is really close to Manhattan. There are good train and bus connections. You don't even have to crowd onto a 'tap-tap'!"

Marie-Noëlle gave her brother a little smile. "The last time I was on one of those, some guy kept trying to feel my boobs."

"Yeah, well, if some guy tries to do that in New York, you just give me a call. I hear New Jersey has a lot of really tough dudes. I'll bring some of them with me, and we'll rough him up!"

She leaned her head on her brother's shoulder. "I wish Isaac had come."

Henri nodded. "He's a smart guy. He'll realize how futile it is trying to change Haiti, and he'll be here in no time. Hell, his dad has money. He can afford Rutgers, even without a scholarship."

Marie-Noëlle sat up and shook her head, "I don't know if I want him to give up on changing Haiti. I don't know what I want."

It was time to have their seats in a "raised and upright position." It was time to get ready to land. Marie-Noëlle was not sure she would *ever* be ready.

Chapter Seven

Ennery, Saint-Domingue, June, 1802

When Isaac Louverture had first come home to Ennery, it had been a peaceful, pastoral place. He and Placide had helped their father with the chores of repairing the property, and tending to the orchards of banana and fig trees, as well as their crop of coffee. Even young Saint-Jean helped. It had been an idyllic time for them all. His father seemed to be forgetting the stresses of leading a war-torn country, and his mother was actually smiling a lot. She often hugged Isaac for no reason at all.

Then it changed. Where once had been only native villagers, there were now swarms of French soldiers. Some he recognized from when he himself had fought in that army, but even these seemed distant and hostile. He had to chase away several who had come onto their property to cut down their bananas and figs. His father asked for an explanation from the French, and received none. Only one French soldier gave Isaac any rationale for their actions: *Just making sure your dad isn't stirring up trouble!*

Isaac had a different idea of who might be stirring up trouble.

"Dad, I don't think you can trust Napoleon, Leclerc, or any of their officers," Isaac said to his father at dinner one day. "They know how much the people respect your leadership, and they are afraid. They can't control you, and that worries them."

Suzanne glared at Toussaint. "You listen to your son on this matter. Your family all agrees." She looked at Placide and Saint-Jean and both nodded vigorously.

Toussaint put down his fork, and looked out a nearby window. Then his attention returned to his family. "I take your warnings very seriously, of course, and I appreciate the love with which they have been given—"

"Love and fear, my husband!" said Suzanne. "We need you here. I do. Your children do. I fear what might happen to us if we lose you."

"But if we go back to war, you might lose me as well," said Toussaint.

Isaac's mother stiffened, and then nodded.

"The people are tired of war," continued Toussaint. "I need to do all I can to make sure peace continues, while making sure our freedom is assured. Having both is not an easy issue."

"No, it is not, father," said Isaac. "You must proceed with caution, either way."

"I have received a letter from Jean-Baptiste Brunet, saying he wants me to come to him to discuss this matter of stationing French troops around Ennery. I want to hear what he says, and what they are willing to do. Perhaps it will clarify the choices I have."

"Or perhaps it is a trap," said Isaac.

"Brunet is a good man," said Toussaint. "I trust his word."

Suzanne stood up abruptly. "Then we will all go with you! Should you be at all delayed, I will not sit around this place worrying with my children about what might have happened. What happens to you, happens to all of us. I will stand with my husband!"

Toussaint slowly rose from his dinner chair, and embraced his wife. She broke down and wept. Isaac considered his mother to be a strong woman, and he tried to remember the last time he saw her sob uncontrollably, as she now did. He couldn't remember it ever happening.

Placide and young Saint-Jean affirmed their resolve to join their mother in accompanying their father, and Isaac was about to do the same when Toussaint broke in. "What kind of leader will I appear to be," he said, "if people think I need my wife and children for protection? It would be like Jacob in the Bible, when he came back to meet his brother Esau. Do you remember that story? I have taught it to all of you many times. Jacob had deceived his brother over his father's birthright, and Jacob knew Esau was angry enough to kill him. But instead of facing his brother like a man, Jacob sent his wife and children on before him! I have never respected Jacob since I first read that story, and I will never do the same as he. You must stay here, and trust I will do my job of protecting my family, instead of the other way around."

Isaac knew that once his father had made up his mind, there was no changing it, especially when he underscored it by a biblical story. All they would be able to do would be to wait and pray.

Toussaint took with him two of his former officers, and left that evening for the plantation called Georges, where he was to meet with Jean-Baptiste Brunet. While he had told his family he was confident the man's intentions were peaceful, in his heart he was not so sure. By that morning there had been 500 French troops stationed near Ennery, and there was no reason for them if Leclerc truly trusted him. That general had even accused him of recruiting armed men to come to Ennery. And yet any fool could see that Ennery had only 50 armed men who were there as a police force for the community. Toussaint had told Leclerc in a letter that he had too much honor to go back on his promise of submission to his authority, but it had not been enough to have French forces removed from the community.

Toussaint paused briefly en route to re-examine Brunet's letter. He read to himself, *"Now is the time, Citizen-General, to make known unquestioningly to the General-in-Chief that those who wish to deceive him in regard to your fidelity are base calumniators, and that your sentiments tend to restore order and tranquility in your neighborhood...We have arrangements to make together, my dear General, which it is impossible to do by letter, but which an hour's conference would complete. If I were not worn out by labor and petty cares, I should have been the bearer of my own letter today; but not being able to leave at this time, will you not come to me? If you have recovered from your indisposition, let it be tomorrow; when a good work is to be done, there should be no delay. You will not find in my country-house all the comforts I could desire before receiving you, but you will find the sincerity of an honest man who desires only the prosperity of the colony and your own happiness..."*

The sincerity of an honest man. Could he believe such still existed in the French army? He wanted to believe. He had no other good choice.

When Toussaint reached Georges, he found General Brunet looking for him. The general smiled broadly, and ran out to meet him as if he were his long-lost brother.

"My dear General, it is good to see you!" General Brunet said. "And you look so well! Have you discovered the Fountain of Youth, and did not tell us?"

Toussaint dismounted, took Brunet's hand and bowed. "Your greeting of me is so gracious, and you lie so well about my appearance. I thank you. I only hope our discussion of the matters at hand can be as uplifting."

"Of course! Of course! The matters at hand. We will get to that soon enough. But how was your ride over? I hope you did not encounter any inconvenience?"

"It was fine."

"Well, then," continued Brunet, "let my men care for your horse. Your officers can wait out here, while we go into my parlor and tend to, as you say, the matters at hand."

Toussaint followed his host into the house, where a servant had laid out some pastries, and was already pouring coffee. The aroma of that hot beverage filled the room. Two comfortable-appearing, embroidered chairs with ornate scrollwork on the mahogany arms, flanked the equally-ornate mahogany table on which the coffee and pastries had been placed. The servant left the room.

"Won't you be seated?" said Brunet, motioning toward the chairs. "You honor us with your presence, and we want you to be comfortable."

Toussaint sat down in the nearest chair. "Ah, yes. Certainly more comfortable than sitting on Bellisarius."

Brunet gave him a questioning look.

"That's my horse. I was making a little joke. I have been sitting on him a while."

Brunet laughed. "Of course. And a good one." He sat down in the other chair. "Are the soldiers stationed at Ennery still giving you and your family grief?"

"Yes, they are," said Toussaint. "And that is what I hope we can remedy with this visit."

His host nodded. "We can remedy that, I am sure. We both want what is best for the colony."

"You have to know that neither the good people of Ennery, nor I, are doing anything to provoke hostilities in the region. As long as nothing foolish is done, such as reinstating slavery, that peace will continue, and without the stationing of French troops."

Brunet nodded. "Ah, but I have forgotten a matter I must discuss with my servants here! Would you excuse me a moment? We can get back to these important matters shortly."

"Certainly."

No sooner had Jean-Baptiste Brunet left the room than eighteen to twenty officers entered from the outside, carrying swords and pistols. Assassins! Toussaint rose quickly and drew his sword, determined not to be easily vanquished. But then a colonel came forward, with his sword lowered.

"General, we have not come here to attempt your life. We have merely the order to secure your person."

Toussaint could see no escape. He put his sword back in his scabbard. "The justice of Heaven will avenge my cause."

In spite of the colonel's respectful words, the other soldiers quickly bound him like a criminal.

"You are only felling the trunk of the tree of freedom," said Toussaint. "Branches will sprout, for the roots are numerous and deep."

"We will tend to them as they come," said the colonel.

And then without so much as another word from General Brunet, they dragged him out the door.

Isaac sought to relieve his mind of his constant anxiety over his father's well-being. He was worrying over nothing. He had been anxious many times before, and his father had always been fine. He was Toussaint Louverture. His ability to escape traps and military challenges was legendary. Even when Isaac had fought for the French, soldiers and officers had spoken of his father's prowess with respect and awe.

So Isaac figured that his challenge was simply to occupy his own mind until his father's return. He found a book in his father's library, a French copy of The Odyssey by Homer. A father takes ten years to return home after a war. Perhaps not a good choice, and yet he began reading it anyway.

All of a sudden he heard the sounds of muskets being fired. Then the cries of both men and women. He jumped up and ran from the room. Everyone was fleeing from the house. He scurried to a window and looked out. From three to four hundred French soldiers pursued and fired upon fleeing household servants and neighbors. Isaac's mother came out from her room screaming. Saint-Jean followed behind her, crying. Placide quickly joined them.

"What's happening?" shouted Placide.

"They're going to kill all of us!" cried Suzanne. "Where is Toussaint? Where is your father? I told him not to go! I told him!"

A servant stopped on his way out of the house. "You must all leave! They are coming to arrest all of you, and shooting whoever gets in the way!"

"Then they must have arrested father," said Isaac. "And we must join him."

Suzanne cried hysterically. "Why did he have to go? Why?"

Placide, fulfilling his role as eldest son, sought to comfort their mother, while Saint-Jean, only twelve, held on to her tightly.

Isaac looked out the window again. "I know some of those soldiers. I fought beside them. Follow me."

While the servant who had warned them fled out the back of the house, Isaac led the family out the front, with his hands held high in surrender. French soldiers swarmed around them.

A colonel whom Isaac recognized stopped right in front of him and pointed his musket at Isaac's face. "You are all under arrest for insurrection against First Consul Napoleon Bonaparte and the French government. Resist and you will be shot!"

"Pierre! You know me!" said Isaac. "Do you truly believe this violence is necessary?"

"Just following orders, Isaac. Just following orders. Which is more than I can say for your father."

Other soldiers rushed in and bound their hands behind each of them, even Suzanne and Saint-Jean. Isaac tried to think of what his father would do in that situation.

He prayed.

Pontarlier, France, April, 1803

Toussaint had heard that when one was near death, one might see visions. Surely that was what this was. What had it been? Nearly ten months that he had been held captive. And in all that time he had not been allowed to see his family. He had been told they had been on board the same ship as he, when it left port at Gonaives. And he had been told they had been imprisoned with him in a different dungeon here at Fort de Joux. But he was never allowed to see those faces which were more precious to him than life itself. Only the guard. Occasionally Mars Plaisir. And on that one occasion, Napoleon himself, when he had come to gloat.

Now, however, a face came to him as through a mist of memory. It was a familiar face. A gentle face. With great effort Toussaint reached out and put his hand on Isaac's head, as the young man knelt beside him. The old general gently stroked his son's hair. He was real.

"Father! Your hand is so cold!"

Toussaint nodded.

Isaac crawled closer on his knees, and looked into his father's eyes. "I would have come sooner, but they would not allow it."

Toussaint nodded again. "I know. How did you manage this time?"

"I know the guard from my days in the army. He had compassion."

Even saying the few words he had spoken had taken away the old general's breath. After a pause, he looked into his son's eyes again. "It is so good to see you. I had come to believe it would never again happen this side of glory."

Toussaint went into a coughing fit, and spit blood into a cup beside where he lay.

"Don't talk, father! It's too hard for you. Can I get you some water?"

Toussaint motioned toward another cup on a small table a few feet away. Isaac walked over and found it had a few swallows of water left in it. He took it to his father, helped him sit up and sip the water. After a few sips, Toussaint grimaced and waved off what remained.

"I was a fool," Toussaint finally said. "You and your mother both warned me, but I didn't listen."

"You wanted to believe."

Toussaint's head was swimming. "Yes," he whispered. He swallowed hard and took a couple of deep breaths. Only then did he feel like he had the energy to speak again. "How is your mother?"

Isaac closed his eyes and shook his head. "She is...not well. She's frightened. She misses you tremendously."

Tears came to Toussaint's eyes. "And I miss her... immeasurably." He coughed a couple of more times. "Son, do not marry until you find a woman like your mother."

Isaac nodded.

Toussaint coughed and spit out more blood. Then he cleared his throat. "Have you heard anything of...Saint-Domingue?"

Isaac nodded again. "Some bad things, some good. The soldiers do talk to me. Did you know Dessalines took part in your betrayal?"

Toussaint attempted to shake his head, but he knew it barely moved.

"He complained to Leclerc that you were not living up to the cease-fire. He knew what they were going to do, and said nothing to you. He was part of the whole plot. It was like Judas in the Garden."

"I hope he got his thirty pieces..."

"No, but I understand he and his wife received some pretty extravagant gifts from Brunet."

"So discouraging," said Toussaint. "I fear for what will happen in Saint-Domingue now."

"But I do have some good news. Much has happened since the defections." Isaac stopped to think a moment. "Well, actually father, the good news happened in relation to further bad news. I must give it first. Slavery was restored in Guadeloupe."

"I knew it."

"But that is what led to good news. When the black soldiers of Saint-Domingue heard what happened in Guadeloupe, they immediately began deserting the French forces. And now the petty officers and generals are following suit. General Clervaux has begun a revolt in the north and Christophe joined him. Indeed, when he heard all this General Dessalines started a revolt in the west."

"Ah! Then he saw the error of his ways. You have learned much."

Isaac nodded. "Some of the soldiers who talk to me are embarrassed. They feel the French army is being made to fight against the very principles of freedom they have vowed to defend."

"They are," whispered Toussaint.

"As you predicted, disease has taken a toll on the French forces in Saint-Domingue. They lost thousands to malaria and yellow fever. Even Leclerc has fallen victim. His command was assumed by Rochambeau." Isaac paused. "Dessalines is taking advantage of their depleted strength. I understand he has vowed to maintain the principles by which you fought and governed. Of course, they think you are already dead."

Toussaint gave a weak smile. "Of course. No one listens to you until you are dead."

Isaac nodded. "I wanted you to know there is hope, that what you fought so hard for still lives."

Toussaint nodded and gently placed his hand over his son's.

"Father, the thing I most want you to know is, I will fight for your cause! And we will win! I will not rest until Saint-Domingue is truly free and slavery is forever banished from our land!"

Tears returned to Toussaint's eyes. "That is what God wants for us: a land where black, white and Mulatto live free, together as brothers. If that happens--" Toussaint went into another coughing fit.

When Toussaint stopped coughing, Isaac finished his father's thought. "If that happens...the name of Toussaint Louverture will be remembered with love and respect throughout the world."

The old general closed his eyes and gently shook his head. "The name...is not so important. The freedom. The freedom." And Toussaint Louverture fell asleep on the cold, hard stone.

Chapter Eight

Port-au-Prince, Haiti, September 2016

Dodging cars and other obstacles in traffic was always a challenge when driving in Haiti, but this was far worse than anything Isaac had ever seen. Angry men were crossing the street, yelling and throwing rocks at every passing motorist. *What did they want him to do?* He couldn't magically leave the road! He needed to get back to Cap Haitien!

Isaac turned the corner, seeking desperately to escape the maze of violence, but there before him in the road loomed a roadblock of tires set on fire. The rancid odor of burning rubber made his nostrils want to close entirely. He stopped in the middle of the street. Suddenly two young men jumped onto the hood of his car and banged large rocks on his windshield. Fishnet cracks radiated across the glass. But even with that obstruction of vision, Isaac saw their eyes. He saw all the anger of their lives exploding at him.

Isaac slammed the car in reverse, spilling his attackers back into the street. He did a quick U-turn, and stomped on the accelerator. Driving faster, he knew rioters would hesitate to get in his way, and each time they did, he swerved or turned down a side street. Still, he hadn't often driven in Port-au-Prince and he had no idea of where he was going or how to get back to the road to Cap-Haitien. Down one street drunken men fired pistol shots into the air. Down another, people brawled in the middle of the road.

Isaac turned down still another side street, and there, near an alley entrance, two young men were assaulting a young woman, ripping her clothes off. Isaac didn't think; he reacted. He slammed on the brakes, leaped out of the car, and ran to where the woman was being assaulted. He grabbed one man and threw him against the side of a building, then turned and punched the other guy squarely on the jaw. Then he grabbed the woman, threw her over his shoulder and ran to his car. He tossed her in the back seat, and got in himself, all before the two assailants could recover enough to pursue. He slammed his foot on the accelerator, and the car careened down the road, as the two men shouted epithets at him in Creole.

"Oh, God! Oh, God! Don't hurt me! Please don't hurt me!" The young woman shrank into a corner of the back seat. "I don't care about politics, and if I can help with your cause, I will—just tell me how. But don't hurt me, okay?"

"I'm not going to hurt you!" Isaac dodged another rioter with his car, then made a hard right turn, for what reason, he did not know. "I got you away from those men. I don't know these roads. If you can help me get out of here, do it."

Isaac looked in his rearview mirror at the tearful, distrustful face of his reluctant passenger. She was trembling.

"I got raped after the earthquake, too," she finally said. "I was only twelve years old, and I was in one of the tent camps. What is it about you men? Anytime you're unhappy about how life is going, you say, 'Well, maybe I should go find a poor, defenseless girl to rape!' That will fix it all, for sure!"

Isaac swerved past a car on fire. "Look, I got you away from the two guys who were trying to do that to you—and you're welcome, by the way—but unless we get out of these riots, we will both be in danger. So, a little advice on where to go!"

The young woman sat up and looked around. "Turn left at the third intersection, then go about two kilometers. That will get us to a U.N. station. The rioters will stay away from there." She hesitantly touched his arm. "And…thank you!"

Isaac nodded. After plowing past burning tires and swerving through a crowd of people chanting against the government, Isaac made the left turn. Within a few blocks the streets began to clear. Up ahead he saw two United Nations vehicles and several officers in riot gear detaining men at the side of the road. He pulled his car over.

A U.N. peacekeeper approached the car with his pistol raised. Isaac raised his hand to show he had no weapon, and spoke to the officer in Spanish. "*Por favor, ayudanos!* I was trying to get away from the riots and came across this woman who was being attacked. She might need medical care."

The officer did a visual check of the car and its occupants, and then lowered his weapon. He peeked in the window at the woman in the back seat, and spoke to her in Creole. "Do you need to get to a hospital?"

"No, thank you," the young woman paused to wipe her tears. "I'm okay now, thanks to this man. I actually work at the hospital in Mirebalais. I was here visiting family, and I would really like to get to them, to make sure they are okay."

"And I was here doing some historical research," added Isaac, "but I need to find a safe way back to Cap Haitien."

"Un momento," said the officer, reverting to his native tongue. He turned and went back to talk to a couple of other officers.

"I'm sorry for including you in with those other guys. You are obviously nothing like them." The young woman reached out a hand to Isaac, who had turned to look in her direction. "My name is Yvette Colbert. And yours?"

Isaac shook her hand. "I am Isaac Breda. And I am glad I got there in time to help."

"I owe you my life." Yvette said. "How can I possibly repay you?"

"Forget it. Just pass it on. Help someone else."

"I will do that," said Yvette. "But that is not enough. How else can I help you?"

Isaac thought a moment. "I'm studying Haiti's history, in order to find some way to make our country better, more like what Toussaint Louverture had in mind when he fought for our freedom."

Yvette's eyes widened. "Wow!"

"Wow?"

"Yes, Wow! You're just out to save the whole world, aren't you?"

Isaac felt a tightening in his stomach. "Well, I'm not a naïve little kid about it. I know I am talking about something really big, and I don't know—"

"I'm sorry!" said Yvette. "I didn't mean to make you feel embarrassed about a big dream. I think it's great! How can I help?"

Even with the remnants of tears still in her eyes, Isaac noticed their beauty. And they now seemed to be looking at him with an interest beyond gratitude. He thought of Mare and looked away.

"I'm not sure what I want to be doing yet," he said, "so how can I know what help I need?"

"Do you have a pen and a piece of paper?" Yvette said. "I had those in my purse, but God knows where it is by now."

Isaac found what she had requested in his glove compartment, and handed them to her. She began writing. "I still have my phone, and here is the number. You can call me anytime…for anything." She paused to think a moment. "Oh, and have you heard of Paul Hansen and his work at Mirebalais?"

Isaac shook his head.

"Well, you should talk to him. He is a doctor from the U.S.—another guy out to save the world. Anyway, he started the hospital at Mirebalais and other places in Haiti. I am writing down his phone number and email address. You should contact him."

The U.N. officer returned to the driver's side window. He held out a piece of paper to Isaac. "Here are directions for how to avoid rioters and get to Cap Haitien."

Isaac took the directions from the officer and the contact information for Paul Hansen from Yvette.

"And for you, senorita," continued the officer, "follow me and I'll take you to an officer who can get you where your family lives."

Yvette looked at Isaac. "Remember you can call me, and that I said 'for anything!'"

Isaac blushed. "Yeah, okay." He never had been very good at interpreting the words or gestures of young women. "Are you sure you're going to be all right? What you went through back there looked pretty scary."

"Yeah, it was, but I'll recover. This is Haiti. It toughens you." She leaned forward and gave Isaac a quick kiss on the cheek, then exited through the back driver's side door. As she walked away with the U.N. officer, she glanced back at Isaac and smiled. It was a beautiful smile. And it made him tremble all the way back to Cap Haitien.

Limbe, Haiti, September 2016

Isaac could not stop his friend Daniel from laughing at him, as they walked to their Freshman class.

"Why are you doing that?" Isaac said. "There is nothing funny about what I told you!"

"Are you kidding me?" asked Daniel, with a smirk on his face. "Some hot girl, who you were brave enough to rescue from her attackers, comes on to you, and you treat that like a BIG SCARY THING! That's as funny as hell, man! Bang her! Let her have what she wants. Don't be such a wuss!"

"When I already have a girlfriend?"

"Up in the United States! Many kilometers away, my friend."

"But I don't want to compromise her trust – just as I don't want her to compromise mine."

Daniel gave another hearty laugh. "She will never know! Besides, if you think a hot girl like Marie-Noëlle isn't going to spread her legs for big modeling agency execs, you're living in some dream world. Grow a pair!"

Isaac clenched his jaw, and said nothing until they reached the steps in front of his class at the *Université Chretienne du Nord d'Haiti*. He paused there and looked at Daniel. "I've got to know I'm not like those guys who attacked Yvette. Taking advantage is taking advantage, and I'm not going there."

Daniel shook his head. "Man, how have you survived in the world this long? You want to save Haiti and trust women. Why don't you just throw in 'make peace in the Middle East and cure cancer' while you're at it? You're such a goody-goody. I've got to watch how much I hang out with you. I've got my reputation to consider."

"Your reputation as…?"

"My reputation as a survivor on the street, man!" Daniel gave a couple of girls a visual once-over as they headed toward their class. They smiled back. "Girls like that wouldn't pay attention to me if I were a wuss like you. They like men! Hell, if I would have been there in those riots, I would have gotten out of the car and joined in on the fun. It's what men do."

"Not this man."

"Yeah, well, you're lucky you have that hot girlfriend I want to steal away from you, because otherwise I wouldn't be seen with you at all."

"Yeah. Really lucky," said Isaac, walking toward the classroom door. "Sometimes I wonder what I've done to deserve a friend like you. Perhaps if I promised not to do it again…"

"Very funny, Isaac," said Daniel, following alongside his friend. "Hey, if I wrote Marie-Noëlle, and described a little of my sexual prowess, I wonder if she would marry me and carry me away with her to the United States?"

Isaac smiled and held the door open for Daniel. "I don't think so. She was really looking forward to leaving all of Haiti's garbage behind."

"Ha. Ha. Ha."

As Daniel and Isaac walked into their class, the room, which held approximately fifty students, was already over half full. Isaac was looking forward to this session. The professor was going to talk about Haiti's history and its implication for the country in the present. This was why Isaac chose the Christian University of Northern Haiti at Limbe. They emphasized training people to make a difference in their own country.

After the room filled up, the professor quietly entered the room, went over to his desk and sat on it. Isaac smiled. He knew this teacher would never do anything so formal and ordinary as sitting in a chair. The professor appeared deep in thought, and the students in the room quickly quieted down in expectation. After a long, quiet minute, he looked at the students.

"Is Haiti a free country?" he asked. "What do you think?"

The students glanced back and forth at each other. Professor Alexandre Gabriel was fond of asking trick questions, and many apparently wondered whether this was one of them.

"Come on, you are smart young Haitians," the professor said, after a prolonged silence. "I really want to know what you think."

Crista, a young woman to Isaac's right, raised her hand. No matter what the subject matter, she always seemed to have something to say. "Well, we elect our own leaders. We aren't forced to do hard labor, like in the days before the Haitian Revolution. So, yeah, we're free."

Arturo, on the other side of the room, laughed out loud. "Come on! Really?"

The professor put up his hand like a stop sign. "This is a big class. We wait to be recognized, to speak. But, go on, Arturo. Tell us more of what you think."

"I think the bitch speaks with the voice of privilege. That's what I think!"

"Whoa! Whoa!" said Professor Gabriel. "We don't need to use that language, and there is no call for personal attack. Avoid doing both, and you can proceed with your thoughts."

Crista crossed her arms and shot a glare in Arturo's direction.

"Sure, sure," said Arturo. "But, look. It's a fact that the only people truly free in this country are the rich. They are the ones who are there pulling the strings behind every President we have had—well, except maybe for Aristide, and they got him kicked out."

Hands shot up throughout the room, and Professor Gabriel called on each one in turn:

"Aristide was a crook. They've all been crooks."

"The United States calls the shots in our country. Once we were subject to France. Now we are subject to the United States. No difference."

"I agree with Crista. We are free. People just gripe over nothing."

"I agree with Arturo. The rich run this country, and the rest of us are no better than slaves to them."

The teacher recognized Isaac's hand. "I've got to say, this whole question has been disturbing me for a long time. I'll admit it: my family is rich, and the rich have had more than their share of the power in this country for a long time. But not all rich are the same. My dad owns a good company, and he really wants things to get better for the people of Haiti—"

"Yeah," interrupted Arturo, "so long as he doesn't have to actually pay them good wages!"

"Now, wait—"

"Arturo!" said Professor Gabriel, interrupting Isaac. "We're avoiding personal attacks, remember? Now, let me see if I can redirect our conversation a little bit. What does true freedom look like? The U.S. President Franklin Roosevelt once gave a famous speech where he talked about 'Four Freedoms.' The first is freedom of speech and expression. We're using that one right now in this discussion. Right?"

Most of the students nodded their heads.

"The second freedom Roosevelt spoke about was freedom of every person to worship God in his own way. We are at a Christian university, and there are Protestant and Catholic universities throughout our country. But many in Haiti believe in Voodoo. So we do pretty well with religious inclusion, too, don't we?"

Arturo raised his hand. "Except I hear that in the United States, they really just want freedom for Christians and Jews, not Muslims or other faiths."

"Some say that," responded the professor, "but we are talking about Haiti here. So, let's move on. The third and fourth freedoms are where things get tricky in Haiti: freedom from want and freedom from fear. How many of you feel like you are free from those two?"

Only two or three raised their hands, but when they saw the absence of other hands throughout the room, they quickly dropped them.

"Yeah, those are tough ones," the professor continued. "But if you are only free to hide from a fear-inducing society and starve while you do it, how free are you?"

Arturo raised his hand again. "You see, that's why I stand with those brothers out on the street in Port-au-Prince right now. We've been poor too long, and nobody in the government seems to give a damn enough to do anything about it."

"Send the police after us – that's what they'll do!" said a male toward the back of the room, without being recognized by the prof.

"You got that right," added Arturo.

"But, wait a minute!" Crista said, as she stood, waving her arms in the air. Professor Gabriel recognized her, probably seeing she was going to speak anyway, but still wanting to maintain some kind of control. "You talk about freedom from fear. You think rich people in Haiti don't have fear? I get afraid when men like those raising hell in Port-au-Prince start taking over the streets!"

"About time, Bitch!" said Arturo. "Share in the fear!"

Professor Gabriel stood up and waved off the other hands which had shot up. "Look, this is an important conversation to have, but I'm going to cut it off completely if we can't be civil. And Arturo, you're the chief culprit here.

Save that rhetoric for the street, if you must, but I don't want it in my classroom! Understood?"

Arturo scowled, but he nodded his head.

Isaac raised his hand quickly and was recognized. He stood up and faced the class. "I know this is going to sound pretty wishy-washy, but I agree with both sides in this discussion. Arturo's right! A small group of rich business people have pulled the strings in Haiti for far too long. And while his approach might not have been the best, he deserves our thanks for being honest enough to say it. Thank you, Arturo!"

There was a smattering of applause throughout the room. Arturo looked around suspiciously, but then smiled a little.

"But I also agree with Crista. Not all rich people are the enemy, and violent protest is not getting us anywhere. With every President, we start out thinking this is the one who will make a difference, but then we get disappointed and people take to the streets to tear things up. We are much better at tearing down than we are at building. How does that help Haiti? So, thank you, Crista, for speaking up against the violence."

Once again there was applause, this time a little stronger.

"But both sides are not seeing something important: whether we are demanding it in the streets, or pleading for it in our legislative bodies, we've got to stop looking for someone else to 'fix' us. If Haiti is going to become what Toussaint Louverture and others envisioned when they fought for our freedom, then we have to look to ourselves!

We have to be the ones to make Haiti into a country of which we can be proud!"

This time the applause was louder and longer, but Daniel stood up from his seat and started waving his hand, and the professor called on him.

"Wow, Isaac! That speech was classic Isaac Breda stuff there—poetic and noble and all that, but you should get your head out of the clouds, because down here on earth, in Haiti, it's not going to work. College students like us aren't going to change Haiti. Right, Professor?"

Professor Gabriel shrugged. "Margaret Mead said, 'Never doubt that a small group of thoughtful, committed citizens can change the world. Indeed, it is the only thing that ever has.' I'm sorry, but she was a lot smarter than I'll ever be, so I'll go with her."

"It's what Toussaint did!" said Isaac, picking up his argument. "When he started out, he was just a slave. Call me crazy, but I think that was a little lower on the prestige list than 'college student'."

"Not much!" said Daniel, and the whole class laughed, even Isaac and Professor Gabriel.

"Toussaint didn't take the attitude, 'Who can I find to change things?' He changed them himself. And he gave his life to changing them."

"Yeah! Take to the streets!" shouted Arturo.

"I don't think that's what Toussaint would do," said Isaac. "Like I said, it hasn't been working for Haiti. But besides that, although Toussaint was a military man, at heart he was not one to tear things down. He was a bridge-builder. He built bridges between blacks, mulattoes and whites. He built bridges between Haiti and the United States, between Haiti and England, and between Haiti and Spain. And he rebuilt our economy by getting workers back to the fields. Yes, Dessalines was a tearer-down. But Toussaint was a builder-up."

"Excellent lesson, Professor Isaac!" said Professor Gabriel. And he initiated applause that spread throughout the class. He waited for Isaac to sit down and the applause to die completely before speaking again. "If I might, let me add to that lesson. This is a Christian University. As such, I want us to consider the case of what Christ did. It was a violent time. The Jewish people had for years been seeking to escape oppression and poverty. Deliverer after deliverer came along seeking to lead the people against Rome, and all of them fell. When Jesus of Nazareth came, many thought he would be the next one to lead a violent revolt. But he didn't. He entered Jerusalem on a donkey, a servant animal we see all the time in Haiti, rather than a war horse. He taught them that movements which live by the sword, die by the sword. Many people were disappointed in this approach, and scholars believe that was a vital factor in getting Christ crucified."

Professor Alexandre Gabriel paused to look at the faces of his class. Isaac turned around and noticed all were quiet and expectant. He could hear birds singing outside the windows.

"When they took Christ to trial, Pilate brought before the crowd another arrested man, and offered to free one of the two, Jesus of Nazareth or this other man, Barabbas. Barabbas was one who had been arrested in violent insurrection. But what a lot of people don't know is that the other man's full name was 'Jesus Barabbas.' The name 'Barabbas' meant 'son of the father.' Since Jesus of Nazareth also called himself the Son of his Father in heaven, the crowd's choice was between two men, both of whom referred to themselves as 'Jesus, Son of the Father.' – one a violent insurrectionist, and the other, the son of a carpenter, one who built things, instead of tearing them down. The crowd chose the man of violence; history has chosen the man of peace."

The bell rang. No one in the class moved. Professor Gabriel looked around at their faces. Then he said, "We'll continue this discussion next week," and he nodded his head for them to go.

Isaac remained seated meditatively in his chair as the rest of the class filed past. Several paused to pat him on the back or say 'good job'. Even Daniel winked and gave him a 'thumbs-up.' But the last two students in the room both pulled around a chair and sat opposite him. Arturo and Crista. They looked back and forth at each other, not without a little suspicion. But then both looked into Isaac's eyes.

"Okay, we're ready. Where do we start?" said Crista.

Arturo nodded his head. "Hey, if the others were honest, they'd say they just want to punch their ticket to get out of Haiti and to the United States. The two of us? Well, we aren't really, shall we say, 'too fond' of each other—"

"You called me a 'bitch' twice!" said Crista. "I'd say we disgust each other."

"Okay, we're a burr in each other's butt," said Arturo. "But we both think you have some good ideas, and we're ready to follow. So, like she said, *Where do we start?*"

Isaac's legs trembled. He had no idea if it was the result of fear or expectation. He had the feeling he would soon find out.

Chapter Nine

Mirebalais, Saint-Domingue, September, 1803

Isaac Louverture had much to regret. His initial choice of fighting for the French, instead of fighting alongside his father. Not accompanying his father to the Georges plantation on that fateful day when he was betrayed into the hands of Napoleon. And now, with his father's death in that cold dungeon at Fort de Joux, he had decided to fight with the forces of Jean-Jacques Dessalines.

The man was a butcher.

Dessalines had, in a letter widely published even in newspapers in the United States, vowed to continue the policies of Toussaint Louverture and never to tolerate the return of slavery to Saint-Domingue. But what he hadn't written about was the violence with which he would fulfill that mission. Isaac had seen mothers and children slaughtered alongside each other, for no strategic purpose other than Dessalines' hatred of white people. Isaac would not take part.

General Dessalines had ordered him to report to his command tent.

"Colonel Isaac Louverture, reporting as commanded, Sir." Isaac saluted as he spoke.

Jean-Jacques Dessalines scowled and returned the salute. "Didn't your father teach you to obey your commanding officers, Colonel Louverture?"

"Yes, Sir."

"Then, why have you disregarded my orders in relation to the throwing out of the white French garbage?"

"Begging your pardon, Monsieur, but my father also taught me the principle of war that you protect the lives of non-combatants."

General Dessalines' eyes blazed as he walked slowly to stand within centimeters of Isaac's now-blanched face. As he looked him straight on, Isaac felt as if that fire in the general's eye would burn right through him. "I have seen women and even children demand the severe lashing of slaves. I have seen them grin like demons at crucifixions of my friends and family. In a war against slavery, there are no 'non-combatants', Colonel!"

Isaac swallowed hard.

After what seemed to him like an eternity, General Dessalines turned and walked away. But then he spoke again, now a little more dispassionately. "Your father was also a biblical man, was he not, Colonel?"

"Yes, Sir."

"And then, did he not teach you about how the people of Israel were commanded by God to totally wipe out their enemy, including women and children, in cities like Jericho?"

"May I speak freely, Sir?"

Dessalines nodded.

"I am familiar with such passages, but my father preferred to emphasize the sayings of Jesus, like 'Blessed are the peacemakers,' and 'Love your enemies.' He believed these sayings taught the principles which would better adapt our country to rebuild and work with the other nations of the world—including primarily white nations—to make us a prosperous nation for all races."

Dessalines nodded again, as he walked away. Then he turned back toward Isaac once more and smiled. "Of course, his beliefs got him imprisoned and killed, while I am alive and now defeating the French. Do you suppose there is a connection?"

Isaac took the question to be rhetorical, and remained silent.

"Of course, there is a connection," said Dessalines. "Of course there is." He sat down in the only chair in the tent, behind a small table. He shuffled through some letters. Then he swiped them all onto the ground. "I hate papers! No one ever won a war with papers!"

"Most certainly true, Sir," said Isaac.

Dessalines stared into Isaac's eyes for perhaps thirty seconds. His expression softened. "I liked your father. I respected him. He was a good general."

"Thank you, Sir."

"For insubordination, I am demoting you to corporal," said Dessalines. "It is for your father's sake that I am not doing worse. That will be all, soldier."

Once outside, Isaac breathed a sigh of relief. It would not have been unlike Dessalines to have him executed. He knew of cases where the general had his own men killed for less. Still, he had to admit that Dessalines was making good progress against the French. His skill as a general was why at a meeting of military leaders on the Arcahaye plain, he had been declared the overall leader of the resistance against the French.

Nevertheless, Dessalines' jab at his father not being able to defeat the French rankled Isaac. His father had said all along that the key to defeating the French was holding them off until disease took its toll with the French soldiers. Previous to Toussaint's arrest, Dessalines had not been patient with that, and he had been among the first to capitulate. But after word of Toussaint's death had spread throughout the country, and after the people had heard of the reinstitution of slavery in nearby colonies like Guadeloupe, the people of Saint-Domingue had once again re-armed and taken to the mountains. When they had, it was quickly discovered how considerably weakened the French forces had become. The yellow fever had killed or placed in the hospital more French soldiers than remained in the field. Isaac had heard that no fewer than fourteen French generals had lost their lives in this plague, including General Leclerc.

The disease was indeed devastating to Europeans who had developed no immunity. It began in the brain with a pain that quickly became unbearable. Soon the victim was devoured by a burning thirst, and fiery veins streaked through their eyes. Sleep would be broken and troubled by convulsions. Their gums would become blackened and they would bleed from the mouth. Those who died quickly were considered fortunate.

Not only did the yellow fever result in depleted forces, but it also meant major disruption in military discipline. Soldiers refused orders that might expose them to the disease. Camaraderie among the troops all but disappeared, as none of the French soldiers wanted to associate with former friends, from whom they might catch the disease.

But of course Dessalines believed his success against these Europeans was only the result of his skill as a general.

Isaac's demotion really didn't bother him. Unlike his father, he was not one who naturally took to commanding others. What he wanted more than anything else in the world, was for the war to be over and for Saint-Domingue to be free. When that happened he would be able to smile and think of his father in peace.

As he thought further, there was one other thing he wanted. He wanted his mother and brothers to return with him to Ennery. Even if victory would come to Saint-Domingue, he doubted his mother would return. She was living now in Agen, France. She didn't want to come back to memories of what no longer was. When he had told her he was coming back, and that he needed to fight for his father's legacy, his mother's eyes glazed over.

"Well…Paris is a beautiful city," she had said. "So, if that is what you want, Dear."

"Not Paris, Mother. Saint-Domingue."

"Paris is a little far to visit often—I am getting old—but you will write, of course." She turned and walked out the back door toward her garden, while still talking. "Your father likes Paris. He told me so. When they let him out of that dreadful dungeon at Fort de Joux, perhaps he will want to visit you there." She bent over some flowers, and weeded around them.

Isaac, who had followed her out, helped her pull weeds. "Mother, I know Father's legacy is important to you as well. You were a slave once. We have a real chance now to end slavery forever in Saint-Domingue."

"Your father loves flowers, too. But they wouldn't let him have any of these at Fort de Joux. At Ennery, he always helped me with my flowers. That's the way he is. That is why I love him so much. Some believe it is below the dignity of a man to help his wife with flowers. But Toussaint is Toussaint. He loves flowers and he loves life, and he loves me. Perhaps I will take some of these with us when next we visit."

Isaac shook his head. "Mother, you know that Father—"

Placide had come out the door, and put his hand on his brother's shoulder. "Don't, Isaac. Let her tend her flowers. Just...don't."

When Isaac finally did leave, Suzanne Baptiste-Louverture, his mother and still referred to in Saint-Domingue as 'Dame-Consort', was again tending flowers. Only Placide and Saint-Jean, sickly ever since their imprisonment, had watched him ride away.

Making his way now down the streets of Mirebalais, Isaac wondered if he would ever see his family again.

Cap-Français, Saint-Domingue, October 1803

It was going to happen, and Henri Christophe knew it. Slavery coming back to Saint-Domingue. No sooner had they heard of Toussaint's tragic death in a cold, dank French dungeon, than white colonists were taking to the streets with a slogan: "No slavery, no colony!" It was frightening. Toussaint had warned about it happening many times. Black leaders of the country, who had wanted to believe the promises of the French, were now slapped in the face with a hard reality: many of the white leaders of the island believed reinstituting slavery was essential to Saint-Domingue remaining as a French colony.

Henri knew that those fighting for the freedom of Saint-Domingue had a big edge: the French forces were seriously depleted because of disease. The French knew of this edge as well, but that knowledge, rather than moving them to surrender or compromise, moved them toward a violence of desperation.

The French began waging war on the women and children of Saint-Domingue. Rochambeau had men, women and children all bound together and thrown into the ocean far from shore. If they managed to get free and approach shore, they were shot. Everywhere were whips, crosses, guillotines, impalement stakes and gallows used by soldiers and white citizens alike on the native populace. Their crime? Refusing to go back into slavery.

But the greater the violence, the greater the courage shown by the black people of Saint-Domingue. They encouraged each other to face death bravely, in the spirit of the early disciples facing the violence of Rome. Chevalier, a black army officer, hesitated at first when he saw what would be the instruments of his death. But the story was told across Saint-Domingue, that when his wife saw this, she said, "What! Do you not know how sweet it is to die for liberty!"

In another story told far and wide, a mother said to her daughters, as they were going to their execution, "Be glad. You will not be mothers of slaves."

Rochambeau could not be allowed to succeed. The martyrs must not have died in vain. The violence of the

French must be met with violence. Only then would the French realize they would never intimidate the black people of Saint-Domingue back into slavery. That's why when he rode to meet General Dessalines, he went prepared to cooperate with his strategies.

"Did you hear that I demoted Isaac?" said Dessalines, as he looked over his troops in the valley below.

"Oh? Why was that?"

"Too squeamish about shedding blood."

"He's a soldier," said Henri. "He's been shedding blood all his life. So, I assume by that you mean shedding the blood of women and children?"

"Correct."

"Yes, well, it is not easy," Henri said meditatively.

"War is not easy!" said Dessalines, as he turned his horse abruptly. The horse reared back, and for a moment Henri thought he would be struck by one of the powerful hooves. "We will win this war! And let me tell you, General, that while I was lenient with a colonel who resisted my order, because he was the son of Toussaint, I will not be so lenient should one of my generals show such resistance!"

Henri Christophe looked at Dessalines, and saw in his eyes a wild animal. Well had he earned his nickname – the Tiger. "General Dessalines, you need not worry about me. I see the necessity, and I will follow your orders unquestioningly."

Jean-Jacques Dessalines calmed his horse. Still, Henri Christophe could feel his superior's eyes staring right through him. For at least a minute he did not even talk. Then he turned and looked down at the valley below.

"Good," he said, "because very shortly you will be given the opportunity to prove yourself. Down below we have surrounded around 400 white colonists. Over half of them are women and children. You will be the one to give the order for their execution."

Henri felt a shiver throughout his body. He hoped it did not show. "As you wish, Monsieur."

From the moment they began their descent into the valley, Henri's head was swimming. Halfway down the mountainside he heard the screams. By the time he reached the place where the colonists were, the screams were deafening. Several women who had not yet been bound, ran up to him with pleading eyes.

"Execute me! Just not my children!" said one. "Please, if you have any compassion at all, not my children."

Henri looked away at once, and from that moment he did not look into the eyes of those who were soon to be victims. He heard their screams, their pleadings, their wailing. He couldn't help that. But he did not look into their eyes.

Then came the moment. All the colonists were bound, and a soldier was stationed behind each one, with a knife at their throat. Dessalines looked over at Henri and nodded. Henri let his gaze lift to the top of the trees which were rustling in the wind. There was a lump in his throat. He swallowed hard. Twice. Then he gathered all the energy he could muster, and shouted into the wind: "CUT THEIR THROATS!"

The screams and the wailing stopped quickly, but they did not so easily leave Henri Christophe's mind. He wanted to get his thoughts off of what had just happened, to fly away to a more pleasant time, a time when he felt proud, like the christening of his grandson, or the first time that grandson said, "I love you." But his thoughts could not long leave that moment, because they were called back by a strong aroma. *What was that smell?* But then Henri realized he most certainly knew. He had smelled it many times before.

The smell of blood. Pungent. Acrid. Offensive. It penetrating Henri's nostrils, as if seeking to worm its way down to a familiar home, his own rapidly-beating heart. Henri violently expelled the air from his nose, and put his gloved hand over that orifice. He would have gladly deprived himself of air altogether if it meant relieving himself of that odor.

General Henry Christophe had always believed he could survive anything the French did to him. What he didn't know was whether he could survive what he had just done to himself.

Cap Haitien, Haiti, January 1, 1804

Isaac knew this day would come, and he only wished his father could have been there to see it. Expectation had been building over several months. Henri Christophe had led his part of the army to some decisive victories in the North; to the West, Isaac had personally fought under Jean-Jacques Dessalines in the battle of Vertières, and they had put that section of the country firmly under the control of the indigenous army; while the forces under Alexander Pétion secured the South. With France increasingly occupied with England, they could afford to send no more reinforcements. The end had been assured.

Rochambeau offered to capitulate. On the 19th of November of 1803, the articles had been signed. The French would have to evacuate Cap-Français within ten days, with all their artillery, ammunition and magazines. They would withdraw to their ships with the guarantee of their personal property, and they would leave their sick and wounded in the hospitals, with black nurses caring for them until they were well. Survivors would be sent by neutral ships back to France. Isaac believed these conditions were more favorable than the invading army had a right to expect.

Now it was all going to be made official. Jean-Jacques Dessalines ascended the recently-constructed platform in front of thousands of people flooding the streets of the city formerly known as Cap-Français. They were cheering and dancing and shouting blessings in Creole. Dessalines raised his hands high and they quieted down.

"This is a great day!" he proclaimed. "On this first day of a new year, I proclaim this to be a new country. This country is no longer France's colony."

People again cheered wildly, and Dessalines waited for them to become quiet enough for him to speak. "This is no longer a white people's country!"

Again came the resounding cheers.

"This is no longer a country that can be owned or controlled by any foreign government!"

More cheers.

"This is, finally and forever, OUR COUNTRY!"

The streets now erupted in dancing and singing, and Isaac wondered if Dessalines would ever again regain control. But with Dessalines and several of his generals jumping and waving their hands downward for calm, the crowd finally quieted again.

"Because this is our country, it can no longer retain a name given it by our oppressive enemy. We are no longer Saint-Domingue. This is a land of mountains. Those mountains sheltered us and nurtured us like a mother during our long and torturous struggle. Therefore, this land needs a name that honors our mountains. The Taino people who lived here before the French invaded, and before we were brought here through French oppression, had a word which meant 'land of mountains.' I therefore declare that word to be the new name for our newly-freed country. I declare the name of our country to be 'Haiti' and the name of this city to now be 'Cap-Haitien'!"

Isaac didn't know if Dessalines had planned to say more. But at that moment the people in the streets went from wild cheering to a repetitive chant that none of the leaders could have possibly wished to quell.

"FREEDOM! FREEDOM! FREEDOM!" All around him Isaac saw eyes which, though they shed tears, were full of hope. "FREEDOM! FREEDOM! FREEDOM!"

Isaac joined in the shouting and he fully believed his father was shouting that word through Isaac's own voice. "FREEDOM! FREEDOM! FREEDOM!"

But as Isaac later left that celebration, a quieter voice came to his head: *Now, make it real. Make it real!*

Chapter Ten

New York City, USA, May 2017

Marie-Noëlle strutted down the catwalk, convinced that every pair of male eyes leering at her were Isaac's eyes. And so she lured in every pair. She wheeled around, smiling, arms held high and breasts pushing against the black sheer fabric of the new lingerie, sure that guy in the third row was Isaac, looking at her with passion and pride. As she swung her near-naked hips saucily down the catwalk, she felt Isaac's appreciative gaze following her every step from behind. And as she stood, proud and erect, at the end of that catwalk, showing no signs of embarrassment or uncertainty, defiantly flipping her jet-black hair back to reveal her glowing face, sitting right below her, she knew, was her Haitian boyfriend, embracing her soft curves with his eyes.

Even the roar of the applause, upon her turning to exit, was his, amplified in her mind.

Still, there were a few things she knew right away were not Isaac's. The arm which swung around her waist when she hit backstage. The hand which patted her bottom. And the cigarette-smoke lips which planted themselves on her right cheek.

"Sweetheart, you killed out there!" the man said, as she gently removed his hand from her derriere. "I can hear all the Tweets already: 'Marie-Noëlle, the new Queen of Fifth Avenue!'"

She smiled stiffly. "Thanks, Eric. I know I owe you a lot for all your help."

"Yeah, you do, but, hey, I have an easy repayment plan. Why don't you come over to my apartment, and we can talk about it?"

Marie-Noëlle grabbed a robe to cover herself and gave him a pouty look. "Sorry, can't. Ashley has been really good about getting me connected with some Haitian people she thought it would be helpful for me to know. Here in a little bit, I'm going to get together with Karissa. I knew about her when I was back in Haiti. She is so beautiful! Most famous model from Haiti ever."

"Well, that can't take long," said Eric. "Afterwards, we could—"

"Afterwards, I promised my brother I would hang out with him and his friends at Rutgers."

"RUTGERS? Isn't that in—"

"New Jersey," responded Marie-Noëlle. "Yes, it is."

Eric appeared dazed. "I don't think I've ever been stood up for New Jersey before."

Ashley peeked around the corner. "Yeah, you don't want to go there, hon. You have a reputation to protect now."

Jessica, an older model standing nearby in the hall, gave her a playful wink. "OMG, yes! Some photographer catches you on the wrong side of the Holland Tunnel, and you'll be peddling flowers in Central Park for the rest of your career!"

Marie-Noëlle rolled her eyes. "He's my brother – I'll risk it."

Eric pulled her aside. "Seriously, I hope you're not saying 'no' to spending time with me at my apartment.

There's a lot I can do for you, but I've got to know that the models I work with are…comfortable with me, personally."

Marie-Noëlle blushed. "Oh, sure, Eric! I want to spend time with you. I mean, who wouldn't? But things are pretty hectic right now, you know? Just give me a little time—"

Ashley put her hand on Marie-Noëlle's shoulder. "Karissa has some time to see you now. Better come right away. She has to head off to a photo shoot."

Marie-Noëlle hoped her sigh of relief was not too obvious. She smiled at Eric. "Gotta go. But we'll get together. Promise."

She kissed him on the cheek, then turned quickly and followed Ashley down the hall. Ashley grabbed Marie-Noëlle's arm, leaned her way and whispered. "Eric doesn't take 'no' easily, if you know what I mean. Not that he hears it a lot." She knocked at Karissa's dressing room door. "Just a word to the wise."

"Come in," came a voice from inside the room. Ashley opened the door and motioned Marie-Noëlle to enter.

"Byenveni, plezi ak sè!" Karissa stood and opened her arms to her guest.

Marie-Noëlle smiled and shut the door behind her. "Oh, my God! To be greeted in Creole and to be called 'sister' by you at the same time! I feel like I am home." She walked into Karissa's embrace.

Karissa was far too animated a person to remain in a stationary embrace for long. She pulled back and eyed her visitor. "Yes! Yes!" she said, motioning toward Marie-Noëlle's physique. "You are every bit as beautiful as they told me!"

"So, how are they treating you around here?" Karissa asked.

"Oh, fine, fine. I mean, they're mostly nice, but I'm not always sure what is expected of me, or how I should act, you know?"

"You're not alone there, that's for sure," said Karissa. "But let me share a perspective which might seem cynical, but will save you a lot of grief, okay? Don't expect to be treated like an actual person! Write that down and refer to it often, and you will be fine. If you expect to be treated as an actual person, you will be hurt. What you are for most people around here is fresh meat."

"Fresh meat?"

"A new body with which to tantalize sexual carnivores."

"Like Eric?"

"Oh, God. Especially Eric," said Karissa. "Has he been pressuring you?"

"That would be putting it mildly."

"Not surprised. There will be others – not all male, and not all as good-looking as Eric. You have some decisions to make."

"Decisions?"

"Damn straight, sister. Decisions about where to put the calluses. I highly suggest you string them from your heart right down to your vagina."

Marie-Noëlle grimaced. "Not a pleasant place for calluses."

"Tell me about it," said the more experienced model. "New York is a tough place to survive for a young Haitian girl who wants to keep her heart and maintain any semblance of romantic sexual relationship."

"You've had difficulty?"

Karissa's expression clouded over. "Got a boyfriend you want to keep?"

Marie-Noëlle nodded.

"Good luck with that. Didn't work for me." She seemed lost in memories. "He couldn't handle it all."

"My boyfriend didn't want me to leave Haiti," Marie-Noëlle said, after a long pause. "He wanted me to stay and help him make things better in our country."

Karissa smiled. "An idealist, huh?"

Marie-Noëlle nodded. "He's actually a descendent of Toussaint, so I guess he comes by it naturally."

Karissa's eyes widened. "Wow!"

"Do you think I should have stayed?"

Karissa shrugged. "I can't answer that question for you. We women still have a lot to learn about balancing career and love life, that's for sure. But, I love all the idealism and love of Haiti I'm hearing. Did you know I produced a video on Haiti?"

"No!"

"I wanted people in the United States to know Haiti is more than just a poor country that keeps going through crises. I wanted people to know there is a lot of beauty – in the land and in the people." She struck a glamour pose, with her hands on her hips and a glint in her eyes. "It was nominated for an Oscar for 'Best Documentary Film!'"

Marie-Noëlle applauded. "You go, girl!"

"And I send half my income back to help family and others improve their lot in Haiti." She sat down again. "So, you can do both—advance your career and help Haiti."

"But Isaac—he's my boyfriend—Isaac thinks what

Haiti needs is for the most gifted Haitians to stop leaving, and to stay there and invest themselves in the country."

"He has a point," said Karissa. "But what are these home-staying Haitians going to do without good jobs or major financial support from the outside, tell me that?"

Marie-Noëlle shrugged. "I guess that's why I'm here."

"And you like modeling?"

"Yeah, it's a kick!" Marie-Noëlle blushed. "I guess I kind of like showing off my body. But sometimes they try to push me a little too far."

"Understood," said Karissa. "I lost a movie part not long ago because I didn't want to take off my top."

"I get it. And then there is the whole thing of being true to Isaac…"

Someone knocked on the door. A voice came from outside. "Karissa, it's time for your photo shoot."

"Be right there," said Karissa. She gave Marie-Noëlle one more embrace. "Hang in there, girl. You're a winner. I know it!"

And the way Karissa said it, Marie-Noëlle believed it just might be true.

When Marie-Noëlle reached the front door of the Chi Psi fraternity at Rutgers, Henri was there waiting for her. He threw his arms around her. Marie-Noëlle could not remember a time when he had hugged her so hard or so long. When he pulled away, his eyes actually looked a little teary, but that did not inhibit his personal style.

"Oh, my God," he said, "is this that bratty little sister I grew up with, or is this Marie-Noëlle, the hot New York model I have been hearing about?"

One of Henri's black American frat brothers came up from behind him, looked over the top of his sunglasses, and smiled. "Hell, no! Ain't no way this babelicious, hot mama is sister to a dork like you." He shoved Henri aside and took Marie-Noëlle's right hand in both of his. "Hey, gorgeous, they call me 'Smooth Bobby.' 'Cuz I am! Why don't you and I leave this stuffy old dork palace, and I'll show you what NJ has that makes that 'Big Apple' look like a shriveled old pea?"

Before Marie-Noëlle could respond, Henri intervened. "Back off! Back off!" He directed the words not only at 'Smooth Bobby', but also several other frat brothers, of various races, who now swarmed around them. "Do I have to ask the groundskeeper to hose you guys down?"

His frat brothers pulled back only a little. "Hey, you going to be in the Sports Illustrated Swimsuit edition?" a short, pudgy Hispanic guy asked.

Marie-Noëlle smiled and shrugged. "They want me to go to the audition, which is tomorrow, so…maybe."

The pudgy Latino got wide-eyed. "Are you going to let them do you in body paint?"

Marie-Noëlle shrugged again and looked at her brother. Henri rolled his eyes. "What Little Ricky over there is talking about is, what Sports Illustrated sometimes does, is take a totally naked model and paint an acrylic 'swimsuit' on them. So you would be out on the beach, in fact, TOTALLY NAKED."

It was Marie-Noëlle's turn to be wide-eyed. "Uh…"

"It's actually just like having a real swimsuit on," said a tall white guy on the periphery. "Very tasteful. At least that's how it looks in the magazine."

She put her hands up like two stop signs. "Hey, I appreciate all this male attention, I really do. But I came here to see my twin brother, and we have limited time—"

"TWIN brother?" said Smooth Bobby in mock horror. "Seriously? You came from the same rock n' roll in the sack by the same parents as SHE did? Did the nurses dip you in UGLY sauce? Really, man. You should file suit against that hospital."

Henri put his hands on his sister's shoulders, and looked her straight in the eyes. "It has been revealed to me from on high that this group of frat brothers is God's way of paying me back for every smart-ass thing I have ever said to you. So, from the bottom of my heart, I apologize for it all."

Marie-Noëlle took her brother's arm, and smiled and waved at the other guys. "Then it seems you guys have performed an invaluable service to the entire world, and I thank you all!"

Henri rolled his eyes, but then, silent and chastened, walked his sister up to his room.

"It looks like you have a really fun group of friends here," Marie-Noëlle said, as Henri shut the door behind them. "I hope you aren't taking too seriously what Smooth Bobbie said about your being ugly, though, because you're not."

"Oh, God, Sis, next to you any guy in the world would be ugly. I've learned to live with that. My ego is not that fragile."

Marie-Noëlle walked over to her brother's window and looked at the sun setting over New Brunswick. "I wish I could make friends as easily as you."

"You've not made any?" He flopped down on his bed.

"One, maybe. Just today. Karissa, another Haitian model."

"Karissa? Wow. Bring her over here, and the two of you will create riots."

Marie-Noëlle sat down on the edge of the bed. "Yeah, she could be a good friend, if we could get much time together. That will be really hard in our business. Everyone else I meet, I'm wondering what they want from me."

Henri seemed lost in thought, and didn't respond to his sister's last statement. But after a minute or so he sat up and looked her in the eye. "Do you miss Isaac?"

Marie-Noëlle nodded.

"I do too," he said. "My frat buddies are great, but we have no history together. I'm not always sure I can trust them."

His sister laughed. "I'm not sure I can trust anyone here." She turned more melancholy. "We talk on the phone every day, and we've Skyped each other a couple of times. But I miss his touch. I miss him holding me. When I'm wearing something skimpy for a shoot, I want it to be Isaac I am showing off my body for—"

Henri stood up quickly and threw his hands over his eyes. "Whoa! Whoa! Too much information! BROTHER HERE!" He looked back down at her. "It was bad enough when that Little Ricky perv was talking about you in body paint!"

Marie-Noëlle rolled her eyes. "Oh, grow up!"

Henri walked over and looked out his window. "You know, looking out this window is not nearly as depressing as looking out my window in Cap Haitien. A lot of nice cars.

Fewer desperate-looking people. No garbage in the streets. Still, I've got to admit, I miss Haiti. Am I crazy?"

"Maybe a little." Marie-Noëlle smiled cockily at her brother. "Of course, if missing Haiti is what makes you crazy, then I'll be right there with you when they ship you to the funny farm. I miss it too. Maybe it's just because it is home."

"Yeah. Or maybe it's a little how people treat you," said Henri. "When you are a young black guy here, you walk in some neighborhoods, and you feel like there are white people sitting at their windows with their rifles cocked."

"A little paranoid, don't you think?" said Marie-Noëlle.

"'Just because you're paranoid—"

"'Doesn't mean they aren't out to get you!' – I know."

They both laughed.

"Did we make a mistake?" asked Henri.

Marie-Noëlle shrugged. "I've been asking myself that question a lot. But I think it's too soon to tell. One thing I know: I can make one hell of a lot of money as a model here, and all that money can do a lot to help in Haiti, to help Isaac with all his ideas of making Haiti better."

Henri nodded. "And Rutgers is a great school. I feel I am running two steps behind all the time, but I sure am learning a lot. The education can give me a good future whichever way I go."

Marie-Noëlle walked over to a row of books Henri had on the top of his desk, and looked them over. "So, for this good education you're getting, what are they having you read? Anything interesting?"

"You're a model. What do you care? So long as you can read the fashion magazines…"

She sent her brother her best glare.

"Only kidding!"

"Yeah, just for that I'm stealing whatever book I want and never bringing it back."

"Well, if you're willing to take my tests for me—"

"The name of a good book – NOW!" Marie-Noëlle placed her hand firmly on a book near one of the bookends. "Or I push all of these books onto the floor – no mercy!"

"Alright! Alright!" He looked over at the titles on the desk. "Okay, I'm taking a class in contemporary American literature, and I just finished a book called *The Invention of Wings*, by Sue Monk Kidd. It's about some women in the American South who fought against slavery. Before their Civil War, but after our Revolution. It wasn't my thing, but I think you would like it. It's there in the middle of the shelf."

Marie-Noëlle picked up the book, glanced at its cover, and then turned to the opening page. It spoke of an African myth where people could fly. She thought of a childhood dream she frequently had where when something scary was chasing her, she suddenly would realize she could soar into the heavens. She would lift her arms and fly above all that was frightening, all that was even unpleasant. How she wished, even today, it hadn't been just a dream.

She was only intending to read a few paragraphs, but one paragraph led to another, and then to another. Before she knew it, she looked up at the clock on the wall and a half hour had passed.

Henri was shaking his head and smiling at her. "Hey, if you were bored with my company, you could have just told me."

Marie-Noëlle ignored her brother's sarcasm. "Did you say you finished this book?"

"Yeah. You want to borrow it?"

"Sure. If that's okay?"

Henri nodded.

She looked out the window and noticed the sun had set. "Wow. It's getting late. Maybe I should get going."

"What did you have in mind for getting back to the train station?"

"Oh, it's not that far," said Marie-Noëlle. "I thought I would walk."

Her brother visibly cringed. "Girl! In these neighborhoods, anything farther than crossing the street at night, is a long walk! Can't you afford a cab?"

"I want to save my money to send to Haiti. Look, I'll be all right."

"Ugh!" Henri shut his eyes and shook his head. "Ain't happening. Me and my frat buddies will walk you there. They'll relish the chance to appear macho."

Marie-Noëlle's eyes widened. "And who is going to protect me from *them*?"

"They'll behave. I'll make them."

Smooth Bobby, Little Ricky and Henri's tall white friend, Johnny James, all agreed to be part of the escort, but they hadn't reached the first street corner before Henri's promise of protection had to be called into play.

"You know, this really is a dangerous city," said Smooth Bobby. "I don't think we should risk it. Your sister should just stay with me in my room and—"

"Cut that crap or go back!" injected Henri. "My sister needs protection here, not harassment."

"All right! All right!" said Smooth Bobby. "I was only trying to be hospitable to an out-of-towner!" He winked at Marie-Noëlle.

The walk was a little longer than the Haitian model had realized, and as they walked past a few nicer homes, she noticed a police car had done a U-turn and was now coming up slowly behind them.

Henri pulled his hood up over his head. "Company!"

"We're not doing anything!" protested Marie-Noëlle.

"Doesn't matter," her brother said.

Smooth Bobby gave Johnny James a firm nudge. "Okay, John Boy, lift your shirt and show them how white you are."

The lights on the police car flashed.

"Too late," moaned Smooth Bobby.

The car stopped beside the road, and two white officers got out. They circled the group of walkers in opposite directions, and eyed each one carefully.

"Something wrong, officers?" asked Henri.

The officers ignored the question. The younger one stopped in front of Marie-Noëlle and smiled lasciviously. The older officer stopped in front of Henri.

"Mind telling us where you kids are heading this late in this neighborhood?" asked the older one.

"We're students at Rutgers," said Henri. "My friends and I are walking my sister to the train station, so she can get back to Manhattan."

"Hey, we would be glad to give ya sista' a ride!" said the young officer, grinning at her from barely a foot away.

Marie-Noëlle didn't smile.

"Don't recognize that accent," said the older officer. "Where are you from?"

"Haiti," said Henri.

"Here legally?"

"Student visa," said Henri. "My sister has a work visa."

The officer nodded. "I'll need to see ID from all of you."

Smooth Bobby's eyes opened wide. "Even the white guy?"

The officer got right in Smooth Bobby's face and scowled. "I know it might not be popular these days among you people, but we expect a little respect for officers of the law. Now, is that a problem for you?"

Smooth Bobby looked down at the ground, and shook his head. "No, Sir," he said quietly.

"Then I'll need ID from ALL of you!"

Marie-Noëlle pulled out her student visa and gave it to the older officer, and the others responded in kind.

"Wait here," said the officer, as he took the IDs back to his vehicle. Marie-Noëlle looked up toward the surrounding tree tops. She couldn't have said why, except that the alternatives seemed to be looking at the younger officer, who was still leering at her, or looking down at the ground. The latter response seemed mysteriously out of character for Smooth Bobby, and she herself would never be comfortable with such a submissive posture.

The older officer returned within 10 minutes, and handed their ID back to them. "Okay, you check out. There have been reports of several burglaries in the area, and so we're keeping a close eye out. Sorry for the inconvenience. You can go now."

"Don't ya think we should search 'em first," said the younger officer, still gazing lecherously at Marie-Noëlle.

She shuddered.

"No, Officer Jenson, I don't," said the one who was apparently the senior partner. "Let's get back to our rounds." Then he looked over at Marie-Noëlle himself, and tipped his hat. "And good luck with the SI audition tomorrow."

Marie-Noëlle cocked her head and narrowed her eyes to slits. "Okay...thanks, I guess."

After the officers pulled away, Henri looked over at his sister. "How did he know about your SI audition?"

"Hey, they probably know what she ate for breakfast this morning," said Johnny James. "It's scary what people know about you today."

"You're not lyin' there," said Little Ricky. "I've been stopped three times by ICE, and I was born in frickin' Queens! Anyway, after the third time I got a little pissed, and I told them that. They not only knew I was born in Queens, they knew the name of the hospital and the doctor who delivered me!"

"First time I've ever been stopped," said Johnny James.

"Surprise, surprise!" said Little Ricky. "Why EVER do you suppose that would be?"

"Hey, we better get moving before the FBI thinks they should question us," said Henri. "Besides, it's getting kind of cold out here."

"Haitians!" said Little Ricky. "It drops below 80 degrees, and you're shopping for long underwear."

They started walking again, but as they did, Marie-Noëlle noticed Smooth Bobby still looking down at the ground. "Hey, Smooth Bobby. What are you thinking, walking over there by yourself?"

He looked up. In the short time she had known him, this was the first time she had seen his face without even the trace of a smile. "Do you guys think I'm a chicken shit?"

"A chicken shit?" said Henri. "Why would we think that?"

"Because I backed down," Smooth Bobby said. A tear escaped from the corner of his left eye. "In the old neighborhood, they would have called me a chicken shit."

"Yeah, well, how many of those guys get out of that neighborhood and end up at Rutgers?" said Little Ricky. "Tell me that!"

Smooth Bobby shrugged. "Not many."

"You did the smart thing," said Marie-Noëlle. "You don't want to get kicked out of school because of trouble with the law."

"True," said the stout young black man. "But sometimes you just get tired of it all – having your nose pushed down into the gutter because your skin isn't the right color."

Marie-Noëlle walked up beside Smooth Bobby, gave him a quick hug and a kiss on the cheek. His smile returned.

They had walked over a full block before anyone else spoke, but then Little Ricky broke the silence.

"You know, I have some 'tough neighborhood' stories as well," he said, while glancing over at Marie-Noëlle. "...for what it's worth."

"I could make some up," said Johnny James, with a sly grin.

Marie-Noëlle rolled her eyes. "What the hell? I'm glad I didn't have to walk this far alone." She gave them both a kiss on the cheek.

"Okay, I'm totally buying the SI Swimsuit edition if you are in it," said Little Ricky. "Totally!"

When they reached the New Brunswick station of the NJ Transit – Northeast Corridor line, the train to Manhattan had just pulled up. Since she didn't want to wait for the next one, Marie-Noëlle hurriedly gave her brother a hug, thanked all her escorts, and rushed to the boarding platform.

It had been a full day, and she still hadn't had a chance to call Isaac. She had much to tell, but also, perhaps, much that would have to go without telling.

Chapter Eleven

Isaac Louverture was so immobile, sitting in the chair in Henri Christophe's office, that he would have understood if an outside observer would have mistaken him for a statue. Getting up close, however, they might have heard the heavy thumping in his chest, and they might have noticed the moisture forming over his reddened eyes.

"I don't think this is what my father had in mind," he finally said.

Surprised by the sudden vocalization, Henri Christophe turned and looked at the younger man. Then he shook his head. "I'm not sure it's what any of us had in mind." He scowled. "Except for, perhaps, 'King Jacques'!"

"He's slaughtered nearly 5,000 white people." Just saying those words took Isaac's breath away for a moment, but he continued. "It's as if he doesn't know the war is over. I know personally that many of those whites supported our cause. If they hadn't, they would have left with Rochambeau."

"Your father would not have tolerated it."

Isaac slowly shook his head. "My heart was so full of pride when Dessalines declared us a new nation. But I can't be proud of this. I couldn't even handle it when he was killing civilians during the war."

Henri Christophe quickly turned away from Isaac, picked up some reports, and shuffled through them in what seemed to Isaac an absent-minded way.

"Did I say something to offend you?" asked Isaac.

"No, of course not," Christophe replied without even turning around. "I simply have many matters occupying my mind right now. King Jacques might think he is running this country all by himself, but there are others of us who have much to do." Christophe tossed the reports back on his desk, and walked over to his window to gaze out at the street below. He spoke now almost as if he were talking to himself, quietly and meditatively. "Do you think...I could rule this country better than Dessalines?"

"Would you kill civilians and work the people as if slavery were never outlawed?"

"Of course not."

"Then you would be a welcome change." Isaac joined his father's old friend at the window. "Are some talking of this change?"

Christophe nodded. "There are many who are unhappy."

"And they want you to take his place?"

The old general shrugged. "Well a few prefer Alexandre Pétion, but what does that man know?"

"And would Dessalines go peacefully?"

Christophe turned and looked Isaac in the eye. "Dessalines does not do anything peacefully."

"The country needs peaceful transition right now."

Christophe nodded. "That's how it would have been had your father been around. Under his governorship, during that too brief time, our country rose from her ruins, and everything seemed to promise a happy future."

Isaac looked out the window at the street below. The people he saw were trudging along, uncertain of where to go. "On that January day when Dessalines declared us to be an independent nation, I heard my father's voice."

"What did it say?"

"He called us to make it real," Isaac said. "He knew the hope in our hearts, and wanted that hope to be based on more than a change of name, and a different oppressor. He wanted to see the smiles in the eyes of all the people, black, white and mixed race, because all would have a legitimate chance at a better tomorrow." Isaac shifted his gaze to Christophe. "Look out this window! Do you see that hope in the eyes of the people?"

Christophe shook his head.

"We must insist on nothing less," said Isaac.

Christophe turned quickly, and went back to his desk. "I have much business to which I must attend. When you write to your mother, please send her my love." He paused and looked back at Isaac. "Oh, and my condolences to both you and your family. I heard of the death of Saint-Jean."

Isaac nodded slowly as he walked toward the door. "Thank you. The prison at Fort de Joux was particularly hard on him. He never fully recovered." Isaac paused at the door, and looked back at Christophe. "And you will at least seek to resolve things with Dessalines in a peaceful way?"

Christophe avoided Isaac's eyes. "I will do what I can do. As I told you, I am not the only one involved."

Isaac found no comfort in that response, but he also knew there was little more he could do. "And congratulations to you, Monsieur, on the birth of your son, Jacques-Victor."

Christophe gave him a stiff smile, and went back to his work.

Near Milot, Haiti, December, 1806

Henri Christophe stood on top of the *Bonnet a L'Eveque* mountain, and looked out toward the sea. *What if they come now?* he thought. *What if French sails spread all across the horizon, with my forces not ready?* He cast a glance down to his left to the path coming up the mountain. Bodies strained to pull the enormous boulders along the path on sleds. Ten men per boulder, moving them perhaps a few meters per minute.

Henri shouted down at the officers who supervised the work. "Faster! They must work faster! By the God of heaven, any day it could be too late!"

Three officers responded quickly, lashing with their whips the backs of the Haitian workers. A fourth looked up at Henri, and ran up the trail to where he stood.

"Begging your pardon, Monsieur," the officer said. "I am Colonel Manuel. Might I have a word?"

"That depends on what you wish to say."

The officer stood speechless for a moment. Henri could see he was trying to suppress his trembling. Then he braved to speak. "Your plan to build a fortress here most certainly shows your genius, Monsieur. Once this is constructed, the French will think long and hard before attempting to invade our beloved land."

"Those are my thoughts, exactly."

"By this plan you have shown you are far wiser than that despot, Dessalines – may his soul now rot in hell."

"I did not kill that man!" said Christophe, defensively. "That was done by Alexandre Pétion, by his own admission!"

"Most certainly, Monsieur!" Colonel Manuel said. "And we all know that the people in the south of our country will soon realize you are a far better ruler than Pétion, and you will rule over all of Haiti."

"And what is your point?"

The officer cleared his throat. "The people of the *Plaine-du-Nord* have been working hard on this project, which you were so wise to propose. They are working hard because they believe in you, and they believe in our new country. However, when you, in your understandable enthusiasm to build quickly, have them whipped and driven hard…well, some are beginning to wonder if you are as harsh as Dessalines. I correct them, of course! I tell them you push them out of your love for Haiti, and your desire to keep them from falling back into slavery. But the task of convincing them would be so much easier—"

Henri felt the rage boiling within him. His angry stare made the officer cringe.

"With all respect, I am only saying—"

The voices came to Henri Christophe's head. *Cut his throat! Spill his blood! You've done it so often now. It's easy.*

"Monsieur? Are you all right?"

Henri's words came out in a growl. "So. You are seeking to kill me now, too…is that it?"

"No! No! Certainly not. I was only saying—"

Henri waved toward a couple of the officer's down below, and they came quickly. "Arrest this man. He is leading a rebellion against me."

143

"No! I—"

The other two officers quickly disarmed Colonel Manuel, which caused the man's rage to break forth. "You arrest me because I warn you of a danger? Then you are the same as Dessalines, and you deserve the same fate! Already hundreds of men have died working on this project, and yet you work them like slaves! Many wonder how this is any different than under the French!"

Henri Christophe pulled out his pistol and shot the man in the face, propelling his body down the side of the mountain. The colonel's blood splattered over the ground and the arresting officers, as well as the hand with which Christophe held the weapon.

He looked around at the other trembling officers, as well as the workers nearby. "Are there others among you who would like to question my leadership?"

All around him shook their heads.

"Then back to work! And leave that man's body there as a warning!"

The men around him immediately obeyed, and once again the boulders moved up the mountain. One officer, however, came up to Christophe and bowed. "A thousand pardons, Monsieur, but if you would, I have been asked to convey a message from a dear friend of yours."

"Yes?"

"Corporal Isaac Louverture, son of Toussaint, would like an audience."

Christophe's body stiffened. "Tell him I have too much to do saving this country, to visit with a demoted corporal."

"As you wish, Monsieur."

And the voices in Henri Christophe's head approved.

Ennery, Haiti, March, 1807

Isaac Louverture loved working outside on their coffee trees. Perhaps it was, in part, because he remembered his father doing it, and that made him feel closer to the man. But there were other reasons as well. He enjoyed knowing he was contributing to the country's economy, and doing so without oppressing the people who worked for him. Isaac worked right alongside them, and when he took a break, so did they. That was the way it should be.

Isaac was proud of Haiti's coffee. There had been a time when Haiti produced over half of the world's coffee. When he had lived in France he would always smile when he heard the French people remark about how much they preferred the Haitian product. Of course, now their share of the market was substantially down. The terror perpetrated by Dessalines on whites had shocked people in the United States, especially in the slave-holding southern part of that country, and that devastated trade. Other countries showed a similar reticence. Strangely enough, only France continued to import such products from Haiti. For them, it seemed, a good cup of coffee was more important than politics.

With the exception of his own farm, however, Isaac had serious concerns about how the crop was being produced. Henri Christophe, in this northern section of the country, sought to maintain the plantation system, with its requirement of forced labor. Isaac was very disappointed in this direction established by the old family friend. It was little different than slavery. While Isaac had his issues with Alexandre Pétion's rule in the south, at least that man had the wisdom to divide the plantations and give them to poor workers.

Isaac wished he didn't have to think about Henri Christophe at all. When the man refused to give him an audience over the abuse of Haitians building the fortress on the *Bonnet a L'Eveque* mountain, Isaac had been crushed. He no longer wanted to fight under him, so he convinced Christophe by letter to allow him to resign from the army to tend his family's farm at Ennery. The production was needed. But even this didn't keep the reports of abuse from reaching Isaac's ears.

Isaac heard a horse galloping toward him and looked in its direction. An army officer was riding his way, and the face was familiar. Simon Armand, a loyal friend.

Isaac turned to a servant working a few meters away on another coffee tree. "Pass the word along to stop work for lunch."

The servant did as instructed, while Isaac walked slowly towards the visitor. "Greetings, Simon!" he said. "To what do I owe the pleasure of the visit of an old army friend?"

"Officially?" Simon said as he dismounted. "Officially, I am here to check on how your coffee is doing. Christophe is interested."

"And unofficially?"

Simon tied his horse to a post. "Unofficially? Can we talk someplace more private?"

"Certainly. Come inside."

A house servant brought coffee and pastries. Both men sat down at the table, but Simon ignored the offerings and leaned in Isaac's direction. "You can't just hide here from what Christophe is doing, Isaac. Your father wouldn't and you can't either."

Isaac felt his body stiffen. "I'm not hiding."

146

"Pardon the brashness of a friend," said Simon, "but you are. Christophe had a good relationship with your father, and because of that, you have influence with him. You must use it. Thousands have died. Thousands!"

"I tried to influence him. You know that! When you told him I wanted an audience with him, he refused, referring to me as 'a demoted corporal.'"

"And so you give up?"

Isaac stared into his coffee. Normally, the aroma alone would calm him. Now that aroma was fighting a losing battle. His gaze shifted back to his friend. "I'm not giving up. I'm simply not sure what to do about it right now. Pétion and his men assassinated Dessalines—"

"...And Christophe knew, and didn't stop him!"

Isaac nodded. "Yes, that's true. But then Christophe became like Dessalines, and Pétion's rule in the south is not much better."

"Pétion does not maintain the plantation system, with its forced labor."

"No, but he does have people killed. And while Christophe at least provides for the education of the poor, Pétion only educates the rich. In French! How will things get better for Haiti if we don't educate the poor?"

Simon threw his hands up in frustration. "I'm not defending Pétion. I simply think we need to get rid of Christophe!"

"But don't you see? That only adds to the instability and chaos. We get rid of the French and get Dessalines. We get rid of Dessalines, and get Christophe. And all the time we are losing markets, because the United States and Europe think we are a bunch of crazy black Africans who don't know how to run a country. There has to be a better way!"

Simon leaned back in his chair. He shut his eyes and slowly shook his head. "I can't stand having to be there. I can't stand myself. What I have to do. I whip poor people for a living. I just want it to stop."

Isaac nodded. He also wanted so much more for Haiti. He wanted his father's vision for the country. But no matter how hard he tried to hold onto that vision, there was something he could not deny. It was beginning to fade.

Milot, Haiti, March 1807

Henri Christophe hated his house. While it was a relatively large plantation home, to him it was too confining, and not at all appropriate for a king. He would have to build something much bigger and more ornate. The leaders of Europe who visited would need to see the power, dignity and accomplishment of a black leader. They would need to know that the architectural taste and genius of his black ancestors who covered Ethiopia, Egypt, and Carthage with their monuments, had not been lost to the world.

He looked out his window at a large open field. That would be where he would build it. He would call it the "Sans-Souci Palace". Carefree Palace. It would be the embodiment of all that he hoped to be, but was not now.

The squeal of a child in another room brought Henri back to present reality. For now, this house would have to do. It was the third birthday of his youngest son, Jacques-Victor. He had two older daughters, as well as a grandson, but this son was special. He would be the heir apparent.

When Henri Christophe walked into their den, little Jacques-Victor immediately squealed again, and ran to his father. Christophe took him into his arms, and held the squirming child. He had never known such pleasure.

His wife Marie-Louise, along with the servants, had decorated the whole house in delightful colors, and friends and family were now dropping by with presents and their own little ones so Jacques-Victor would have playmates for the special day. But somehow as more mothers arrived with their children, the more uncomfortable Christophe became. His heart raced and his head throbbed. The mothers' voices grated against him. The children's squeals mutated into screams from his memory. He shut his eyes and held his hands over his ears.

"Quiet!" he shouted. In the sudden stillness, he opened his eyes and looked around. All were staring at him. But even though the voices still screamed in his head, the mouths in the room were silent and motionless. His own eyes opened wide and his terror reached a crescendo.

From the neck of each mother and child, he saw the blood streaming down.

Chapter Twelve

Port-au-Prince, Haiti, May 2017

Isaac and Arturo hadn't wanted to be out walking quite this late, but there had been a good turn-out at their recruitment rally, and many people asked questions. The rally had been at the Statue of the Unknown Slave at *Champs de Mars*, and Isaac had seen the statue as an invaluable visual aide to what he needed to say. They wanted to help Haiti rise to its feet and claim a new vision of the hope for which so many slaves had died. They had acquired names and contact information for nearly a hundred people, mostly men and women about their age. Isaac was excited.

Parking, however, had been scarce around the park, so they had to walk a little farther than they wanted in order to get back to Isaac's car. In the dark.

As they passed an entrance to an alley, several figures leapt out of the darkness. They grabbed Isaac and Arturo, dragged them into the alley and threw them to the ground. Isaac felt the barrel of a pistol against the back of his head.

"You are both under arrest!" said the man with the gun aimed at Isaac. "Fight us, and you will not see tomorrow."

Isaac's mouth was pressed into the dirt and excrement of the ally, and he feared that if he opened his mouth, he would choke on the garbage. But he had to speak. He lifted his head off the ground just enough.

"Okay, okay," he said. "Show us your credentials as Haitian National Police, and we will go quietly to wherever you wish!"

The man smashed his face back into the dirt and grime.

"Not those police," said Arturo. "These police have more street cred. They're the MVSN – the Militia of National Security Volunteers. Am I right?"

"You've got it!" The man grabbed Isaac by the hair, and pulled back his head as far as it would go, to leer maliciously into his eyes. "Or, as we prefer to say, the *Tonton Makout*, the bogeyman of voodoo, 'Uncle Gunnysack', the one who grabs unruly children and puts them in a gunnysack to eat later for breakfast! What do you think of that, unruly child?"

"I thought they had disappeared with the Duvaliers," said Isaac. It was only after he said the last word that he thought of how unwise his response had been. The man slammed his face into the ground once again.

"What have we done to offend the *Tonton Makout*?" asked Arturo.

"We are the true protectors of national security in this country!" The man speaking was the one who held Arturo down. "We heard you speaking in the park. Talking your talk of revolution. That would never have been tolerated under the Duvaliers."

"We weren't talking about a political revolution! We were—"

Isaac's captor slammed his face back to the ground. "You would be wise, unruly child, to let your friend do the talking!"

"What my friend says is true," said Arturo. "We were not talking against the government. We were calling for a new attitude. A new patriotism. We agree with you. We should bring back the secure order of the Duvaliers."

"Good!" said Isaac's captor. "But still you must pay a fine for your insolence!"

"Of course, of course," said Arturo. "You have some money with you, don't you Isaac?"

"I…uh…maybe."

"How much?" said the captor.

"You have to let go of my arms, so I can check my money belt."

The captor kept his gun at the back of Isaac's head, but loosened his hold on him.

Isaac checked his money belt. "I've got about a thousand rials and a little over a hundred U.S. dollars. I—"

"Give it to me!"

Isaac did as he was told, and the captors released both Isaac and Arturo. But before leaving, Isaac's former captor pointed the gun at him one more time. "In the future, we might not be so forgiving. Support François Cambronne for President, if you know what is good for the country. And tell everyone you know the Tonton Makout has returned!"

The captors ran down the alley.

Isaac wiped blood off his face with his sleeve. "Why did you have to tell them I had money?"

"Because otherwise they might have killed us!" said Arturo. "I've dealt with these guys before. Be glad I didn't tell them you have a rich Daddy and a famous girlfriend, or they would have held us for ransom."

"I'm so very lucky," said Isaac, rolling his eyes. "Thank you for not revealing those little bits of information."

"Damn straight," Arturo said, as he stood up. "And speaking of your girlfriend, isn't she flying in tomorrow morning? Once she takes one look at that stomped-in face of yours, she's going to get on the next flight back to New York."

Isaac also stood up. "That bad, huh?"

"Your eyes look like a zombie's and your nose like a frickin' hemorrhoid."

Isaac looked at the shadows around them, and began the trek to his parked car. "God, you sure knew a lot about the Tonton Makout."

"My grandfather belonged. It was when he was young, and thought they were going to 'straighten out' Haiti by force. I started out that way, too. But now that you mention it, you sure as hell need to leave talking to anyone on the street to me. I know all about that shit. You and *Mademoiselle Prissy-face Moneybags*—"

"Crista!"

"Whatever. You two can talk to the rich people who pull all the strings. You'll do better at that."

Isaac had reached the car. He opened it and got in quickly. Arturo followed suit, and Isaac immediately locked the doors. Still, he felt compelled to respond to Arturo's last statement. "You need to ease up on the derogatory rhetoric toward Crista. Her contacts with the business community will be invaluable, as will mine. She's recruited some people to join us when we visit the hospital at Mirebalais next week. A big part of our challenge will be to get rich and poor on the same side."

"Yeah, yeah, I know. I'm just not used to playing kiss-ass with rich people. But you get what I'm saying about people on the street, right?"

"Right," said Isaac. He started the car, and pulled into the street. "I need to plan to have you around whenever I get abducted by street thugs."

"You know these guys weren't just ordinary street thugs, right? The *Tonton Makout* was a badass organization, and if François Cambronne is really behind reviving them, then we've got problems. He's the grandson of Luckner Cambronne. You've heard of him, right?"

"Only in history class."

"Yeah, I could have taught that frickin' history class. You know what I'm saying? I know you are smarter than I am in most ways, but I've studied a lot about this. The *Tonton Makout* was created by Papa Doc Duvalier in 1959 to suppress political opposition, and Luckner Cambronne was put in charge. How many people they murdered and raped is unknown, but conservative estimates are they killed between 30,000 and 60,000 Haitians. He died in exile in 2006. But if his grandson -- who has declared himself a candidate for President – if he is seeking to revive the *Tonton Makout*, we've got major problems."

"There are people who really want to bring back Duvalier and the *Tonton Makout?*"

"Yes!" said Arturo. "In spite of all the murder and extortion, there are those who now look at that time as 'the good old days.' Duvalier was in power for 14 years, and if you include the time of his son 'Baby Doc', it was a period of 20 years of stability. That's a long time for Haiti. 'Papa Doc' got his name because as a physician, previous to his political ascent, he did a lot to halt the spread of typhus, yaws and malaria. His strength was among the blacks of rural Haiti, where many still remember him with fondness. Not only that, but previous to him, political power was always in the hands of a light-skinned mulatto elite. Duvalier won because he advocated black nationalism. He got his power legitimately, but maintained it by violence, especially against mulatto opposition."

Isaac shook his head. "Man, sounds like Dessalines, come back to life."

"In many ways," said Arturo. "I understand that in the U.S. many complained about the waterboarding torture technique. Under Duvalier, Haitian dissidents were immersed in sulfuric acid."

For a long time, Isaac couldn't talk. Haiti's whole history was immersed in violence. Was he being naïve to think he could lead them in another way? It wasn't until they were almost out of Port-au-Prince that Isaac spoke. "Wasn't much better under Baby Doc, was it?"

"The violence and oppression?" said Arturo, who had been immersed in silence himself. "Afraid not. He personally profited from selling the body parts of dead Haitians."

Isaac batted his eyes a couple of times, as if clearing them of irritants would similarly clear his mind. But in a way, it did help. He let his spirit be reinvigorated by a new energy, the source of which was uncertain, but the power of which grabbed hold of him. "Well, we never thought this would be easy!" he said. "At least now we see more clearly what we are up against."

Arturo reached over with his closed fist, and Isaac bumped it. "In it together, Bro!" said Arturo. "We're in it together."

A smile slowly spread across Isaac's battered face.

Cap-Haitien, Haiti, May, 2017

Isaac had to fight for standing room in the baggage claim area of the Cap Haitien airport. Not only were there all the men seeking tips for carrying baggage for foreigners, but on this occasion there were many other men as well – men seeking a glimpse of a Haitian cover girl, returning from the United States.

Isaac hated having to share the moment.

"There she is!" shouted one man, and the men crowded together even more. Isaac strained to look past all the heads, and quietly cursed his parents for not passing onto him genes for height. At 1.77 meters, he was just a couple of centimeters taller than Mare.

"Gentlemen! Gentlemen!" shouted an airport official. "You must make room for these passengers to reach their luggage! I have been assured that Marie-Noëlle will sign autographs for all who would like, out in the parking lot. Please wait there, if that is what you seek!"

Isaac was almost trampled. He knelt down and threw his arms over his head until the crowd of men – along with some women -- passed by. When he stood up and looked in the direction of the arriving passengers, he saw her. Misty eyes. Wide open. Gazing at him.

Mare ran toward him, threw her arms around his neck, and kissed him all over his face. His lips hungered for hers, and pulled those lips toward his like a vacuum. The warmth of her mouth was like an anesthetic to his troubled spirit, while the softness of her body, pressed against him, brought his body to life.

As Isaac pulled away from the girl he missed so much, he looked into her eyes and saw the reflection of his own love. But then her eyes began surveying his face, and registered concern. Of course – he had forgotten.

"Just a little disagreement with some street thugs," he said. "I'll be fine."

Isaac's eyes were pulled away by the presence of two men standing behind Mare.

She turned around and saw the men's less-than-enthusiastic glares. "Oh…uh…Isaac, these are two men who came down with me," she said, speaking in English. "The man on the right is my agent, Carl, and the one on the left is Jesse, who the modeling agency sent down as a bodyguard."

Isaac looked askance at the second man. "Bodyguard?"

"Just a precaution," said Jesse. "There was a previous incident."

Isaac pulled Mare close again, and smiled at her. "I am the only body guard Mare needs."

Mare returned the smile. "I agree! But the agency is a little protective. There was a minor thing that happened when I visited Henri in Jersey a while back. Nothing too bad – I'll tell you more about it later. But—"

"Just protecting our investment," said Jesse.

Isaac scowled at the much larger man. "Investment? She's not property, you know."

"Of course, of course," said Mare's agent, Carl. "But we are not the enemy here, Isaac. We are protecting her for you, too."

"Nice of you," Isaac said with no little amount of sarcasm.

"But Marie-Noëlle," Carl continued, "I do have to say that it's in our interest to encourage your male fan base down here, and…well…PDA's with your boyfriend don't encourage their illusions of your eligibility."

"She's not eligible."

"I understand, Isaac," said Carl. "But with beautiful celebrities, there is an illusion they like to maintain. Every guy out there imagines, given half a chance, he could win her for his own—"

"That's not happening. I—"

"I understand. It's just—"

Mare put her hand on Isaac's arm. "Carl, you're not trying to keep Isaac and me away from each other, are you?"

"Just in public, with your fan base around. In private, well—"

"And we'll have that privacy?"

"Of course," said Carl. "Providing it's safe—"

Just as Isaac was getting in Carl's face, Mare stepped in between them. "Isaac, we'll have our privacy. I'll make sure of it. But for now, could you wait in your car? It's like a performance for an actor. I need to play the role. Okay?"

Looking in the eyes he had so longed to see, there was no way he could refuse her request. Still, that did not prevent Isaac from shooting nasty glances at the two interloping men, before turning and heading back to his car. He opened the driver's side door and sat down, then looked over at the crowd of men and women gathering on the other side of the parking lot. Several held U. S. magazines with the increasingly famous Marie-Noëlle on the cover. Isaac suspected that many did not have the money to actually purchase such magazines, and they held pages ripped out of the magazines of others. Isaac saw the excitement in their eyes and momentarily felt guilty for his possessiveness. The men longed for what they could never possess, and the women longed for the excitement and freedom of what they could never be. In a land where there was so little to excite, his girlfriend now embodied possibility.

When Mare came out to the lot, the crowd flocked around her, but Carl and Jesse got them to line up. Isaac saw immediately what Mare meant by a "performance." She smiled and twirled, strutted and flirted, and the men especially followed every move. It was clear this had become her element.

Isaac sat back in his chair and sighed deeply. When even that did not release all of the tension in his body, he jumped out of the driver's side door, and jogged around the part of the parking lot farthest away from where Mare was holding court with her fans. Then he danced around like a prize fighter, sparring with shadows.

It helped, but not enough.

Isaac knew he must love Mare, because he really did not want to take her away from all the pleasure and success she was obviously experiencing as a model in New York. And he felt pride that the name of Marie-Noëlle was gaining world-renown, earning her a place among such previous one-name celebrities as Cher, Madonna, Prince, Bono, Beyonce, and Adele.

Still, he hated how much he wished it were different.

He wanted her beside him in the fight. *Was that backward and macho?* He wanted her to come home to when he became stressed and worn down, and needed arms to hold him, and soft kisses to soothe his soul. *Was that stifling her freedom and ambition as a modern woman?* He looked over again at the crowd surrounding Mare, especially the two men who had traveled with her. *Was it selfish that he didn't want to share her?*

Isaac longed for simplicity.

He was not aware of how long he had struggled with his soul. It might have been over an hour, or perhaps it was only ten or fifteen minutes, when he finally saw Mare walking his way. The beauty of her smile revived his spirit.

Isaac looked past Mare and saw a few of her fans, along with Carl and Jesse, looking his way. Remembering the concerns expressed over public affection put a little scowl on his face, and yet, wanting to respect Mare's feelings on the matter, he ducked into the front seat of the car, and opened the passenger-side door.

Mare got in the passenger side, shut the door, and took Isaac's hand. "I told Carl and Jesse we would wait for them to get in their rental, but...DRIVE!"

Isaac backed out and then the spinning wheels of his car spewed gravel as the vehicle lurched forward. Isaac could see Carl and Jesse in his rearview mirror, as they waved desperately for him to stop. He did not. In less than a minute he was out on the main road, dodging Haitian traffic.

Mare eased over next to him, and nibbled on his earlobe, even as Isaac could feel her warm breath on his neck. "Find someplace private," she said, "...quick!"

In the middle of Cap Haitien, few places were private. Still, he knew of a beach not too far from the edge of the city. "Quick" would also be a challenge, and yet, with that word still floating softly through his inner ear, he squealed around corners, left the street to drive on sidewalks and miniscule yards, and played "chicken" with several motorcycles and "tap-taps," before finding the dirt road that led to the water's edge. He shut off the car's engine, and turned to the girl he loved, meeting her full, moist lips with his.

Mare moaned softly. She opened her eyes and looked out the front window at the beach in front of them. The sun was setting, and, miraculously, no one was around. The leaves of mango and banana trees fluttered nearby, and Isaac smelled the sweet-salty aroma of the ocean.

"Nice choice!" she said in a whisper.

Before Isaac could respond, Mare flung open the passenger-side door, got out and ran toward the beach. He followed right behind. She stopped and turned quickly, ripping off her shirt, kicking away sandals and quickly dropping her shorts. Underneath was the sheerest, most ornate black lingerie Isaac had ever seen, even in a magazine.

Mare danced and twirled across the sand, before stopping and looking back at Isaac. "They were part of a photo-shoot and now they're mine!" she said in a sing-song voice. "What do you think of my career now, huh?"

Isaac smiled and walked a little closer. "Come closer, to let me get a better look."

Mare playfully shook her head and backed away. "No, no! You want me, you have to COME GET ME!" Then she ran.

Isaac followed quickly, and with long strides developed in high school distance running, was upon her in no time.

He grabbed her by the waist, but she spun and twisted, and fell to the ground. She rolled over on her back, and smiled up at Isaac. "Close enough look for you now?" Then she jumped to her feet, reached behind her back, unfastened her bra and draped it over his head. "Or is that better?" Isaac was too fixated on the beauty of her naked breasts to respond. She pulled off her bikini panties and flung them into Isaac's face. "How is your view now?" she whispered seductively. Then she lay back in the sand.

For the next moments of Isaac's life, no words are adequate. His fantasy and his reality melted into an amalgam in the passionate fire. The hardness of his body caressed the softness of this magical girl who enveloped him into herself with her legs, and Isaac wondered how it could be that such intense physical pleasure could at the same time feel so spiritual. Their bodies twisted into one, her breath became his breath, and Isaac felt as if his whole self had exploded into her inner warmth.

As their passion subsided, Isaac breathed a contented breath. His senses became more aware of what was around him. He heard the lapping of the waves against the shore nearby, and the calls of several gulls overhead. He felt the still-warm sand between his toes. He lifted his head and looked to the horizon. Layers of color – red, purple, pink and yellow, shot out across the water from a sun that had just dipped below that horizon.

When his gaze returned to Mare as she lay underneath him, he saw tears rolling down from her eyes onto her cheeks. But there was a smile that shone from those cheeks, as well as from the eyes shedding the tears.

Isaac cocked his head and gave her a questioning look. She shook her head. "They're happy tears," she whispered.

He smiled and kissed each one off her face. Then he stared into her eyes. "I've always loved your eyes," he said, "but I am amazed how when I get this close, what an amazing variety of subtle shades are in them. You really are a work of art, you know."

Mare's face shone for a moment, but then retreated to a more sober demeanor.

"Okay, now what's wrong?" Isaac asked.

"You know I have to go back, don't you?"

Isaac felt as if he had been punched in the gut. He rolled over off of Mare, and looked up at the darkening sky. "I was trying not to think about it."

"I mean, we can still enjoy the time we have—three days this time," she said while caressing the hair on Isaac's chest. "And there will come a day when I don't have to go back at all. But I do now."

"Why?" Isaac asked. "Why do you have to go back? Just have them come down here and do their shoots in Haiti."

"I'm not there yet. Sure, my career has had a great start, but I am still relatively new, and I have to develop my contacts in New York. I can probably fly down here more frequently, but—"

"I need you here, Mare. Personally," said Isaac. "Toussaint had Suzanne. I need you."

Mare stiffened, and she glared at Isaac. "So, I don't have my own story; I'm just supposed to play my role in your little historical re-enactment?"

"That's not what I meant!" said Isaac. "It was only a comparison. I know you have your own life."

Mare was still bristling. "Isaac, I told you before I came that I would be going back, so why are you emotionalizing everything? I'm helping with your work financially. You got the check I sent, right?"

Isaac nodded.

"Then, let's leave everything as we agreed," Mare said. She grabbed his hand. "I just want to enjoy this time with you. PLEASE!"

Isaac squeezed her hand. "Just one more thing," he said. "If I send you back the check, can I have you instead?"

Mare smiled and shook her head.

"Can't blame a guy for trying."

Isaac's father had always told him, *If you can't get all you want, take care to hold on to what you already have,* and Isaac put his whole self into that that goal for the rest of the time Mare was in Cap Haitien. He knew that any further attempt to grab hold and keep her there, might in fact be the act which would make her shake free altogether. She was a wild Mare after all. So, when he took her to her parents' home and found Carl and Jesse there, fuming, he did not try to grab hold. When he went around with her the next three days, he savored each moment, and spoke nothing of his desire that she stay. And when the time came to go with her to the airport, he let his tears flow, but he did not cling.

Desperately, he hoped setting her free would be the way to hold her close.

Chapter Thirteen

Ennery, Haiti, June 1816

Isaac Louverture sat on the porch of the family home at Ennery, staring into the distance, at nothing in particular. One of the servants appeared in his line of vision, less than a meter away, looking into Isaac's eyes.

Isaac blinked. "What do you need, Antoine?"

"Pardon the intrusion, Monsieur Isaac, but the other servants and I – well, we know you need your solitude right now, but the coffee, it will not wait…"

"I can't…"

"Of course, Monsieur Isaac, we understand. We know that normally you always work alongside of us, and we love you for that. But, given the circumstances of your loss, we think it wise for us to go on with the work without you. With your permission, of course."

"The coffee…of course. As you wish."

"Thank you, Monsieur Isaac." Antoine turned to leave, but then hesitated and looked back. "Monsieur Isaac, if you will permit, one more thing…"

Isaac nodded.

"We loved her, too. All of us. She was a wonderful woman who loved your father with all her heart. He could never have done what he did without her."

Tears came to Isaac's eyes. "Thank you, Antoine."

"And Monsieur Placide, will he be joining us here any time soon?"

Isaac shrugged. "After her memorial, I tried to convince him to return with me. He wasn't ready then, but he might come later. I just don't know."

"Of course. We will pray for the both of you. Oh, and one more thing." He pulled a rumpled letter out of his pocket. "We received this letter from…well, from King Henri. I didn't know what you wished."

"His condolences, no doubt. Right now I can't think of anyone whose condolences would mean less to me." Isaac sighed deeply. "But I suppose you can toss it in the pile with the others."

"Most certainly, Monsieur Isaac." Antoine went inside the house to toss the letter on the dining table, where Isaac knew still lay perhaps 100 more unopened letters.

Isaac whispered a thank-you prayer to God for Antoine and the other servants. They were all that kept him from feeling completely alone. Yes, people sending letters of condolence was nice, but those people were not family. His grandparents died long before. His dad and mom were both dead now. Even his Uncle Paul and younger brother Saint-Jean were dead. With his brother Placide still in France, the household servants were his sole family in Haiti. A whole generation had passed away.

How does that happen? Wasn't it just a few weeks ago he played among these trees? His mom would have to call several times to get them to come in for dinner. They never had to worry about the market for coffee in France or the

United States. That was his father's job. His father and mother talked to them at dinner about the time of their enslavement, but that was from another world and another time. The only freedom he needed was enough freedom from chores to play with his friends.

Wasn't it only days ago he was so angry with his father for sending him to France?

Wasn't it just yesterday they had reconciled and he was helping his father on this very plantation, tending to the coffee trees, chasing French soldiers away from the banana trees?

Wasn't it only earlier that day he knelt with his mother in a garden in Agen, France, helping her to pull weeds and remember.

How could remembering be so easy, and yet so hard?

How would people ever remember what it was all really about?

How would they remember a man who gave his life to free a country from slavery and make it a beacon of hope for racial brotherhood?

How would they remember a woman who not only stood by his side, but infused his very soul with love?

How would they remember what the revolution had been about at its very beginning?

Isaac found himself growing increasingly restless with all the unanswered questions. He rose abruptly, went into the house, ran into his father's library, and rolled back the top of his roll top desk. He grabbed the quill, and found some paper in one of the drawers. He sat down.

There was only way to make sure they would remember. He would write the story himself. The first things he wrote would be easy – the title and the date he was starting: *Mémoires d'Isaac, fils de Toussaint L'Ouverture*, 5 June, 1816.

The rest would not be easy. It would be written in his sweat and blood, but regardless of how long it took, it would be the act which would redeem his life.

He could not wait to begin.

Milot, Haiti, 8 October, 1820

Henri Christophe looked out of a window of the palace dining area. He did not find what he was looking for, perhaps because he had no idea what it was he was seeking. All he really knew was what he was looking for was not inside this palace.

Sans-Souci Palace. "Carefree" palace. But it had not made his life carefree. The Haitian people had complained even more about building the palace than they had about building the Citadelle Laferriere. And the walls simply were not thick enough to keep out the cares he faced: plots against his life, lack of support or recognition from the United States and Europe, a shaky economy.

Oh, well, what did it matter? Nothing was forever.

All he had really wanted was to secure Haiti's freedom and to bring his country respect in the community of nations. Why did people not see that what he sometimes called the Citadelle Henri was needed to secure Haiti's freedom? Sure France had not attacked, but that was because they had heard about the huge fortress shaped like a ship of war, positioned on a mountain to see all around. And why did the people not see that the palace in which he now stood was not for his own glory, but for the prestige of Haiti? Visitors from the United States and Europe had stood in awe. It was a monument to the capability of the whole black race.

Still, the people of Haiti hated him. They would feel differently when he was gone.

The problems Haiti faced were not his fault. The United States would not recognize Haiti's independence because of the way Dessalines had slaughtered the white population of the island. That was not his fault. France would not recognize Haiti's independence because they held that Haiti owed them "reparations" of millions of francs for their "loss" of slaves and property used to oppress slaves. He would never agree to that! Still people thought their economic losses were all his fault. Racism was behind the way the United States and many European countries now got their sugar and coffee from countries like Brazil who were not under black rule.

Oh, well, what did it matter? It would no longer be his problem.

He still heard the voices, of course. The voices did not understand why he had done it. There was Dessalines. There was the violence of the French who opposed them. There was...all the confusion.

The voices, too, were something he could leave behind.

Henri Christophe, former slave, former general and friend of Toussaint Louverture, and now King Henri I of Haiti, took a pistol out of a desk drawer. A pistol and a silver bullet.

He walked slowly and quietly to his bedroom door, opened it, and looked in. Marie-Louise slept quietly. She was a strong and capable woman. She would do well. He proceeded down a long hallway and came to the door of Jacques-Victor. He opened the door a crack and looked in there as well. His son also still slept. Now 16 years old, and strong and competent. He would make a great heir. He could figure it all out. Help the country start anew. Memories of holding him, playing with him as a child flashed through Henri's mind, but he quickly shut them out. He could not live on memory of the past. It all had to be about the future.

A servant had fetched his favorite horse and he now left the palace to mount the steed. And no, he did not wish for anyone to accompany him. He was simply riding up to the Citadelle. The servant could return to his other chores.

Henri had always loved the ride up to the fortress on the mountain. Haiti's beauty was all around him. The view was especially peaceful this morning. Birds were singing. The cool breeze brought the aroma of fish from the ocean. Mountain goats scattered in front of him, as if knowing one does not get in the way of a king.

Henri left his horse with a guard at the gate, entered the fortress and walked deliberately through the labyrinthine halls and up the stairs. He did not pause or hesitate. The more he walked, the more he felt the stone walls of the fortress taking him into its womb. He stopped in front of a small windowless room. They normally used it for storage, but he had it cleaned out the day before. He shut the door behind him. The darkness felt inviting, friendly. He pulled out the pistol, placed the cold barrel against his temple and smiled.

There really was a way to be carefree.

Ennery, Haiti, 19 October, 1820

Isaac Louverture's heart was weighed down with an overwhelming sadness. His friends and some of the household servants didn't understand. They thought he should be happy. Not long before he had married his cousin Louise Chancy. He had gone searching for a woman who, as his father had suggested, had the loving qualities of his mother Suzanne, and many people saw these qualities in Louise. But what the others did not know was that Isaac could not say he truly loved her. To love was to risk losing. She could be a comfort to him, and he a source of security for her. That was all.

Many thought he should be happy because of the news about Henri Christophe, but that news, fully understood, made his blood run cold. There had been a time when Henri Christophe had been like an uncle to him. His father's right hand man. One of the few men his father completely trusted. Now dead.

There had been a time when Isaac had shared the hope of the nation that freedom from the oppression of France would mean freedom from all oppression, that the black people of Haiti would govern themselves with justice, and violence would no longer hold sway in their land. But the oppression of France had merely given way to the oppression of Dessalines, and violence had replaced Dessalines with Christophe, and now again replaced Christophe with Jean-Pierre Boyer. Henri's 16-year-old son, Jacques-Victor, had been assassinated only 10 days after his father's suicide.

The blood of Haiti was crying out to God from the land.

Isaac walked slowly back to his father's study. He did not have energy to do more. There on the roll top desk sat the memoires. They had been published and distributed throughout both Haiti and France. But what good had they done? This was still not the Haiti his father had died for, and prospects for improvement were, if anything, looking worse, not better. France was still refusing to recognize Haiti's independence, and rumor had it that they were demanding an indemnity of millions of francs as a condition of such recognition. Toussaint would never have agreed to such a travesty. Jean-Pierre Boyer probably would.

Isaac thought of all the people he loved who had died. He had mourned so many times. But how do you mourn the death of a revolution?

Part II
DEFENDING THE CASTLE

Chapter Fourteen

Isaac was stunned by his first view of the hospital at Mirebalais. Yvette Colbert had set up a meeting with the famed medical doctor, Dr. Paul Hansen, and Isaac had known from her and from what he had read, that this was a first-rate facility. Still, seeing it in person took him to a whole new level of understanding.

The Mirebalais University Hospital, located about an hour and a half outside of Port-Au-Prince, was treating close to 700 patients a day, with an emphasis on child and maternal health services. That it was at Mirebalais was significant to Isaac, for he knew it was near that town the Haitian Revolution first organized back in 1791. What was especially impressive to Isaac was that all services were free after an initial registration fee of about $1.15, U.S. The building featured four wards surrounding a central courtyard, and housed six operating rooms with advanced technology. Built-in cameras transmitted live video feed of surgeries to other hospitals for learning and consultation. Along with advanced technology, 1800 solar panels made Mirebalais the largest completely solar run hospital in the world. *And this was in Haiti!*

Of course, Isaac would never have had this opportunity if it not been for Yvette, the young woman he had rescued from the street riot in Port-au-Prince four months earlier. It had taken a while to arrange, and he had found out in his reading about the man what an incredibly busy person he was. Isaac felt fortunate.

As Isaac and his companions were ushered into one of the conference rooms to wait for the doctor, he immediately noticed Yvette was there waiting for them. Isaac smiled and held out his hand. Yvette rushed up to him, brushed his hand aside, threw her arms around him and kissed him on the cheek. Isaac's friends responded with a series of whistles and catcalls.

"Whoa!" said Rene, a recent recruit from Port-au-Prince, "I thought this was serious politics, not a booty call!"

Isaac blushed. "Hey, wait, I—"

Arturo stepped in between Isaac and Yvette. "Now, listen girl, I'm here to tell you that if you are interested in this guy, you have some serious competition." He sidled up next to her. "On the other hand, if you'd like to share a little of that Haitian sugar with me—"

"You wouldn't have any competition at all!" interjected Crista.

Arturo scowled.

For Isaac, it made for an exceedingly uncomfortable start to a crucial investigative experience. Yvette was even more attractive than he had remembered, and Mare's return to New York still weighed heavily on his heart. In his worst moments he wondered if he had lost her forever.

As Isaac was reflecting on this future prospect, Dr. Paul Hansen entered the room and everyone turned his way.

"So, which one of you is Isaac Breda?" he asked.

Yvette stepped in right away, putting her hand on Isaac's arm. "This man right here, Dr. Hansen. And let me say again how grateful I am to you for consenting to meet with us."

Dr. Hansen reached out his right hand to Isaac. "Yes, I understand you have a little hero in you – rescuing our damsel in distress, huh?"

Isaac looked down and shuffled his feet. "It was all reaction, doctor. I'm not sure what I would have done if I would have actually stopped and thought it through."

"So it is with most heroes. I also understand you are a descendent of Toussaint Louverture. Then the name 'Breda' has some real meaning, doesn't it?"

"I am very proud of it, Monsieur."

"How can I help? Are you looking for a list of helping organizations making a difference? There are a lot of them. Or are you looking for something more, a vision perhaps?"

"A little of both, I think," said Isaac, now speaking more assertively. "We aren't looking to start another NGO, and we aren't wanting to start another political campaign. We are wanting to step beyond all of the things that haven't been working, and do nothing less than start a second Haitian revolution."

"I hope you're talking figuratively."

"No guns and street violence. Just change that has some bite to it."

"Then I'm with you," said Dr. Hansen. "Again, how can I help with this little insurrection?"

Isaac looked around at the members of the group who had come with him. There were twelve young men and women who had set aside their normal lives to join him in this place. Another 200 were now on the contact list of what they were calling *The Sons and Daughters of Toussaint.* "We're all tired of people in other countries just thinking about Haiti as the poorest country in the Western Hemisphere. We're also tired of all of our friends and family members, giving up on Haiti and leaving for the U.S." Mare's image quickly flashed in his mind, but he shut that image out just as quickly. "We want Haiti to be what Toussaint had envisioned when he initiated the Haitian Revolution. We want a Haiti that can take a place alongside the great nations of the world, and not be simply a poor stepchild."

"I'm with you there, as well," said the doctor.

"And, yes, we do want to find out about what is already going well, like your hospital, to give people in Haiti a sense of hope and pride."

"Well, then, let's sit down and talk."

Chairs had been set up in a circle, and each person took a seat, with Isaac sitting by the famous physician on one side and Yvette on the other. "I think you are starting in the right place when you talk about the vision of Toussaint and what he sought to accomplish. I love what he said after being trapped by the French: 'In overthrowing me, you have done no more than cut down the trunk of the tree of black liberty in Saint-Domingue. It will spring back from the roots, for they are numerous and deep.'"

"I had to memorize that back in grade school," said Crista. All around the circle, heads nodded in agreement.

"But for a new revolution in Haiti to grow from those deep roots, it has to be about more than changing the people to whom the nation is subservient," said Dr. Hansen.

"You got that right," chimed in Arturo.

"It has to be about even more than well-meaning foreign organizations," the famed physician continued. "Church groups have done some great things in this country, especially in education and medicine. And many NGO's have also contributed greatly. Even this hospital in which we meet came about because of the actions of foreign groups like Partners in Health and the American Red Cross. Haiti needs such help. But it cannot be dependent on outside help.

Haiti has for a long time been called 'The Republic of NGOs'. NGOs are like a drug, and Haiti needs to be weaned off of that drug!"

"Preach it, brother!" said Arturo. "The United States and the rich people of the world are frickin' drug pushers, handin' out their goodies so the people of Haiti will kiss their rich asses!"

"Oh, get a grip, Arturo!" said Crista.

"I wouldn't go as far as our friend – Arturo, is it? – I wouldn't go as far as Arturo, but I certainly would agree that the patronizing approach of wealthy countries has often been part of the problem. Former U.S. President Bill Clinton admits it himself. Not long after our earthquake he said that the United States took the wrong approach by sending us their food, instead of helping us produce our own. It made us more dependent, and Clinton flat-out admitted he was wrong in being part of it."

"But can Haiti really produce the food our hungry people need for themselves?" asked Tina, a young woman sitting on the opposite side of the circle.

"Not entirely, perhaps," said Dr. Hansen. "But with help we can do much better. Not long after the earthquake we helped Haiti produce a vitamin-enriched peanut butter which proved to be a miraculous treatment for childhood malnutrition, while at the same time creating jobs and stimulating local agriculture."

"How did things get this bad in Haiti?" asked Isaac. "Our nation once had a lot of economic promise."

"Richest colony of the New World at the beginning of the 19th Century," said Dr. Hansen. "But oppression isn't always in the form of being formally governed by a foreign power. Sometimes oppression is economic. When Haiti gained their freedom as a country, many countries would not even recognize them. My own country didn't recognize Haiti's independence until the presidency of Abraham Lincoln sixty years after the Haitian Revolution. France recognized Haiti much earlier, in 1825, but only because they finagled a deal where Haiti had to pay them 150 million francs as 'restitution' for the slaves and equipment they lost in the war. Remember President Aristide?"

Everyone nodded.

"When he was President of Haiti he told the French government they should pay that back to Haiti, at that day's monetary value, and with interest -- $21 billion US dollars!"

"Gee," said Arturo, "I wonder why he isn't around anymore?"

"Exactly!" said the doctor. "Aristide's demise was a direct result of pressure against him by France and the other wealthy countries of the world. Anyway, Haiti struggled to pay off this indemnity. The US and Europe were taking their coffee and sugar business elsewhere, largely because of racism against the black-led Haitian government. So they ended up selling timber from their forests. This was the beginning of a long process of deforestation. With increasing poverty, the people of Haiti burned more trees to make charcoal to use in cooking, and to sell, and this deforestation accelerated. At one time the nation was about 90% forested. Today it is more like 2%. Deforestation has led to soil erosion and less land to be used for agriculture. Haiti's poverty, then, also has deep roots."

"So how can we change all of this now?" asked Isaac. "Another way of asking that is, how do we go about our new revolution?"

Dr. Hansen took a deep breath and thought a moment. "Reviving Haiti means strengthening the country in several areas: medical services, education, infrastructure and the overall economy." He pointed at the walls around him. "Let me start with the medical aspects, since we are here, and since that is what I know best!"

"Makes sense," said Isaac.

"The earthquake of 2010 absolutely devastated Haiti's medical resources. One assessment at the time found that about half of all public-sector health facilities in Port-au-Prince collapsed or were found to be unsafe. And as far as rural areas were concerned, even before the earthquake, most studies showed that the majority of Haiti's physicians and nurses had left the country altogether, and that those who remained were concentrated in the capital city. And then came the earthquake, centered in Port-au-Prince, and many of those physicians and nurses died. Those who were left were seriously overworked during the crisis, and some left for other countries afterward. As a result, Haiti was made extremely dependent on foreign healthcare workers like myself.

"How could Haiti get back on its own feet in relation to healthcare? Our response to that question has been this teaching hospital. It had been in the planning as a regular hospital since 2008, but after the earthquake the Haitian Minister of Health convinced us to aim higher. He convinced us to make this a teaching hospital where nurses, young doctors and other health professionals, like your friend Yvette, could be trained, and to also provide support for other hospitals throughout the country."

Yvette, put her hand on Isaac's arm. "You see? This is why I wanted you to come here. I love this place! It's a revolution in itself."

Isaac looked down at the hand resting on his arm. Her soft touch sent chills through his whole body. He loved Mare so much, and yet...she was gone, and Yvette was here. He didn't remove her hand.

"And I would also say," continued Dr. Hansen, "this hospital has had a positive economic impact on the community. This facility has created thousands of jobs, many of them permanent."

"Tell us more about the economy and jobs," said Tina. "Not having money or jobs is what drives so many people to the violent kind of revolution."

"There really is a lot happening in the area of economic improvement, but most people, even in Haiti, aren't even aware of it. After the earthquake the movement was to

'Build Back Better', and this meant encouraging industry away from the most earthquake-prone centers such as Port-au-Prince. There is now a new industrial park at Caracol, near Cap-Haitien, which could eventually employ as many as 100,000 people."

"I have friends who work there," said Pierre, a friend of Isaac's who had come down with him. "They are very hopeful."

"The Clinton Foundation has done a lot for Haiti in terms of economic improvement," continued the doctor. "After the earthquake Bill Clinton was among the first world leaders to respond. He pointed to the possibility of providing jobs in reforestation and public works, as in the American Great Depression. Since then the Clinton Foundation was also instrumental in the development of the industrial park at Caracol and in efforts to revive Haitian coffee production. They are working on what they call the Haiti Coffee Academy with international coffee company La Colombe Torrefaction. Just like this hospital has become a model teaching facility in medicine, this academy will be a model coffee farm and training center serving rural coffee growing communities with the objective of improving crop yields, the quality of coffee grown and access to markets and investments. The recent emphasis in the US of buying fair trade coffee is also helping."

"Haiti's economy at the time of the Revolution was built on coffee and sugar," said Isaac. "Do you know if there are similar efforts with sugar production?"

"Some, though not as much. There is a sugar refinery down at Darbonne. For many years it struggled to make a profit. Imported U.S. sugar was much cheaper, due in large part to subsidies given to US farmers. Now, however, after a loan from Cuba, and after a deal to use their sugar in biofuels, it seems to be getting back on its feet. Still, employment in sugar production is nothing like it was during the early Nineteenth Century."

"What about education?" asked Crista. "I mean, we are students who are getting our education in Haiti, and we want to think there will be a lot of others following right behind us."

"It's an area of challenge, of course. Those of you who have reached postsecondary education in this country are the lucky ones. Most don't make it through grade school, because of the need to help support their families financially. Churches help a lot in this area, of course—"

"The university some of us go to in Limbe is a church-supported university," said Isaac. "And I know that the same church groups support several elementary schools. And they even give children goats to raise to pay their own expenses."

"Church-supported schools really do help," said Dr. Hansen. "But if Haiti is going to get fully on its feet in education, the public sector needs to do a big part. Even though several presidents of Haiti have talked of improving public education, implementation has been uneven at best. Again, the Clinton Foundation has worked hard, funding the building of schools, and working with the Haitian government to make progress toward their goal of universal primary school enrollment."

Arturo squirmed in his chair. "But what do we do?" he finally said. "I'm ready to act! I'm ready to do something! I don't want to just sit here listening to what others are doing."

"On this one, I've got to agree with Arturo," said Crista. "Let's get this party started!"

"The one thing I would say is missing right now," said Dr. Hansen, "is a movement of the Haitian people to take ownership of their own betterment. The Clinton Foundation is involved. Why not a Toussaint Louverture Economic Freedom Foundation? Run by young Haitians! Instead of waiting for an NGO or church group to build their schools, why don't Haitians get in there and build their schools? No waiting around for someone else to do something! Haitians could band together and clean up their streets of both garbage and violence. Put their lives on the line for it, if need be. It's what Toussaint would have done! If you could lead Haitians to take initiatives, I would bet others would rush to your aid."

"Now you're talking my language!" said Arturo. "Let's do this!"

"This is getting scary, but I agree with Arturo again," said Crista. "That foundation idea? Both my dad and Isaac's dad have businesses. I bet they would buy in. Don't you think so, Isaac?"

"Definitely," said Isaac. "And...uh...I know someone else who can help also." *Why didn't he specifically mention Mare?* He looked over at Yvette. She was smiling at him.

"Getting the people on the street to put their asses on the line to help will be the hard part," said Arturo. "They've been screwed over by new movements too many times. But I could help with that. I know some others who might help also."

185

"So we could get a lot of help," said Crista. "That's the good news."

"Yes," said the doctor, "but the not-so-good news is that it can all go back to square one, not because of some untimely earthquake, which we are learning to plan for, but due to the less controllable violence of the political process. The Haitian people have been violently switching leaders since the Haitian Revolution. And people who are seeking violent revolution often sabotage progress in order to foment discontent."

Isaac put his head in his hands and moaned. Yvette placed her hand gently on his shoulder. "Arturo and I have already had to deal with that violence. After our rally last week, we were accosted by some men who claimed to be the revived *Tonton Makout*—"

Reactions came from everyone in the circle.

"Oh, my God!"

"Sweet Jesus, preserve us!"

Tina pulled out a rosary.

Rene leaned back and shook his head. "My grandparents were killed by the *Tonton Makout*."

"We want to take the country back to the compassionate brotherhood of Toussaint," said Isaac, "and they want to take it back to the violence of the Duvaliers, inherited from Dessalines and Henri Christophe."

"A good comparison," said Dr. Hansen. "Do you know that just as you are descended from Toussaint, Baby Doc Duvalier was married to a woman named Michèle Bennett, who was the great-great-great-great granddaughter of Henri Christophe?"

"This version of the Tonton Makout wants to elect François Cambronne," said Isaac, "who is the grandson of Luckner Cambronne, head of the *Tonton Makout* under Papa Doc."

"I'm not going up against those guys," said Rene, and he stood up and left the room. Four others joined him.

"'Narrow is the way...'" said Crista.

"The way of violence and authoritarianism often gains support during times of economic uncertainty," said Dr. Hansen. "Eric Fromm, a psychiatrist at the time of Hitler, wrote a book called Escape from Freedom, in which he told how it worked under the Nazis. People sometimes feel insecure with freedom, but reassured by someone who purports to have all the answers and demands obedience. Even former President Michel Martelly, while he did some good things for the country, supported bringing back the Haitian army, whose only enemy historically was the Haitian people. He also was not averse to the *Tonton Makout.*"

"Arturo and I agreed that the *Tonton Makout* was not going to intimidate us," said Isaac, "and that is how I still feel. How about the rest of you?"

Those who remained looked back and forth at each other in uncertainty. Isaac got up and walked to the center of the circle. "Who will join me?" He held out his right hand, palm down. Arturo, Crista, and Yvette quickly rose, walked over and put their right hands over his. "I'm in." each said. Slowly the others rose and joined their hands in the circle. Then last of all, the famous physician also rose, walking over and putting his hand in the circle as well.

"Ayiti p'ap peri" the doctor said.

Isaac remembered the saying his father had also spoken. *Haiti is never finished.*

"Ayiti p'ap peri" he said, and the others nodded their heads in agreement.

Isaac wished that it was Mare in the circle with them, with her hand joined with his. As it was, Yvette left her hand on his after the others had already broken away. He simply could not pull his hand away from hers.

Chapter Fifteen

New York, June 3rd, 2017

The moment Marie-Noëlle left the catwalk, she rushed past Eric and every other fashion executive and peer, with the single-minded goal of reading a newspaper. More specifically, an article in the "World News" section.

She had been alerted to the article by her friend Karissa.

"Have you seen it?" she had said, as Marie-Noëlle made her way toward the catwalk.

"Seen what?"

"The article about your boyfriend in the New York Times: 'The Heritage of Toussaint.' It's all about what he is doing to bring change to Haiti. They're calling him 'Haiti's Martin Luther King.' You should read it!"

Marie-Noëlle paused long enough to glance at the article which Karissa held up before her eyes. All she really saw was the accompanying picture. Young Haitians were gathered in front of the *Statue of the Unknown Slave* in Port-au-Prince. In the middle of the group was Isaac. To his right was a girl. A pretty girl with her arm around his waist.

"Yeah…uh…no time to read it now, but for sure when I get back."

She had rushed toward the catwalk, making every effort to shut the picture out of her mind. She had been only partially successful.

"Hey, that was a different look for you out there," said Eric, who had caught up to her at Karissa's door, just as she prepared to knock.

"How so?"

"More aloof. Less the sexy girl next door."

"I guess I was a little distracted."

"Don't apologize," said Eric. "I kind of liked it. So, tonight at my place?"

Marie-Noëlle's eyes glazed over. But then she shrugged and smiled. "Sure. I'll look forward to it. Uh…but right now I've got to see Karissa."

Eric winked and turned away. Marie-Noëlle knocked on the door, and Karissa opened it immediately.

"I was thinking it might be you!" she said, as she grabbed Marie-Noëlle by the hand, and led her to a corner table where a newspaper lay. "Read it, quickly! I was so excited when I saw it – I said to myself right away, I've got to be the one to share it with Marie-Noëlle!"

Marie-Noëlle gave Karissa her best effort at a smile. "The people in my life who are really special to me call me 'Mare'. Would you do me the favor of calling me that?"

"'Mare' it is!"

Mare picked up the paper and found the article right away. She tried to look past the accompanying photo and actually read the article. She tried. It didn't work. It was that girl. Something about the way she had her arm around him and looked up at him so admiringly seemed so possessive. Like he was hers to be proud of.

"Mare?"

What seemed equally disturbing was that Isaac didn't seem to be pushing her away.

"Mare?"

There were other girls in the picture, and none of them seemed to be staking a claim to this emerging Haitian leader.

"Mare!"

Marie-Noëlle woke up. Karissa stared at her with a puzzled expression. "Your face is not exactly showing the positive feelings I was expecting to see. I'm feeling deprived of my joy here! What's up?"

Mare screwed her face into a pout. "The girl."

"Girl?" Karissa looked over Mare's shoulder at the picture. "Oh...the girl. Hey, you can't let yourself get all worked up about shit like that. That's what drove my boyfriend away. I would be with a guy in a photo shoot – playing on a beach, out on the town in a cool car, getting proposed to with some beefcake placing some monster diamond on my finger. It was all staged!"

"Yeah, but Isaac isn't a model, and this isn't staged."

Karissa rolled her eyes. "Not by a modeling agency anyway. But I don't know about her. Look, trust the guy. Trust your love. If it's real, ain't no social action groupie going to steal it away. Call him if you're worried. Show some genuine interest in his achievements. Ask how you can help. Then, if you're still worried, ease in a question about who's the little slut? – only don't call her that."

Mare nodded.

"Of course, to show genuine interest, you have to actually READ THE ARTICLE!" Karissa pointed at the text as she spoke.

Mare complied, and as she read, she felt more and more ashamed of her jealous response. Isaac was getting international attention for building a sense of pride and hope in Haiti. Wasn't it being petty to look past his achievement all because of jealousy over what could be nothing at all? She thought of the novel she had borrowed from Henri. *The Invention of Wings*. If he could be the person to give the people of Haiti wings…WOW! That would be something.

She looked up from the article and smiled at her friend. "Thanks for showing me this, Karissa."

"That's better!" said her friend. "For a moment there I thought in order to get any joy out of this I was going to have to steal Isaac myself."

Mare laughed. "Yeah, like I couldn't whoop your ass!"

She gave Karissa a hug, kissed her on the cheek, and headed out the door. She couldn't wait to get to her dressing room to have a little privacy to call Isaac. She punched in the number and paced the floor while it rang. By the time it rang four times, she was getting anxious and when his voice mail came on, her spirit crashed again. He hardly ever didn't answer her call.

Where could he be? And with whom?

Cap-Haitien, Haiti, June 4th, 2017

Isaac didn't like the expressions on the faces of some young men along the fringes of the rally. Most eyes were hopeful, joyous even. These eyes were guarded, threatening. Most eyes were focused on him as he stood up front. These eyes surreptitiously looked back and forth at each other.

Isaac glanced over at Arturo, caught his eye, and nodded in the direction of the interlopers. Arturo grabbed Crista and a couple of young men nearby and headed in the direction Isaac had indicated.

Trusting their response, Isaac took a deep breath and looked out at the crowd gathered before him. He guessed the numbers to be around 5,000 people and growing. He stepped up to the microphone, and spoke in Creole.

"Ayiti p'ap peri!"

Those gathered shouted approval of this expression of confidence in Haiti's future and raised their fists in the air. After a pause to let that shouting subside, Isaac continued, still in Creole.

"You know our story, and that is why you are here. We are not here for another meaningless political campaign. We are not here either to blame a government or beg to a government. We are here for nothing less than to reclaim a vision for a new Haiti!"

Applause broke out throughout the crowd.

"We are tired of being a poor country. We are tired of being an impotent country, pitied by the world. We are tired of being a despised pawn in the chess game of the powerful. We are here to take control of our own future. *Ayiti p'ap peri! Ayiti p'ap peri!*"

The crowd joined together in the chant. *Ayiti p'ap peri! Ayiti p'ap peri! Ayiti p'ap peri!*"

"We can do this! Our future is in our own hands. We can clean up our streets. We can clean up our politics. We can restore the prosperity of our country, so that all Haitians, rich and poor can stand proud and take care of their families!"

More applause.

"We don't need to be strong-armed by those who want us to fear them, whether it be a foreign government or the *Tonton Makout!*"

The applause now thundered throughout the crowd. People resumed the chant, *Ayiti p'ap peri! Ayiti p'ap peri! Ayiti p'ap peri!* Isaac looked toward the back of the crowd for the suspicious men he had seen along the fringes, but they were no longer evident. *Had they simply blended into the crowd?* Arturo, Crista and Arturo's friends were searching them out, but with no luck. Arturo looked up at him and threw his arms into the air in frustration.

There was nothing for Isaac to do except continue. "When the black people of the United States wanted to claim their part in the future of that country, they followed a man named Martin Luther King. He did not call for the overthrow of their president. He did not lead people into the streets with the weapons of violence. He led people with the weapons of faith and moral courage. He taught the people that if they stood together, no one could defeat them! Violence did not intimidate them. Many had to bravely face death, even as many of our ancestors did in our revolution over 200 years ago. If we stand together, we also will have to confront violence against us and even death. But I stand before you today to declare, we shall not be moved! We shall overcome!"

People throughout the crowd began dancing and shouting. *Ayiti p'ap peri! Ayiti p'ap peri! Ayiti p'ap peri!* And for a moment, Isaac smiled.

Then came an explosion in the middle of the crowd. People screamed. Gun shots rang out from several directions. It was difficult to tell where they came from, but several people fell to the ground. Isaac saw Arturo and his friends bravely running toward where they had heard gunfire. Another shot popped in the crowd and Crista fell to the ground. Arturo quickly knelt by her side. U.N. police cars pulled up at the edge of what had quickly become a chaotic melee. Isaac's heart raced.

What could he say? What could he do? He quickly grabbed the hands of two supporters near the stage. He looked briefly for Yvette to join them, but he saw her running away from the stage with her arms over her head. Isaac lifted the arms of the other two high, and sang in Creole:

"We shall overcome, we shall overcome,

We shall overcome someday…"

Throughout the crowd people stopped, took each other's hands and joined in the song:

"Oh, deep in my heart, I do believe,

We shall overcome someday…"

More people joined in the song, even though several fell by bullets:

"We are not afraid, we are not afraid,

We are not afraid today,

Oh, deep in my heart…"

Isaac saw U.N. soldiers taking a couple of shooters to the ground, but even so the shots kept coming. Semi-automatic rifle fire strafed the stage. Isaac felt a burn in his leg and the left side of his chest. Weakness swept through his body and he fell to the ground.

Next came a confusion of voices. People hovering overhead. Distant sounds of gun shots and singing. Then silence and blackout.

New York, June 4th 2017

Marie-Noëlle stepped into the plush Manhattan apartment. Eric said something about how beautiful she looked, but she could hardly believe it. She knew her makeup could not have covered it up that well. She had cried all afternoon.

He had never even returned her call.

She could not think of any reason why he would not have called, except if he was with that girl. Now she would be with someone else, too.

"Can I fix you a drink?"

Marie-Noëlle smiled, mostly to herself. "I could use one. Make it a bourbon on the rocks."

Eric brought her drink, and as he handed it to her with his right hand, he eased his left around her waist, and kissed her on the neck. "I've really been looking forward to having you here."

She sighed. "'Having me', huh?"

Eric chuckled and nodded.

Marie-Noëlle surveyed his apartment. She saw a posh loft with original art by Gerhart Richter, and an eclectic mix of furnishings dividing up the open space. Through a door she could see a four-poster bed with mirrors all around. Nearer by she noted an ornate, hand-carved medieval style chess set in ebony and oak.

She sidled up to Eric and breathed in his ear. Then she whispered, "You know, real men prefer a little challenge to win a woman, rather than having everything be too boringly easy. Would that be true of you?"

Eric gave her a sly smile. "What kind of challenge are you proposing?"

"I notice you have a gorgeous, hand-carved chess set over there. Is it just for show, or do you play?"

"I play."

"How about we play each other? I win, and I get the chess set. You win, and you get...me."

Eric laughed. "Challenge accepted! But I must warn you that I was President of the Princeton Chess Club!"

Marie-Noëlle smiled coyly. "Oh, my! I hope I will be enough challenge for you."

Eric sauntered over towards the board and pointed toward the set. "White or black?"

Marie-Noëlle followed him across and put her hand on his. "It would seem nature has already determined that. I have always been, and will always be black. You must be content with being white."

"Most would say that in chess, white has the advantage."

Marie-Noëlle sat down in front of the board. "As in life, of course. But I have always done well being black. So, I believe yours is the first move."

Eric sat down opposite the Haitian model. "Hey, I always like foreplay. So let's get to it." He moved his king's pawn two spaces ahead to e4.

Marie-Noëlle smiled. *A standard first move. Good. She loved attacking the standard with the unexpected.* She moved her bishop's pawn to c-5.

Cap-Haitien, Haiti, June 5th, 2017

Isaac opened his eyes to a swirling blur. Someone was speaking to him.

"Monsieur Breda! Can you hear me, Monsieur Breda?"

The blur cleared, and the room stopped swirling. A man in a surgeon's gown leaned over him. Two nurses, one male and one female, stood on either side of the bed.

"Monsieur Breda, if you understand me, squeeze my hand," said the surgeon.

Isaac cleared his throat. "I don't need to do that. I can talk."

"Monsieur Breda, do you remember what happened?"

Isaac coughed, and pain shot through his leg and chest. He nodded. "I was shot."

"Yes, you were," continued the doctor. "That bullet in your chest just missed your heart, and you lost a lot of blood. But you are in the hospital now. We're watching you carefully. It's important that you get some more rest."

Isaac frowned and cleared his throat again. "My throat is...sore."

"That's from the tube when we anesthetized you for surgery. We had to sew up your leg and get that bullet out of your chest."

"The others...I, uh...I need to talk to my friends. Arturo, Yvette and Crista."

"Yes, Arturo and Yvette have inquired about you. And Crista – well, she was shot also, and she's getting the best of care in another room. None of them can see you now. Like I said, for now you must rest."

"Oh, you have also had some calls on your cell," said the female nurse. "From someone your caller ID labeled as…'Mare'? Anyway, I'm sure she can wait too."

"No…she…where is my cell?"

"Monsieur Breda, seriously!" said the doctor. "We can't have you thrashing around with these injuries. Nurse, he needs that shot now."

"No, I—" But then it all faded away.

New York, June 5h 2017

Marie-Noëlle woke up and stretched. She sat up in bed and looked around the room, the room of her own modest flat in Manhattan. And there it was, beautifully carved out of ebony and oak, her prize from the previous evening.

She had thought about letting him win. She really had. Who was she saving herself for – Isaac? Well, maybe. She had gotten really angry, but she still didn't know what was happening there. She was irritated enough at Isaac to jump into bed with some other guy, but she didn't know if that irritation had any factual basis behind it. Besides, she didn't want to be another notch in a playboy's bed post.

Of course, Eric had gotten pretty angry. Part of that was pride. He considered himself too good a chess player to lose to a Haitian girl. When she told him she had twice won the Haitian Chess Federation Tournament as a teen, and had done very well in international competition, he accused her of hustling him, and tried to renege on their agreement. Only when she massaged his ego and promised him a chance to win back his chess set…and her…did he agree to let the chess set go. Yeah, that wasn't a man she wanted to go to bed with.

She picked up the television remote and clicked on CNN International. The first report was on the tension in the Middle East. As always, that concerned her. Fighting and hatred with such deep historical roots.

But then came the next report. Marie-Noëlle's eyes opened wide, and her heart raced. Violence at Isaac's rally, and he had been shot. She turned up the volume.

"A rally meant to spur hope and renewal in Cap Haitien, Haiti turned violent yesterday evening when a bomb exploded and hooded men began peppering the peaceful crowd of over 5,000 with semi-automatic gun fire. Order was restored by U.N. troops, but when it was all done, at least 150 people lay dead and hundreds of others were wounded, including organizer and speaker Isaac Breda. He is reported to be in serious but stable condition at the *Hôpital Bon Samaritain*, Limbe."

Marie-Noëlle grabbed her cell phone and punched the button to speed-dial Isaac. She reached his voice mail. The newscaster continued.

"Supporters of Breda believe the assault was carried out by forces loyal to candidate for President, François Cambronne, grandson of Luckner Cambronne, head of the notorious *Tonton Makout* in the days of the Duvaliers. Here is reporter Carlos Morales at the hospital in Cap Haitien."

The screen switched to a young Hispanic reporter standing next to a tall Haitian male. "I'm here with Arturo Pamphile, and first of all, Arturo, we want you to know our prayers are with you and your friend Isaac Breda after this vicious assault."

Arturo's eyes were red, and he looked back at a door behind him for a brief moment, before returning his focus to the camera alongside the reporter. "Yeah. Thanks. And Crista, too, please. Crista Patrice. I don't know if she's going to make it."

The reporter nodded. "Certainly. Our prayers are with her as well."

Arturo folded his arms and looked down at the floor.

"But, now, Arturo, what makes you and your group think the ones who attacked you are associated with François Cambronne and a revived *Tonton Makout*?"

"Well, the main reason is that they told us they were going to do it. They attacked Isaac and me in an alley weeks ago, told us they were *Tonton Makout* and that we better support François Cambronne. I'd say that was a pretty strong indication!"

"And why would they attack you, a group peacefully working for the betterment of Haiti?"

"Look, man, I'm just a street guy who also happens to know some things about recent history. Take those Contras down in Nicaragua back in the 80s. What did they have against nuns and poor villagers? They were all peaceful. But the Contras did all that shit to them! Killed a lot of people. They wanted to get people all scared so they would listen to them instead of the Sandinistas. And what about the Taliban and ISIS? Hell, it's just the same song, second verse. They always attack peaceful people who are just trying to live their lives and make things better. It's the only way they can be in control."

"You have been teaching non-violence," said the reporter. "Will this attack make you re-think that strategy?"

Arturo looked down at the ground again, and shifted his weight. "Isaac is in charge here, and I'll do what he says. But if he doesn't survive, or if Crista doesn't survive, all bets are off. I'm going out and kick myself some *Tonton Makout* ass."

Marie-Noëlle jumped out of bed and began to pace the floor as the TV screen returned to the newscaster.

"There is, of course, another side. We go to Marie Darcisse in Port-au-Prince."

The TV screen now showed a young woman standing by an older, slightly graying Haitian man. "I'm here with François Cambronne, candidate for President of Haiti. François, you heard the accusations made against you and your group. How do you respond?"

"Marie, thank you for giving me a chance to comment on these ridiculous charges. Of course, we feel for the families of those who died in this incident, and pray that Isaac Breda and his followers recover quickly from their injuries. But it is simply not true that my followers attacked a peaceful demonstration. I understand from some of my people who were there, seeking to keep in touch with what was going on, that an argument broke out between street thugs, and they began firing at each other, and people got caught in the crossfire. This is the type of thing that happens every day in Haiti! That's why I support bringing back our national army and the *Tonton Makout*. We need them to control the street violence we see around us. Isn't it time we had peace and political stability in our beloved country?"

Marie-Noëlle was getting so upset by the broadcast she turned the television off.

How could François Cambronne attack peaceful Haitians and then claim such violence was why he was needed? She continued pacing the floor, while occasionally staring at her cell phone. *Why didn't it ring? Why didn't Isaac call to tell her he was really okay, and she had nothing to worry about?*

She stopped pacing, and abruptly turned and went into her walk-in closet. There on the floor. Behind two rows of shoes. Underneath her collection of skirts. Her suitcase looked up at her expectantly.

Cap-Haitien, Haiti, June 6th, 2017

Isaac awoke again. He looked around the room. His father and mother rushed to his side, and Arturo and Yvette quickly joined them.

"Isaac! Thank God, you're awake," said his father.

Isaac blinked his eyes. He looked over at Arturo. "Crista? How is she?"

"She seems okay," Arturo responded. "I talked to her earlier. The crazy bitch is ready to get back out on the street again. Her parents are trying to talk some sense into her."

"As well they should," said Isaac's mother. "Isaac, you've got to give up all this political stuff and come home. Please tell me you will!"

Isaac looked at his father. He smiled and shrugged. "She's your mother. What can I say? She wants you safe."

Isaac cleared his throat. "Mom, Dad, could you let me talk privately to Arturo and Yvette? It won't take long."

His mother cried and shook her head, but his father gently led her out of the room. Isaac turned to his two friends. "Are both of you still on board?"

Arturo nodded.

Yvette looked down at the floor. "I…I don't know. I mean, I don't know if you noticed, with all the commotion. I ran." Tears streamed down her cheeks. "I ran away screaming while you were on stage getting shot. I didn't even notice where you were or what was happening to you until I was lost in the crowd and looked back toward the stage. Maybe you shouldn't even want me 'on board'."

Isaac wasn't sure if his response was a grimace or a smile, but he hoped Yvette received it as a smile. "Well, there are those who would say you were the smart one."

"Some are asking if we shouldn't arm ourselves," said Arturo. "For defensive purposes only, of course."

"Once we do that, we've lost," said Isaac. "The *Tonton Makout* will always be able to come up with more arms than we will – and they will be in the hands of better-trained fighters." Isaac coughed a couple of times, and then refocused on his friends. "Our example has to be that of Martin Luther King and the U.S. Civil Rights fight. Our weapons must be the weapons of nonviolence: truth, faith, and courage."

"King had the support of the Kennedys and the national media," said Arturo. "Federal troops had their back."

Isaac nodded. "And we should do a better job of communicating with the U.N. and the Haitian National Police. They will help us. But, above all, we cannot let fear win."

"My presence will help with the media coverage," said a familiar voice from the door.

Isaac looked that way. He feared that the one he saw was an anesthetic-produced hallucination. Then the voice came again, soft, gentle and, above all, real.

"After all, an internationally-known model standing with you, one loved in Haiti, and valued by international corporations with an investment in her image, might make even the *Tonton Makout* hesitant to fire."

"Mare!" Isaac attempted to sit up, but he could not.

Mare rushed to his side, and kissed him gently all over his face. "Lie down. It's okay," she said soothingly. "Don't worry, I'm not going anywhere."

"Your modeling…"

"Hey, I'm not giving that up! The agency gave me some time to come down here. They decided it would be good for publicity. Maybe they will want to do some shoots down here after all."

Isaac glanced at Yvette. She had turned away and was looking out the window. He refocused on Mare. "I could sure use you with me. But, it's going to be dangerous."

"I know. We will face the dangers together." She shifted her gaze toward Yvette, who turned to face her. "We will confront them with your friends. Your friends will be my friends." They smiled at each other. Mare turned back toward Isaac. "I heard when you were being fired upon, you started singing 'We shall overcome.' I thought of the verse which says, 'We are not afraid.'" She walked to the door, where she had dropped her carry-on, unzipped it, pulled out a t-shirt and held it up. "So I put that phrase on this shirt in Creole: *'Nou pa pè.'* I thought Creole was best. This country is already too full of used American t-shirts, written in English."

"I love it!" said Arturo. "You got one of those for me?"

"Yes, but not this one," said Mare. She walked over to Yvette and held out the shirt. "This one is for you – if you want it."

Yvette smiled and took the shirt. "Yes, I do. I could use a brave t-shirt."

"But you are still on board?" asked Isaac.

Yvette, with her eyes on the Haitian model, nodded.

Mare looked back at Isaac. "I had a thousand more of these shirts made, and shipped here. All have the phrase, *Nou pa pè* on the front, and the Haitian flag on the back. They will be here by the end of the week."

"It will take much more than t-shirts," said Arturo. "But they will help."

Isaac was feeling both exhilarated and exhausted at the same time. Still, he sought to focus, because he knew there was much to do. "Arturo and Yvette – I need you to contact our supporters right away, to let them know we are not intimidated. Tell them we will rally in front of the hospital at Mirebalais one week from today." He gave a loving glance toward Mare. "Oh, and tell them the famous Haitian model Marie-Noëlle will be there with us. Let them know we will gather to take charge of the country of Toussaint. Tell them to come prepared to be put to work."

"And give them a message from me as well," said Mare. "Tell them I personally am guaranteeing media coverage from the U.S., as well as Haiti. Tell them the media will be here if I have to strip naked to make it happen!"

Isaac laughed, in spite of it causing pain in his chest. Then he shared a smile with the group gathered. "Maybe don't tell them that, okay?"

Mare looked at him with an abundance of attitude, the sassiness he had become so used to in her. "Unless it is necessary, of course!"

Isaac shifted his gaze to Yvette, who blushed and looked down at the floor again. "Thanks to all of you," he said.

Yvette nodded, then looked over at Arturo. "Come on, Arturo. We have work to do. And Isaac and Marie-Noëlle deserve some time alone."

Isaac felt a little embarrassed that Yvette had to be the one to say what he so desperately wanted, but he was not going to contradict her. As the others left the room, Mare put her hand on his, and that moment became frozen in time.

Chapter Sixteen

Isaac slowly ascended the stairs to the makeshift stage. His chest and leg both ached, but no pain could ever be enough to keep him from this moment. The t-shirts Mare had ordered had arrived on time, and throughout the crowd he saw light blue shirts with the red and blue Haitian flag on the back. The words on the front nearly moved Isaac to tears: *Nou pa pè.* We are not afraid. An easy thing to say, but so much harder to live. And yet before him he saw at least 3,000 people ready to live those words. Mare had already ordered more t-shirts.

He stood on the stage, surveyed the milling crowd and reflected. Over 200 years before, the ancestors of those gathered here had faced execution by the French. They had done so, standing proud and declaring how sweet it was to die for liberty. And now these descendants were standing ready to do it again, to make liberty real.

Arturo and Crista sat near the stage, signing people up for projects of renewal for Haiti. Crista struggled to sit up for such a long period of time. But periodically Arturo would reach over, stroke her hair and kiss her lovingly on the cheek. Isaac smiled. How had he missed that coming?

Not far from Arturo and Crista, Mare and Karissa were signing autographs on t-shirts and pages from fashion magazines. Then they would direct their admirers to one of the many project sign-up stations.

Still, Isaac's eyes had learned too much from their last gathering to focus solely on the positive. They scanned the crowd for what he hoped they would not see. But there it was. A man polished a semi-automatic rifle, and smiled at him. And over there – two men who looked very much like the ones who had assaulted Arturo and him in the alley. He wouldn't even count the numerous others who stood around the periphery, arms folded, scowling at him.

Isaac rose and walked to the microphone. He only grimaced slightly as he held his arms high in the air. The still -bandaged wound on his chest throbbed, his injured leg wobbled, but his heart held steady.

"Nou pa pè!" he shouted.

The response was thunderous. *"Nou pa pè! Nou pa pè!"* People throughout the crowd danced around and thrust their fists in the air. "Nou pa pè! Nou pa pè!" Then another shout arose from the crowd. "Vive Isaac! Vive Isaac! Vive Isaac!"

Isaac signaled for quiet, and slowly it came. "I can never thank all of you enough for the many prayers said for me as I lay in the hospital in Cap Haitien. They say I am a man of great words, but I do not have the words to voice my love and gratitude for all of you!"

"Vive Isaac! Vive Isaac! Vive Isaac!"

Again Isaac called for quiet. "But these are no longer days for words. These are days for action. We are going to put our country back together piece by piece! The Tonton Makout does not want that. They want chaos and despair, so the people of Haiti will think we need them to hammer the country into submission. But we are the sons and daughters of Toussaint! We will not be intimidated! We will not fear!"

"Nou pa pè! Nou pa pè!" The crowd danced and shouted. *"Nou pa pè! Nou pa pè!"*

"We are not going to sit around passively and wait for someone else to help us," Isaac continued when the shouting subsided. "We will be the ones to build schools for our children! We will be the ones who are going to clean up our streets and neighborhoods. We will be the ones planting the trees our agriculture needs. WE will do it!"

The crowd applauded.

"And if any of you have been involved in the violence that has wrecked our country – kidnapping and mugging people in the street, *because you needed to feed your families –* vow this day to turn away from all of that! We cannot pay you, but we will provide food for you and your families while you work on these projects!"

As the crowd applauded once again, Isaac looked down at Mare, who smiled and gave him a "thumbs up". She had gotten contributions from wealthy New York friends to supplement her own financial investment and those of Haitian supporters, to pay for food for workers.

Isaac now shifted his gaze back to those suspicious faces around the periphery. UN officers circulated throughout the crowd. "You do not have to turn to violence in order to eat. Join us! Make Haiti better!" The chants started up again, but Isaac squeezed in a few more essential words. "Enough talk! Let's get to work!"

"Nou pa pè! Nou pa pè! Nou pa pè! Nou pa pè!"

Before descending from the stage, Isaac surveyed the sign-up stations and other happenings all around him. Long lines formed in front of the work stations. Off to the right were a fleet of motorcycles and tap-taps recruited to take workers to the sites. Nearby was also a handful of volunteers from the U.S.NGO, the Central Asia Institute. This group, originally headed by Greg Mortenson, had used local volunteer labor to build many schools in Pakistan and Afghanistan, and now they had volunteered to help build schools in Haiti. Employees of *Ramase Lajan,* which picks up plastic trash and recycles it into polyester thread for fabric, were also there to take volunteers to the streets of Port-au-Prince to pick up plastic trash. Leaders from *The Eden Projects* stood by to train and assist volunteers in growing trees, and not far from them representatives of *Sun Ovens International* talked to people about solar-powered ovens as an alternative to burning down trees for charcoal for cooking food.

Television reporters from the U.S. and other nations roamed throughout the crowd, followed by television cameras. A flock of these reporters and cameras gathered around Dr. Paul Hansen, in front of the hospital. He beamed with pride as he spoke to them.

All of these happenings were a little surreal to Isaac. He and his friends had worked so hard to make it all come to pass, and yet that it was happening still had a dream-like quality to it, like it could vanish in the mist of a moment.

Isaac descended from the stage, and people swarmed around him. Some were asking for outright hand-outs, and Isaac had to tell them that was not something they would be doing. But most spoke how his approach had revived their hope for Haiti. They felt like their children now had a chance at a future, and they thanked him.

Isaac came to a man he thought was another well-wisher. The man smiled and held out his hand. Isaac took it. "Great gathering!" the man said. And then he stopped smiling, and added, "Enjoy it while you can, because you are going to die." Isaac tried to take his hand away, but the man gripped it tightly. "After you are dead and rotting in the ground," the man continued, "the world will know who really controls things in Haiti." His smile came back and he released Isaac's hand. "Have a nice day."

Isaac trembled.

Cap-Haitien, Haiti, June 13th 2017

Marie-Noëlle's head throbbed. Word of the threat against Isaac and the dangers they faced had reached New York. She was on the phone with Eric.

"I can't go back to New York right now, Eric. We had an agreement. Karissa and I could come down for a month, and you would arrange a shoot while I am here. That's what you promised."

"But the dangers there have gotten worse!" he said. "We can't afford—"

"Have you forgotten what nearly happened when I went to New Jersey? There are dangers in the U.S. as well."

"Yeah, well some of our photographers don't even like going to New Jersey. But Haiti right now? That would be a tough sell."

"Tell them it will be a lot of good publicity! People like to hear about celebrities making a difference in the world. Think about Angelina Jolie, Sean Penn, George Clooney, Penelope Cruz—"

"It's dangerous!"

"It's exotic!" Marie-Noëlle reached into her cabinet and pulled out a bottle of maximum strength Ibuprofen. She took three. "Hell, tell them I will stretch out on a cannon at the *Citadelle Laferriere*, in the sheerest negligee they can find. Talk about a phallic symbol! People will eat it up!"

"Yeah, well, then I'll come too. We could—"

Marie-Noëlle rolled her eyes, and made a gesture with her middle finger, which she was glad could not be transmitted through a cell phone. "I don't know, Eric. You're really needed there. But just let me know when people are coming. I've got to go. Things are getting hectic around here."

Marie-Noëlle hit "End" before she received a response from Eric. She took three deep breaths and looked at the time on her cell phone. 4:30 PM. Just enough time for a quick nap before a dinner meeting with the Toussaint Louverture Economic Freedom Foundation. That was what they had decided to call the financial support group for *The Sons and Daughters of Toussaint*. It included Isaac, his father, Crista's father, Dr. Paul Hansen, as well as Karissa and her. She and Isaac were going to grab some private time afterwards. She could hardly wait.

Mare curled her left arm around Isaac's right and laid her head on his shoulder. Isaac's father, Pierre, was staring down at his plate. He hadn't touched a bite of food. The expressions on the faces of the others ranged from Karissa's empathetic smile at her friend Mare to Paul Hansen's pensive surveying of the other restaurant patrons, to the matter-of-fact, set-jaw glare on the face of Crista's father, Manuel Patrice.

"What did you expect?" Manuel asked. "This is Haiti! You get threats against your life for swerving your car in front of a tap-tap."

"That's not the same," said Pierre quietly.

"No, but he's right," said Isaac. "This should not have been unexpected. We are fighting violence with non-violence. We are modeling our movement on that of Martin Luther King. He was threatened many times before—"

"Before he was killed," said Isaac's father.

Isaac nodded. "But I will not back down. We have chosen the motto, *Nou pa pè!* How can I not live that motto myself?"

All except Isaac's father nodded. Isaac looked at him. "Father! You understand also, do you not?"

Tears welled up in Pierre Breda's eyes. He clasped his hand over Isaac's so firmly that he thought his bones would be crushed. Pierre looked his son in the eye. "You are my brave, beautiful boy! I, the father, proudly follow you, the son, *anywhere!*"

No one spoke as the gaze of a son penetrated to and massaged his father's soul, and a father's trembling emotion vibrated in sync with his son's courage.

Manuel Patrice broke the silence. "Well, we came here to talk about funding, and we better get to it."

Isaac nodded. "I have given all of you a copy of our income and expenditures to date. The bottom line is that in spite of costs for the t-shirts, food and material for all our projects, and subsidizing the purchase of over 500 solar cookers, we have about $1,000,000 U.S. more than when we started. That's due in large part to generous gifts from the friends of Mare and Karissa, along with some positive publicity in the U.S."

"And there is more coming in each day," said Karissa.

"I've got to tell you," said Mare, "the responsibility for handling that much money on the behalf of the people of Haiti makes me more than a little nervous."

"If that much makes you nervous," said Manuel Patrice, "then you are going to have a real mental collapse when we start doing 100 million, because I believe that is where we are heading."

"So, what's next?" asked Isaac.

"Many people working with countries struggling economically have found that the best way to help is by helping the women," said Paul Hansen. "The saying is 'Give to a man, and you help one man; give to a woman, and you help the whole village.' That is because women share what they are given, and make sure that it benefits not only their families, but the families of their friends. For instance, when Rwanda was recovering from the devastating economic effect of tribal genocide, when the country was pulling together, it was on the backs of women the country was rebuilt. Many of these women had been victims of rape and physical violence, and others had been abandoned by husbands who were imprisoned or fleeing imprisonment. Now that country is doing remarkably well."

"Yeah, I know of some missionary workers around Cap Haitien who give micro-loans to female entrepreneurs," said Isaac, "and the approach seems to be working well."

"I would certainly put more of my money into that," said Karissa. "Maybe it's just because I am a little distrustful of many Haitian men—"

"Hey! Tender male egos here!" said Isaac, with a smile.

"Okay, present company excepted! But it's also true, I know, that women hold the purse strings in many Haitian families."

"Wouldn't such an approach alienate a lot of the men?" asked Manuel Patrice. "Take Arturo, for instance. I know my daughter seems to have become...well, somewhat attached to him. I can't say I'm overly excited about that, but—"

"He's a good guy," said Isaac.

"Yeah, well, she's my little girl! But put that aside for the moment. He was very good to her when she was recovering in the hospital. I know he used to be just another street thug, but now he seems to be committed to making a real difference. I don't want to turn off guys like him."

"That's a good point," said Isaac. "Perhaps we can focus on female entrepreneurs, but be open to male applicants as well. The point is, we should be supporting projects that help whole communities, and not just giving hand-outs to individuals."

The others nodded.

Isaac looked at Mare. "So, what's the status of the photo shoot here in Haiti?"

"It's still on," she said. "But some people within the agency are getting nervous. Worried about 'their property', I guess. I just talked to Eric a couple of hours ago, and I haven't even told Karissa yet."

"It's not unexpected," said Karissa.

"I think they're still coming down," added Mare. "But I can't say how long they are going to be patient with our being down here."

Isaac felt a tightening in his stomach. "I really need... uh...the project needs you. Both of you."

Mare smiled and Karissa giggled. "Can I assume you don't need me in the same sense you need Mare?"

Isaac shrugged. "I don't know. What are you offering?"

Mare slugged him on the arm, and Isaac winced. "Too much. I can see that now." He rubbed his arm and looked at Mare. "Man, I knew they had you working out, but for what? – a TITLE FIGHT?"

Mare smirked. "Let's just say in my line of work, I have plenty of opportunities to punch cocky men who step over the line. And thanks for the additional practice."

"Are we done?" asked Manuel Patrice dryly. "Or are we needed here to referee?"

"No, we're done," said Isaac, while lost in Mare's sassy, but passionate gaze. "I know I have other things to do."

Isaac didn't know who said what after that, what others said about where they planned to go, or who left first and who left last. He was lost in the eyes of the woman he loved.

Being lost there was a safe place.

Cap-Haitien, Haiti, July 2017

Isaac gazed out the bedroom window of his parents' home on a hill overlooking the city of Cap-Haitien. Out front was a car from the Haitian National Police. Just down the street he also saw a car marked "U.N." This security was necessary now, he realized. He had moved back into his parents' home because that way security could be provided for his parents as well. His father especially might be a target.

He shook his head and moaned. How long will I have to live like this? he thought.

Mare came up behind him and put her hand gently on his shoulder. "Hey, Nerd! When you asked me to come here after the meeting, I didn't know it was to watch you stare out a window. I guess I have to tell you everything!" She pulled him toward his bed. "This is how it works: a guy asks a girl to come to his room to see his 'etchings' or some other dumb thing. Then he throws her on the bed and attacks her passionately. That's what my body was ready for. You are wasting the moment!"

Isaac wanted to join Mare in her 'moment', but his mind still lingered outside the window. What was out there spoke of the limitation of moments one has in life. It could all be gone in the blink of an eye. Then he thought of what he had put in his right front pants pocket earlier that day.

"Wait! Wait!" he said. "There is something I need to talk to you about."

Mare sat on the bed with a look of mock despair on her face. "Oh, God! This is my life. I fall in love with the only guy in the world who gets propositioned by his hot girlfriend, and wants to TALK!"

"No, look, this is important," Isaac said. "We don't know what is going to happen to us, and we can't just ignore that fact. I have been threatened by men who have the reputation of following through with such threats. You, on the other hand, are being pressured to go back to the U.S., leaving me here without you again."

Mare rolled her eyes. "Wow. Great pep-talk so far. You should copyright it. Really."

Isaac got down on one knee, and looked into his girlfriend's eyes. He pulled a small box out of his pocket.

"Oh, God!" she said, now wide-eyed. "Are you sure?"

"If a moment is all we have in this life, then I want mine to be with you, Mare. I can face anything if it is with you as my wife. I could face death itself. I could even face you going back to the U.S. for a while. I want to tell the world that God made us for each other, and that nothing will ever pull us apart. Will you do it? Share this adventure with me! Be my wife!"

Isaac had the ring poised at the end of Mare's finger. She trembled, but he held steady. Tears formed in her eyes, and she tried to brush them away. "I...I...Oh, God! Oh, God! Oh, God!"

"Is that a 'yes' or 'no'?"

Mare jumped up from the bed and began to pace the floor. "That's a *give a girl a little warning, okay*?! You are such a dork about this! What a guy is supposed to do is to invite a girl to some romantic place, and tell her he has something important to talk about. That's called giving a warning. I mean, it could have been the beach where we first made love...or, or...that cannon room in The *Citadelle Laferriere,* or even a nice restaurant. But, no, you propose to me in your bedroom! God, I can see the headlines now: *Famous Haitian Model Marries Total Nerd."*

"So...that's a 'Yes'?"

Mare squealed and did a little pirouette. Then she jumped into his arms, threw her legs around his waist and covered his face with kisses. "Of course it's a 'Yes'! I mean, you are a nerd, but the words were nice."

Isaac laughed, as he held her body which still wrapped around him, and jumped in a circle.

Mare giggled. "Hey, what is this, kinky sex? You could at least throw me on the bed!"

No sooner had those words left Mare's mouth than Isaac did exactly as she suggested. As he slid up next to her, he had to pause as their eyes met. Even though it was Mare's body and spirit that ignited his passion, nothing grabbed hold of him like her eyes. And all the time he was furiously pulling off her clothes, he didn't break that connection. They were one. When he penetrated her warmth, it simply completed the connection. The vows would say, "'Til death do us part." Isaac knew that the future promise was already a present reality.

Chapter Seventeen

Cap Haitien, Haiti, July, 2017

Everyone on the camera crew was talking about how much brighter and more alive Marie-Noëlle's smile was. One photographer told her he had always seen her smile as the finishing artistic touch on a great work of art. Now her smile had become even more. Now her smile was the window through which the perfection of her beauty shone.

Of course, only Marie-Noëlle and Karissa knew the secret of how this new smile had been birthed.

The two Haitian models pranced and played along the beach at Labadie, as the photographers' cameras clicked and whirred. They had contracted to do three photo shoots in Haiti. They had previously done one for lingerie at *The Citadelle Laferriere,* where the agency had indeed arranged for Karissa and her to be photographed draped across cannons, while wearing flimsy lingerie. They had also done one in more modest sportswear, riding a motorcycle together through the streets of Cap Haitien. This was then the third shoot, featuring the models in swimwear by several designers.

Marie-Noëlle couldn't say when she had more fun just being pretty.

Eric, however, was most certainly not having fun. Every time Marie-Noëlle looked his way, he was glancing around nervously at every Haitian native looking on. When a man started hammering on the roof of a nearby lodge, Eric went into hysterics. "Everybody down! We're taking fire!" He ran to the parking lot and rolled under their rented van.

Marie-Noëlle put on her robe, walked calmly over to the van, knelt down and looked under it. "Find any snipers under there, Eric?"

"Get down! The *Tonton Makout* are after us!"

"Don't think so, Eric. They prefer AK-47's to roofing hammers."

"To what?"

"Hammers, Eric," said Marie-Noëlle. "You're hiding from a roofer with a hammer."

"Well, I should never have let you convince me to come down here!" said Eric, as he crawled out from under the van. He looked around at various camera crew members who tried to suppress their laughter. "It's dangerous down here. You know that!" He stood up and brushed himself off. "Let's finish this up, and get out of here. And that means you and Karissa, as well. The models are not in charge here. I am! Models are in this world to look hot and do as they are told. Not plan shoots and publicity."

"Come on, Eric, lighten up," said Karissa, who had joined them.

"I will *not* 'lighten up' I am the head of this agency, and you've got me hiding under vans, with my models and camera crew laughing at me!"

"Well, you have to admit—"

"I didn't come down here for this!"

"So, why did you come down here?" asked Karissa. "You didn't have to."

Eric looked at Marie-Noëlle. "Well—"

"He was trying to get into my pants, of course," said Marie-Noëlle.

"That's not true!" protested Eric. "I am not so desperate that I have to—"

"Well, I'm done with your antics! I am getting married, Eric! To a guy I actually care about."

"Married...?"

"Yes! And I am going to stay in Haiti, changing the country I was born in, as long as it takes. If that doesn't work for you, then you can go and find yourself some other piece of 'eye-candy' who doesn't care about anything but looking pretty and pleasing you!"

"That's it!" said Eric. "You're fired! Stay down here and starve with the other Haitians! I can get another model."

"Then you have to get two," said Karissa, "because I'm staying also."

Eric's eyes widened and his nostrils flared. "All right, we're done here!" he shouted. "Pack it up, and let's get out of here!" He lowered his voice, as he focused on the two models. "And in case you are thinking you can get on with some other agency, you are underestimating my influence in the industry. Influential people throughout New York are quickly going to know how difficult you are to work with. They might even hear how your attitude endangered this whole crew. You are finished! Enjoy your new poverty!"

"Don't you mean 'Enjoy your new freedom?'" said Marie-Noëlle. "That's what I plan to enjoy!"

Marie-Noëlle and Karissa stood there staring at the modeling executive, as he strutted away. When he was out of earshot, Karissa leaned toward Mare. "Do you think that was B.S. about bad-mouthing us to the other agencies? I mean, because I really don't do well without nice things."

"Yeah, me too, but we'll figure it out." Mare crossed her arms, and stool tall. "I'm sure we're not the only ones in the business who know that Eric is a pompous ass sleaze. And Eric will use this shoot. With the expense of coming down here, he can't afford not to. People will see our work here, and they will be calling."

"You really think so?"

"We have no other choice, at this point – we need the money, and so does our work in Haiti." Mare held Karissa close. "And thank you so much for backing me up down here. It means a lot to share all of this with you."

"Sure, we're sisters and we share," said Karissa. Then she giggled. "Does that include Isaac? Because he's really cute!"

Mare pulled back and flashed her most beautiful smile. "Not a chance, Bitch!"

The two friends laughed, and jostled each other like guys all the way to the car. Mare knew just below the surface of their revelry, they were afraid to let go of the laughter, lest the fear break through and slay them.

Cap-Haitien, Haiti, July 2017

The sweat poured down Isaac's forehead, quickly infiltrated both brows, and seeped into his eyes. He was just thankful he did not normally have to do construction work like this in the oppressive heat of the Haitian summer. He desperately sought to find a dry cloth to wipe away the stinging streams of salty sweat, but to no avail. His shirt, emblazoned with the Haitian flag and the motto of *The Sons and Daughters of Toussaint,* was sopping wet with perspiration and caked over in places with mud and flecks of concrete. His blurry eyes couldn't see clearly more than a few feet away, and he moved along blindly. Then he felt the soft touch of a dry cloth on his face.

"It looks like you could use this." It was the voice of Yvette. "I brought along some extra dry cloths, just for this purpose."

Isaac took the cloth from her hand, and continued to dab the sweat from his forehead. "Man, you are a lifesaver! I was beginning to feel like I was drowning in salt water."

"I have some bottles of Gatorade here as well. You better drink up, or you will be keeling over into wet cement."

Isaac smiled at Yvette as he took the drink she offered him. "Thanks. I do have a tendency to overdo it, sometimes. Goal-driven and all that."

"I can't criticize your ambition," she said. "Those goal-driven tendencies are driving projects like this one forward."

Isaac looked around as he drank. A six-room primary school had risen in two short weeks on this previously neglected lot, and now volunteers were mixing water, cement and aggregate into liquid concrete and passing it up in old buckets to five men on a ladder, so it could be used on the rebar-enmeshed roof. No cranes or power equipment. All human power. Often a project like this would take years in Haiti, due to lack of funds. So this was amazing. Isaac shifted his gaze back to Yvette.

"You know, I must confess I underestimated you," he said. "When Mare came and we started... being together, I thought we might not see you again."

Yvette nodded and looked away.

"Anyway, I'm really glad you are still with us. You add a lot to the team."

"I believe in what we are doing," said Yvette. She started to walk away, but then she turned back toward Isaac. "Marie-Noëlle is really nice. But I would be lying if I didn't say I wish she weren't. I wish she was this bitch I could feel good about driving out of your life. Of course, if anything changes with you two…"

Isaac nodded. The hurt look in the young woman's eyes pained him. He never thought it would be this stressful being wanted by two beautiful young women. Isn't this the kind of situation most young men dream of? He remembered reading Victor Hugo's Les Miserables and envying Marius, loved as he was by both the beautiful Cossette and the also attractive, but rejected, Eponine. Now the tragedy of their story infected him.

He smiled at Yvette. "Thanks again for the refreshment. And by that I mean the cloth, the drink and your company."

Yvette returned the smile and walked away toward another group of workers.

Isaac shifted his gaze toward the school, and as he did, his eyes were drawn to a commotion just beyond that building. A man with an AK-47 was running toward him. Beyond him were two U.N. officers in pursuit, and coming in from his right were a handful of Haitian National Police. But the man was now close. Unless someone fired on him, the man would be within easy firing range in seconds. Isaac fell to the ground and rolled behind a stack of concrete block.

"Stop, or we'll shoot!" The words had come from one of the Haitian National Police. Isaac looked in the direction of the would-be attacker, and saw his hands, minus his weapon, raised in the air.

"Please, please!" said the man. "I mean you no harm. I want to surrender my weapon. I want to join you!"

The Haitian National Police reached him first and threw him to the ground. One of them held a pistol to the man's head, and might have shot had Isaac not intervened.

"Stop! Stop! Let me talk to him," shouted Isaac. He ran to where the man was restrained, and he looked down. "All right, start talking. Why should I believe that a man who was running toward me with a semi-automatic rifle meant me no harm?"

"Check it," he said. "It's not loaded. I tried to tell that to the U.N. officers, but they wouldn't listen."

A UN officer who had picked up the weapon now confirmed the man's claim.

"And besides," the man went on, "if the *Tonton Makout* had meant to attack you, they would have sent more than just me. I want to leave them. I want to join your work!"

Isaac visually surveyed the work site. Indeed, there didn't appear to be any other threats. He nodded toward the law enforcement officers. "Many thanks to you for responding so quickly to this situation. If you could take his weapon, and any ammunition he has, and leave him here to talk with me, I would greatly appreciate it."

"This could be a *Tonton Makout* trick!" said one of the police officers. "I wouldn't trust him too far if I were you."

"Once again, I appreciate your vigilance," said Isaac. "But without a weapon, there isn't much he can do. I have appealed to members of the Tonton Makout to join us, and so I need to trust this man for now."

The officers slowly dispersed, along with a number of workers who had been drawn to the commotion. Isaac looked at the newcomer, who had risen to his feet. "Next time you defect from a terrorist group, you might consider not running from the police with an assault rifle. I'm a little disturbed you made it this far."

"I was not thinking."

"What is your name?" Isaac asked.

"Ricardo Sante," the man replied. "I have done building before, so I can help around here."

"Do you have a family, Ricardo?"

"Yes, and they are always hungry. I remember you mentioned food…"

Isaac nodded. "A good hot meal is always served at noon. They are welcome to join us. And for today, workers are allotted leftover food to take home."

Ricardo furrowed his brow as he stood staring at the ground.

"I suspect you are in danger of retaliation from the *Tonton Makout*." said Isaac.

Ricardo nodded. "My family as well. Everyone here is in danger, especially you."

Isaac's right eyelid quivered. Everything around him suddenly seemed to be nothing more than a projection on a giant curved screen. It wasn't real. Just a story. Certainly nothing that really endangered him. *How could a world be real that seemed to be on the verge of going on without him?*

Ricardo had not said anything Isaac hadn't known previously. He had proposed to Mare because he knew his time could be short. But to hear it from someone who had been part of a group out to kill him, that penetrated to his soul. *How much longer could he keep the truth of his endangerment at a distance from his heart?*

"We will be in danger," he said in a whisper. He straightened up, and drew a deep breath. "Okay, then we will be in danger. That's all there is to it. It's what has to happen to change Haiti."

Ricardo also straightened up and smiled. "That is true. It's why I came. I want a better Haiti for my children."

"Then let's get to work!"

Isaac took Ricardo to join the bucket brigade.

Cap-Haitien, Haiti, August, 2017

Karissa slammed her cell phone down on the bed. Then she walked to a corner of the room and curled up in a ball on the floor. Mare wandered over, sat down beside her and put her arm around her friend.

"You know, Sister" Mare said, "just because I'm staying here, doesn't mean you have to. You could go back to New York, get on with an agency, and contribute financially, like you did before."

Karissa shook her head. "I can't do that now any more than you could," she whispered. "It's in my blood now."

"Are there any agencies we haven't tried?" Mare asked. "Surely we have established enough of a reputation that someone would take us on."

Karissa shook her head again. "Only if we commit to staying in New York. Marcel at the last agency I called really liked our Haiti shoots, but Eric scared him off about Haiti and our commitment down here. He likes more control – just like the rest of them."

Mare stood up and walked over to the window of Karissa's hotel room. "You have a beautiful view from here. A great beach. Nice homes. The Caribbean, as people in the United States imagine it. No garbage around. One could almost forget the problems of Haiti."

Karissa joined her friend by the window. "Yeah, expensive motels can afford to manipulate the view around them. They can create an illusion. But without a job, I can't afford to stay in this hotel much longer."

"It does remind you, however, that there is a lot of beauty in Haiti."

Karissa nodded.

Mare gave her a sly grin. "I even heard someone once made a video about Haiti's beauty and it was nominated for 'Best Documentary Film.'"

Karissa couldn't help but smile at the reminder of what she once accomplished. "Yeah, but it didn't win."

Mare shrugged. "You took things into your hands, and did something that needed to be done." Mare's eyes opened wide. She heard the words she had said to the one who had become her sister. "'You took things into your hands!' Why didn't we think of that before?"

"What do you mean?"

"We need to take things into our own hands!" said Mare. "Form our own modeling agency right here in Haiti! We could design and model our own clothes, and market them to Haitian ex-patriots in the States."

Karissa's eyes widened. "That just might work!" She pranced and spun across the room. "I know a Haitian fashion designer in Manhattan who might even come down and help us. We can put together a collection with a distinctive Haitian flare – declare fashion independence from the United States!"

Mare put her hands at the sides of her head as if to prevent it from exploding. "And my brother, Henri! He's studying marketing at Rutgers. I could get him to help. And Yvette and Crista – they could definitely help us model!"

Karissa returned to look out the window, as if her room were too small for her to visualize the future she wanted to see. "We could call our company 'The New Haitian Revolution.'"

Mare looked out the window with her friend. "We will make clothes for every economic class. Everybody out there will soon be wearing our clothes instead of second-hand t-shirts from the United States!"

Karissa stepped back from the window. "Everybody? Are we getting a little carried away here?"

"Yes! But that's okay. That's the trouble with Haitians – we think too small. We need to think big and act big!"

Karissa gave Mare a high-five and then firmly grasped her friend's hand, holding it high while looking into her eyes with a fiery gaze. "'Think Big! Act Big!' I love it. It will be our company motto."

Tears flowed down Mare's cheeks, settling on the lips of an ear-to-ear smile. "Look out world! There is a new Haiti coming, and these sisters are going to model it!"

Mare embraced Karissa and marveled how it felt as if she had known the woman her entire life. She felt Karissa's heart beating rapidly, and knew their hearts were beating as one.

Chapter Eighteen

Milot, Haiti, September 10th 2017

Isaac Breda looked down from the window in the stone wall, a window which was once used to look out for an approaching enemy, a window once used perhaps by Henri Christophe himself, a window once used in fear. But all he chose to see at this moment was hope.

Below people ascended the steep trail to the *Citadelle Laferriere*, to the place where he and Mare would soon become one in marriage. They could have stayed home in fear, but they did not. They were ascending to a mountaintop, ascending to a fortress built by slaves to see a land of promise and freedom, a land where love could win.

"If you are looking for a way to escape, I wouldn't advise that window." Isaac turned around and saw Henri, grinning from ear to ear. "It's a long way down, and if you survive the fall, my sister will find you and kick your ass all the way back up the mountain."

Isaac ran to his old friend and embraced him. "Man, it is so good to see you! How was the trip from New Jersey?"

"Fine. Except the strip search at security was kind of interesting. I had seen a hot female TSA agent and asked if she could do the search, but the guy who was frisking me had no sense of humor about it. I guess he figured that if you're a black guy from New Jersey and flying out of Kennedy to a God-forsaken place like Haiti, you're probably a terrorist anyway. He kept banging his fist against my balls like he was testing to see if they would explode. They didn't, in case you were wondering. Although if that hot TSA agent had been doing it—"

"Okay, enough!" said Isaac. "We brought you here to be my best man, not do a comedy routine."

"Is there a difference?"

Isaac ignored the question. "Did Mare talk to you about marketing her idea for a modeling agency?"

"Yeah, that was the first thing she wanted to talk about. Before she even asked how I was doing! Anyway, I don't know if I can help her with marketing. I'm literally at a 'Marketing 101' level. What she needs is definitely graduate level."

"Maybe one of your profs can help. Or you can make it the subject of an independent study."

"I might have considered that…except it goes against one of my basic, heart-felt principles – 'greed is good'! Gordon Gekko in *Wall Street*. I am going for the money in the States, instead of trying to save Haiti."

"Yeah, but we're going to talk you out of that attitude. Still, we can work on that later," said Isaac. "Have you met the rest of the wedding party?"

"Not yet. Any hot young women?"

"As a matter-of-fact, yes," said Isaac. "But I'm not sure I want to expose them to you—"

"Really? And this from a guy who wants me to help his fiancé market her new business? Interesting."

Isaac laughed and threw his hands up in surrender. "All right! All right! The Maid of Honor is Karissa, the model. She is a little older than you, but—"

"Yes!"

"But, now that I think of it, she is rather particular about men—"

"Yes! I said 'Yes!' You can't back out now!"

"Then there is the fact she is going to be a partner in this new modeling business, and she would be really impressed by a guy who helped them market it."

"I'm reconsidering as I speak. An independent study on marketing a modeling agency in Haiti – what an excellent idea!"

Isaac grabbed Henri's hand firmly and shook it. "We've got a deal! Of course, to be truthful, Mare was already going to have you sit next to Karissa at the reception. But now, I'll also lie and say good things. Is that better?"

Henri punched him in the arm. "Yeah! Was that so hard?"

Isaac rubbed his bicep. "Let me take you over to where my groomsmen, Arturo and Professor Alexandre Gabriel, are helping with preparations. Arturo can be a little crude, so I think you will like him. Professor Gabriel is older, but I've learned a lot from him. Maybe he can even teach you something."

"Yeah, I'm on a break from school, so…"

"Of course, they also have access to the alcohol."

"Well, why didn't you say so? A crude street Haitian and a college professor. Interesting combination. Show me the way."

Isaac led his old friend downstairs to the courtyard where the reception was being set up. Professor Gabriel was helping to arrange tables and chairs. Arturo's hands, however, were otherwise occupied – with Crista. They were making out in a corner by a pile of old cannonballs.

"Hey, Arturo!" said Isaac. "You are supposed to be helping Professor Gabriel with the reception set-up, not checking out the bridesmaid!"

Arturo removed his lips from Crista's long enough to respond. "Yeah, well, Crista needed someone to check out the fit of her dress, and I stepped up. Duty, you know."

"Truly, a man after my own heart," Henri said, aside to Isaac. Isaac ignored him.

"I appreciate your sense of sacrifice, Arturo, but the women can take care of each other's dresses just fine. You need to help with chairs and tables for the wedding reception."

Crista smiled mischievously as she pulled away from Arturo's lips and looked into his eyes. "Arturo and I are rehearsing for our own wedding, thank you."

"Really?"

"We've set it for next March."

"Personally, I would prefer to rehearse for the wedding night," said Arturo, "but women, you know – they got to have the ceremony!"

Crista gave Arturo a playful shove. "God, you're such an animal!"

Isaac loved the banter. Such talk made it seem like this was a normal joyous wedding at a normal time in a normal place. The playful sexuality was life bursting forth, protected from a land of death and threat by high, thick stone walls. *The Citadelle Laferriere* was not a typical place for a wedding, but there was no doubt that it was the right place for this one.

"Hey, Isaac! The minister was looking for you." Professor Gabriel paused in his work setting up chairs, and looked Isaac's way. "With the wedding less than an hour away, I guess he wanted to make sure everything was ready. Speaking of which, I could use some help. I'm too old to do all this by myself!"

Isaac nodded toward Henri and Arturo. "You heard him guys, play time is over." Then he looked at Crista. "And my guess is, Mare could probably use your help right now."

All three relented, and Isaac was left free to seek out the minister who was to perform the ceremony. People called him Pastor Ronald. Isaac had met the man only twice. Once when he and Mare had decided on a whim to attend the minister's church, and the other when they had met with him in preparation for the wedding. Isaac had never been a frequent church-goer. He believed in God. He believed in God because he believed life was meant to be good, and to have a purpose. But the church services he had attended had never really caught hold of his spirit. That is, not until he attended this man's church. The minister had talked about Jesus' passion for the poor, and he quoted Jesus' saying about the poor "inheriting the earth." Pastor Ronald made Jesus' vision seem as present as Isaac's own far-fetched dreams of a renewed Haiti. He knew this was the one to perform their wedding.

Early-arriving guests roamed throughout the fortress, some apparently experiencing the historical site for the first time. Not surprising, since the entry fee was normally $20

US, a sum equal to a week's pay for most Haitians. Isaac's new influence had gotten that fee waived for the wedding.

Isaac found Pastor Ronald talking with several of the early arrivals near the main gate.

"Ah, there you are, Isaac!" said the clergyman. "I was beginning to wonder if you and Marie-Noëlle had decided to elope."

Isaac smiled. "Yeah, that would have been easier, but I would miss seeing the envious looks on all the guy's faces when Mare walks down the aisle!"

"Hell, I hear you on that one," said Ricardo Sante, who had just walked through the gate. "I tolerated getting grilled by all those security dudes outside just to see that hot babe in a wedding dress. Got nothing to do with you being here, that's for sure. I'd steal her for myself if it didn't get me arrested!"

Isaac had forgotten about all the security they had set up to protect against the Tonton Makout, the group from which Ricardo had defected. "Yeah, I should talk to those security guys to find out why they ever let you through!"

Ricardo smiled. "Don't worry, my wife is already here somewhere. And she is scarier than any security guy. She'll hang me up by my balls if I so much as smile at another woman!"

"You have a few minutes to talk?" asked the minister, interrupting the banter.

"Sure," said Isaac. "That's why I came looking for you."

Pastor Ronald grabbed him by the arm and led him down the hall and up a stairway. "This really is a fascinating building," the minister said. "I must confess I have not been here since I was a teenager and used to escort tourists, in order to make a few bucks."

"Then you must know a lot about the history."

The clergyman laughed. "What I didn't know, I made up." He took on the demeanor of a tourist's guide. "And this VERY ROCK in this VERY WALL was found splattered with Henri Christophe's blood!"

"That exact rock, you say?"

Pastor Ronald spoke aside to Isaac, as if in confidence, "I can sell you a piece for a very small sum!" Then he motioned dramatically toward a cannon. "And I have it on good authority that this cannon was fired by no less than Toussaint Louverture himself, as he repelled the French!"

Isaac threw his arms up in a mock show of surprise. "Why, I never knew Toussaint was even alive when this fortress was built!"

"Ah, yes. There is so much that the common lay person does not know about this place. I only wish I had time to tell it all."

Isaac laughed. "And tourists actually believed what you told them?"

Pastor Ronald shook his head. "Say it with a straight enough face, and with swagger and confidence, and people will believe anything. Politicians have taught us that oh, so well."

The minister led Isaac into the same cannon room where he and Mare had once played at defending the fortress.

"Marie-Noëlle told me this room holds special memories for the two of you."

Isaac nodded. "Yes, it does. That was back when the dangers beyond these walls were more of a game we could play like children."

There was a twinkle in the minister's eye. "Yes! Playing like children is an essential part of any marriage. That might be my most important marriage advice. Never forget it."

"Good advice. Thanks."

"But that part about the dangers beyond these walls," Pastor Ronald continued, "that is what I wanted to talk to you about. Do you realize how short your lives together might be?"

It was virtually all Isaac had thought about the last several weeks, but this minister was still a stranger to him, and he did not wish to confess that, even to a clergyman. "None of us know how long we have in this life. Is that not the case, Pastor?"

The minister nodded. "Of course. But I hardly believe you think the likelihood that you might die tomorrow is the same as any other person on the street. You are one of the most targeted persons in Haiti. Respect me – respect *your-self* – enough to acknowledge that!"

Isaac leaned against one of the cannons. "Okay, I grant you your point. But what should I do about that? Cut and run? Or maybe you're just trying to book me a reservation to heaven? A little 'Come to Jesus' moment?"

"This isn't about a religious sales pitch, Isaac. I always like to say I am in the 'service' department of the church, not 'sales'. I believe God is a gracious God, as far as the eternal is concerned. But I'm not talking about the hereafter. I'm talking about the here and now. I believe in what you are trying to do. However, the threats are real, and I am afraid you're thinking there are only two ways to deal with the fear – to run from it or to try to ignore it. Am I right?"

Isaac walked over to the same meurtrière, the same opening in the wall, he and Mare had looked through months before. Below he saw the coast in the distance, the coast that Henri Christophe once vigilantly surveyed for signs of the invading French. Nearer by were the hills of Haiti, covered with Haitians even now enslaved to poverty and fear.

He turned and looked at Pastor Ronald. "Okay. I do need another choice. What have you got?"

"It's not what I have, Isaac: it's what you have already. You have been modeling your movement on the work of two men, Toussaint Louverture and Martin Luther King Jr. Am I right?"

Isaac nodded.

"Neither of them would have accomplished what they did if they hadn't tapped their deep faith in God."

Isaac rolled his eyes. "Ah! And now, the sermon."

"Hear me out on this. I'm not just saying this because I am expected to. I am saying it because I believe you really need to hear what I am saying."

Isaac sighed. "Okay. What do I need to hear?"

"I'm not trying to sell you a faith, I want to point to a faith you already have. It's what King and Toussaint had – not a faith that God would give them some kind of special protection from death, but a faith that helped them believe what they were doing would make a difference, a faith that would be with them in the trenches of warfare against evil.

King knew there was a strong chance he would die in the battle, but he battled on because of his faith and vision: 'I might not make it there with you, but I have been to the mountaintop, and I have seen the Promised Land!'"

"Toussaint also," said Isaac quietly.

"That's right. I think that was the main difference between him and others like Dessalines and Christophe. They were driven by their fear and hate. He was driven by faith in a God who held something better."

Isaac shut his eyes and shook his head. "I'm not a church-going man, Pastor."

"Doesn't matter. The world isn't changed by the church-going. It's changed by the faithful."

Isaac focused again on the view out the ancient meurtrière of the fortress. Mare and he had looked out that opening in the wall once, and felt weaponless in the face of the threats Haiti faced. At least this minister was seeking to offer him something for his limited arsenal.

He looked back at Pastor Ronald. "This is something to think about, Pastor. But not now." He smiled. "I have something more immediate on my mind."

"Ah, yes! A wedding I believe?"

Isaac put his hand over his heart. "I confess, right now I love her more than God. Of course, I've never seen God naked…"

The clergyman laughed. "Sounds like I need to get you two married – quick!"

Those were Isaac's sentiments exactly.

The bride's room for a wedding normally would have been a classroom or a parlor at a church, or even a conference room at a courthouse. Marie-Noëlle's was a 200-year old ammunition storage room. She had smiled when first told. "How appropriate!" she had whispered to herself. She examined herself in the mirror. "Girl, you are positively lethal!" She had said the words to herself, while examining how she looked in her wedding dress, but immediately there was a chorus of agreement from friends and photographers in the room.

A photographer from *Brides* Magazine snapped pictures from every angle. "This is the look brides from around the world are going to emulate for the next decade!"

A Haitian photographer, taking pictures for their new Haitian fashion company, chimed in: "With these pics, Cap-Haitien will once again be called 'The Paris of the Antilles'!"

Her wedding dress was a light pink gown of her own design, that followed and caressed her curves, and was covered with intricate lace, including see-through lace arm coverings, and see-through lace to both sides of her waist. The gown had a V-neck which showed her cleavage enough to draw every eye, but still retained enough modesty for the dignity of this moment. In her hair was a cluster of crimson hibiscus, Haiti's national flower.

"Can I borrow that dress for my wedding?" asked Crista. "And while we're at it, can I also borrow that BODY?"

Karissa shook her head. "Not a chance of that happening, Crista. There is only one Marie-Noëlle in all the world." She winked at her friend and business partner.

Yvette threw her hands up in resignation. "This was what I thought I could compete with. I surrender!"

Marie-Noëlle smiled. "You were a very worthy opponent. One day you will rock your own wedding dress!"

Yvette returned the smile. "Well…if the right guy comes along."

Marie-Noëlle exulted in the moment. She had looked forward to this day since she and Isaac had first fallen in love, and she wanted to experience every precious minute. She didn't want it to go by too quickly, moving on to being a memory before she was ready; nor did she want it to go by too slowly, keeping the reality of their marriage too long at a distance. She wanted nothing to rob her of the fullness of her wedding day joy.

Marie-Noëlle noticed the Haitian photographer had withdrawn to herself. Her brow was furrowed, and she was staring at one of the stone walls.

"Hey, Suzanne," Marie-Noëlle said, "have we lost you somewhere along the way? What's up?"

Suzanne shook her head and shrugged. "No, I'm sorry. I will get back to taking pictures. This will be a wonderful wedding. I want to help preserve it for you."

"Is something heavy on your mind?" the Haitian bride asked.

"No, nothing. It's nothing at all. I just worry about things sometimes."

"This is my wedding, and it's an important time for me," said Marie-Noëlle. "However, I am not the only one here who is important. If something is worrying you, I want to know. Perhaps I can help."

The photographer now stared at Marie-Noëlle, who noticed tears filling the woman's lower eyelids. "Hey, no need to hold back feelings like that. What is it?"

Suzanne shook her head a couple of times. Then she finally spoke. "I don't know. It's just…This is all so beautiful, but…what happens if he dies?"

Marie-Noëlle shuddered. "Wha…what?"

"I'm sorry! I'm really sorry!" The photographer squirmed. "I know you don't want to think about this. But I hear rumors. People say the *Tonton Makout* want to kill him! Everything was so perfect. I started thinking. What if it's true?"

Marie-Noëlle tried to focus on the mirror again, but her eyes were already turning red, and the corner of her mouth twitched. *Why did this girl she hardly knew have to bring this up?* It wasn't like Marie-Noëlle hadn't thought about it herself. Ever since she learned Isaac had been shot, and rushed back to Haiti, the very same question had been trying to sneak into her mind. She always shut it out. But how do you shut out a question raised, not in the dark recesses of your mind, but in the blinding glare of a public moment?

"I think I am going to need about fifteen minutes to myself, so could you all leave the room?" she said. "Check and see if everything is set up, and how many guests have arrived." She smiled weakly at Suzanne. "Then when all of you get back, I am going to want a few more photos before the ceremony begins."

"Whatever you want, Mare," said Karissa. She punched Suzanne on the arm and pointed toward the door. "We'll all be back in exactly fifteen minutes."

Before leaving, Suzanne touched Marie-Noëlle lightly on the arm and looked into her eyes. "I really am sorry, you know. Sometimes I have a hard time keeping my mouth shut."

Marie-Noëlle nodded and quickly returned her focus to the mirror.

When the others had left, Marie-Noëlle sat down on a stool and cried harder than she remembered having cried in a long time. But then, as quickly as she started, she stopped. She stood up and looked back at the mirror. Her eyes were puffy, and her mascara was streaking down her cheeks. Still, this damage could be repaired.

She wasn't so sure about the damage to her heart.

Finally, the music started. "Canon in D" by Pachelbel. Violins and a portable synthesizer lifted the soothing notes of the 300-year old composition into the air to caress the walls of the fortress, a young 200 years by comparison. Isaac opened the door leading to the courtyard a crack and looked out at the crowd of guests. He saw a mixture of friends from the college, family members, political dignitaries and even a few international celebrities. Most of the latter were friends of Mare's, and had contributed financially to their cause.

An usher escorted in his mother, accompanied by his father. His heart filled with love for them. Isaac's mother cried virtually every day for him, mostly out of fear for his well-being. But her tears now flowed through a smile, and he knew they came out of happiness for this moment in her son's life. His father was not crying. His pride wouldn't permit it. Still, he walked proud and erect, and that posture was his way of expressing the same joy his wife felt.

Isaac knew the moment he had been waiting for was very near, and that realization brought with it both excitement and anxiety. What was about to happen was going to change his world.

The next events in the evolving ceremony floated through Isaac's awareness in slow motion. Mare's mother was ushered in, strutting down the aisle like the Queen of the World. Beyonce, who had become friends with Mare while she was in New York, sang *At Last,* and Isaac felt the words of that classic song come alive for him even more than when she had sung them at President Obama's inauguration:

"At last my love has come along

My lonely days are over and life is like a song, oh yeah

At last the skies above are blue…"

And the skies above that day were blue. What they might be like tomorrow simply didn't matter.

Before Isaac realized it, the song was over and the music stopped. For a moment all was quiet, except for the sounds of murmuring anticipation in the gathered crowd. *What was coming next?* Isaac could not remember. Just then music began again, the violins and synthesizer playing an instrumental piece that he quickly identified. How could he have forgotten this was next? Wagner's *Bridal Chorus.* Better known as *Here Comes the Bride!* It was time for Pastor Ronald, him, Henri, Arturo and Professor Gabriel to enter and take their places. Mare and her entourage were about to enter!

People had asked him earlier that day if he was nervous, and he had said no. Now was a different story. As he reached the place he had been told to stand, by the front platform near the center aisle, shivers were going up and down his spine. His legs felt weak and his balance uncertain. It took all the strength he could muster to hold himself erect. Yvette, Crista and Karissa seemed far more composed as they swayed, one at a time, down the center aisle to their places stage right.

After the wedding party was in, the wedding march hit a crescendo, and Pastor Ronald motioned for those gathered to stand. Rose petals, shot up into the air from air cannons on the fortress wall, descending onto the courtyard like pink snow, and Marie-Noëlle – he really couldn't think of her simply as 'Mare' in this moment – entered escorted by her father.

Isaac stood looking with his mouth hanging open. He could not believe the beauty of this woman he was about to marry. From dry ice to either side of the entry came up a gentle fog that made it appear to Isaac that Marie-Noëlle was coming to him out of a dream. As she came closer and closer, Isaac could see a demure smile on her face, as her eyes focused on him. He trembled.

Isaac would never remember exactly all that happened next. Mare's father withdrew, leaving her gently touching his arm. The minister said some words. Isaac was sure that they must have been wise, but they came to him as white noise. Before he knew it, a question was being posed to him, but at first he did not hear it. His eyes, his heart and his ears were all focused on Marie-Noëlle. The question came again: *Do you, Isaac Breda, take this woman, Marie-Noëlle Raimond, to have and to hold, from this moment forward, in sickness and in health, in good times and in bad, 'til death do you part?*

Isaac's response at first came as a whisper, said only loud enough for Marie-Noëlle to hear: "I do!"

Pastor Ronald cocked his ear toward Isaac. "Excuse me?"

Isaac spoke louder. "I do! With all my heart, I do!"

Isaac was more alert now to what was being said, and he heard the question posed to Marie-Noëlle: *Do you, Marie-Noëlle Raimond, take this man, Isaac Breda, to have and to hold, from this moment forward, in sickness and in health, in good times and in bad, 'til death do you part?*

A shadow came across Marie-Noëlle's face, and tears flowed instantaneously from her eyes. She shook her head. "No!"

Through some miracle of their spiritual connection, Isaac picked up right away that there was more to this unexpected answer, but the minister did not. "What?! Did you say, 'No'?"

Marie-Noëlle kept shaking her head, but a tearful smile was focused on Isaac. "'No' to 'til death do us part'," she said. "'Yes' to 'I take you Isaac Breda in this eternal moment, that our spirits will never ever be apart. Here I promise you, Isaac, by the grace of God, even death will not end us!"

And suddenly Isaac felt a deeper peace than he had ever felt in his life.

Chapter Nineteen

Cap-Haitien, Haiti, September 11th 2017

Isaac awoke to playful eyes. They sparkled and danced as they flitted back and forth between Isaac's tussled hair, his still sleepy eyes, and his sinewy, flat abdomen.

"Good morning, Madame Breda," Isaac said.

Mare smiled, slid onto her back and stretched, causing the sheet to slip down her naked breasts to unveil her nipples. She gave Isaac a coy look out of the corner of her eye. "Good morning, Monsieur Marie-Noëlle. Are you up for anything...mmmm...special this morning?"

Isaac eased over next to his wife and pulled her close. "Hey, if it's anything like last night, I could get up for that again...and again...and again!"

His cell phone called out from his bedside table with the ringtone he had assigned to Arturo.

"Oh, man! I told those guys not to call me unless it was an absolute emergency. Maybe I should just turn it off."

Mare nibbled on his ear. "You'll get no complaint from me on that," she whispered.

"...unless it really is an emergency."

"Ah, you know Arturo," said Mare. "He just wants to give us a hard time on the morning after our wedding night."

"I better get it," said Isaac. "I don't want to take any chances. I'll make it quick." He touched the 'accept' button and brought the phone to his ear. "Hello."

Arturo's voice responded right away. "Good! You answered. I was afraid you wouldn't. Hell, I don't think I would have. Look, I hate to bother you like this, but you've got to get over here. The *Tonton Makout* has been ambushing our volunteers on the way to worksites. We have at least thirty dead!"

Isaac sat up quickly in bed. "Dead? Are you sure?"

Mare bolted to a sitting position, her eyes wide. "Who's dead?"

"Yes, I have been to two of the sites already and Crista was at another," said Arturo, "and we saw the bodies."

"Do we know any names?" asked Isaac.

"Only one so far, and you're not going to like it," said Arturo. "Ricardo Sante, the *Tonton Makout* guy who defected. I had the misfortune of being around when his wife got there and saw him. God, it was horrible!"

Isaac opened his mouth, but couldn't speak.

"Isaac, are you still there?"

"I'm here," said Isaac. "Were the attacks only in Cap Haitien, or—?"

"No, they hit some sites in Port-au-Prince and Mirebalais as well."

"Where are you now?"

"I'm at our school project in Limbe near the *Hôpital Bon Samaritain.*"

"I'll be right there." Isaac ended the call and looked over at Mare. "The *Tonton Makout* ambushed volunteers on their way to our worksites. At least thirty people are dead, including Ricardo Sante."

"Oh, my God!"

"I told Arturo I would meet him at our school project in Limbe. You stay here and I'll get back as soon as—"

"No way!" said Mare as she jumped out of bed, and grabbed her clothes. "I'm not some delicate flower wife who hides in the safety of a luxury hotel, while her husband goes out and risks danger!"

"It's really not—"

"We're in this together, right? Besides, Ricardo Sante's wife will need comforting, and you suck at comforting, face it!"

"I don't suck at—"

"And get going!" added Mare. "I'm halfway dressed and you're still sitting naked in the bed."

Isaac knew better than to argue with his new wife when she was like this. And besides, she was right. Calming and comforting a frightened people would be a big task, and he needed all the help he could get.

Limbe, Haiti, September 11th, 2017

As Marie-Noëlle looked down at the broken woman beside her dead husband, she couldn't help but envision herself, with Isaac's bloodied, lifeless body lying on the cold, hard ground. The woman wailed with all that was within her, as she stretched her hands and lifted tearful eyes to heaven. She seemed totally unaware of Marie-Noëlle's presence.

The new wife knelt down and gently stroked the hair of the new widow. Isabelle Sante looked into Marie-Noëlle's eyes like a fallen child seeking comfort from her mother.

"Why did they have to do this?" the mourning woman said. "He was so good to me…to our children…to everyone!"

Marie-Noëlle shook her head in bewilderment, and continued to caress the widowed woman's hair.

Isabelle Sante's eyes opened wide, and she stood up abruptly. "We must never let them win this way!" She pointed to the words on her t-shirt, the words Marie-Noëlle had designed to go there. "Nou pa pè!"

The widow yelled the words at the top of her lungs, and people all around the work site looked her way.

"Nou pa pè! Nou pa pè! Nou pa pè!" she repeated.

Workers and mourners throughout the worksite took up the chant, declaring their determination that they would not fear: "*Nou pa pè! Nou pa pè! Nou pa pè!*"

Off to her left, U.S. camera crews were taking footage of the defiant crowd. Mare felt she could hear the message of refusal to fear resonating throughout her country, and the woman's courage brought tears to her eyes. She realized she had thought that victory in their battle depended on her and Isaac and their leadership. It didn't. It depended on women like this finding courage from God to face fear and death. She lifted her eyes to the heavens.

Isaac stood by an old Haitian widow kneeling by the crumpled body of her dead son. Her last family member gone. He recognized the young man as one he had seen around the University, and who had joined them early in their work. Isaac's heart sank.

The old woman did not cry. Rather she simply touched the cold forehead of her son, brushed back a shock of hair from his head, and whispered something inaudible.

"I am...so sorry for your loss, Mama Jo," said Isaac. "I am sure your heart is broken."

The woman shook her head. "Not broken. Not broken." She looked into Isaac's eyes. "Why should I be sad? He is with his God now. We are the ones who remain in Hell."

The woman's words reminded Isaac of what Pastor Ronald had said to him prior to the wedding. Faith to deal with the fear. The faith of Toussaint.

Just then Isaac heard the chant building across the worksite and smiled. *Nou pa pè!* After this most recent round of attacks, he even found it hard to believe himself that fear was not winning. His marriage to Mare made him acutely aware of how much he had to lose; but the chant from these mostly impoverished people also raised his awareness of his country's passion for freedom.

Before encountering Mama Jo, he had been talking with other leaders of *The Sons and Daughters of Toussaint*, including Arturo, Crista, Yvette, and Crista's father, Manuel Patrice, about the effect the attacks might have on the movement. The chant had come as a resounding response to their questions.

Isaac shoved his fist in the air and joined in. "*Nou pa pè! Nou pa pè! Nou pa pè!*" The others with him also picked up the chant. "*Nou pa pè! Nou pa pè! Nou pa pè!*"

Isaac noticed a group of men about a hundred meters to his right, who were not joining in the chant. He also saw that most of them were armed, and that at the center of the group was a man with graying hair he had previously seen only on television.

Isaac nudged Arturo and pointed in the direction of the group he had spotted. "Hey. Isn't that—"

"François Cambronne!" exclaimed Arturo. "Standing there with his thugs, acting like he owns the whole frickin' place!"

Isaac thought of Toussaint, riding to meet Jean-Baptiste Brunet. "We can't let him believe we are intimidated by him," he said. "Let's go pay him a visit."

François Cambronne broke out in a big smile when he saw Isaac, Arturo and Crista coming. "Why, what do we have here?" he said. "We have the honor of being greeted by the Boy Wonder himself. And his little friends as well!"

Cambronne held out his right hand in Isaac's direction. Isaac ignored it. "Just wanted to make sure you heard our chant, old man. I know sometimes when a person gets older, the hearing goes first."

Cambronne withdrew his hand and folded his arms in front of him. "Getting older is not so bad – not that you will ever know. Unfortunately, some young people simply don't have the intelligence to live that long."

"But we believe the world is changed by those who place more importance on living right than on living long," said Crista. She motioned toward the building project rising nearby. "And as you see, what we believe is paying off."

Cambronne's face and voice displayed mock sorrow. "Ah, but I understand you have lost some workers today. How sad. It's hard to do such good work with dead people."

Arturo got into Cambronne's face. "If I thought you had the balls, I would say 'Go fuck yourself!' But, *unfortunately* I know some old men can't get it up anymore! How sad, indeed."

Cambronne's associates raised their weapons, and Crista grabbed Arturo and quickly pulled him back.

"If you are here to intimidate us, Monsieur Cambronne," said Isaac, "I'm sure you can see it's not working. So, why don't you—"

"No, son, look – we got off on the wrong foot with each other. I'm not trying to intimidate you; I'm trying to help you! I hate violence. I'm as sorry as you are that these poor workers were attacked. We didn't do it." Cambronne motioned toward his armed associates, who all shrugged and shook their heads. "What can I say? We live in a violent country. These things happen in violent countries. I know you are trying to do good things for Haiti, and I actually want to be on your side. I'm here to make a proposal. You support my candidacy for President, and I will make sure that nothing like this happens to your friends again."

"Or," Isaac said, "we could just keep on doing the good work we are doing, we could vote our conscience on the Presidency, and you could still see that nothing like this happens to us again."

François Cambronne sent Isaac a sardonic smile. "That's not the way the world works, son. If by some miracle you get a few more years under your belt, you will come to understand what I am saying is true."

Officers from the United Nations swarmed the area and surrounded the confrontation. More officers from the Haitian National Police were not far behind.

"Glad you could make it, friends," said Isaac. "although you are a little late to the party. We were just finishing a little discussion."

"Lo Siento mucho, Señor Breda," said one of the U.N. officers. "There have been many attacks, and we could not respond to them all. We were able to stop an assault on some volunteers going to one of the tree planting sites, but the attackers got away."

"That's good news!" said Cambronne. "But, of course, you were not needed against us. We are not the ones perpetrating violence in this country—"

"Which is why you are packing so much heat," said Arturo.

"We are armed to protect ourselves from all this violence," said Cambronne. "The UN officers and the Haitian National Police work very hard, but they cannot do it all. That's why our campaign wants to get them help. The *Tonton Makout*—"

"We don't need your kind of help," said one of the Haitian National Police. "Everywhere you go, death follows."

Cambronne's jaw hardened, and he glared at the police officer, with his eyes on fire. "I will overlook that remark," he said after a long pause, "since you are obviously ignorant of what is really going on in this country." He pointed at the Haitian police, while looking around at his supporters. "Where do they recruit these guys, anyway? Grade school dropouts, with friends in an incompetent government!" He shifted his focus back to Isaac. "Well, I'm running for President in order to change that. You better hop on board the bus, or it's going to run you over!"

François Cambronne turned and walked away, and his supporters followed walking backwards, with their eyes and weapons still trained on the gathering.

The police officer who had stood up to Cambronne turned toward Isaac. "Cambronne is right about one thing, Monsieur Breda. We cannot do it all. With all of your work sites, and with the other violence in the country, we just can't cover it all."

"*Es verdad,*" said the U.N. officer who had spoken earlier.

Arturo put a hand on Isaac's shoulder. "Hey, man, I know what they're talking about. You know, with King, U.S. federal troops generally only had to protect one big gig – a protest march, the desegregation of a school or one of King's speeches. Even then, they got to King when he was at his hotel. There's just too much shit that can happen when we are working at sites all over the whole damn country."

"So, what do you expect us to do?" asked Isaac. "Limit ourselves to one or two projects? There is simply too much to do!"

"I don't know," said Arturo. "Maybe have them focus on protecting you and Mare—"

"Not happening! No way I'm going to ask others to take risks, while I have protection."

"Well, then, what do we do?"

Isaac became conscious again of the chant resonating all around them. He smiled. "There's our answer! What do we do? *Nou pa pè*! We will keep on doing what we are doing, in spite of all the risks, and we will not give in to fear." He looked at the Haitian police and the UN officers. "You men and women keep on doing the best you can. We appreciate you so much! You Haitian police are a credit to your country. I don't care what Cambronne says. And members of the UN forces stationed in our country? You are helping hold this fragile world together. I know you are here with us, even though you have problems and needs in your own countries."

"*Es verdad tambien,*" said the U.N. officer who had been speaking for the group. "In my home country of Chile we just experienced an earthquake. My family seems to be okay, but I worry about aftershocks."

"Our deepest gratitude to all of you," said Isaac. "*Nou pa pè* is a message for you as well."

Mare came up from behind Isaac, put an arm around his waist, and leaned her head on his shoulder. She was crying. Still, she managed to speak. "And our deepest gratitude also to…to those who died or lost loved-ones today. They are so brave! I don't know that I could be so brave."

She could say no more. Her tears had evolved into deep sobs. Those tears were contagious, and no one was immune. Not Crista, with her face buried in her hands. Not Arturo, although he turned away to hide his own grieving. Not the most hardened male or female law enforcement officer.

And not Isaac.

Chapter Twenty

Port-au-Prince, Haiti, October 2017

As Isaac surveyed the waters of the Artibonite River, he had to smile. Yes, this was a river that had carried the ravaging disease of cholera to much of his country, but his smile came from what he did not see at this moment: garbage. He was used to seeing Styrofoam containers floating like toy boats making their way to the Gulf of La Gonâve, surrounded by an armada of dirty plastic bags and soda bottles. Such scenes had been emblematic of the nation's despair. Now all he saw was water. A new Haiti was coming.

Hundreds of volunteers had removed debris from this and other rivers for weeks. And still other poor Haitians had picked up plastic trash from the streets, putting it in bags and transporting it by tap-tap to Ramase Lajan, where it would be turned into plastic thread for polyester-type fabric.

Manuel Patrice shook his head in wonder. "Now I can die in peace, having indeed seen a miracle," he said. "People who have lived their lives in hunger, picking up the trash of those who have eaten."

"A miracle?" asked Isaac, mostly to himself. Then he focused on the others. "Yes, I suppose it is. Miracles happen when people step up and take on the work of God."

Mare took hold of his arm, "I have another miracle to bring to everyone's attention. Henri is still here! And he's going to meet with Karissa and me about marketing our Haitian fashion business."

"Really?" Isaac looked toward the heavens. "Then we should prepare for the sky opening up and a host of angels descending on Haiti!" He looked back at Mare. "Of course, I suspect his interest in Karissa might also have had something to do with that."

"Karissa? Oh, no," said Mare. "She blew him off right away. But my brother is resilient. He rebounded right into the arms of Yvette. When he found she was going to be one of our models, suddenly he saw the light."

"He's not going back to school?"

"Oh, of course he is. He got approval to stay a little longer and work on this as an independent study. He'll have to head back next week."

"Enough about your brother, and his romantic escapades," said Manuel. "I am a busy man. We came here to take a look at our projects in Port-au-Prince. I like what I see in cleaning up this river, but I want to see more, so let's get to it."

"I'm afraid I've decided not to go with you to see the other projects," said Mare. "I need to get back to start work with Karissa on our fashion business. You can tell me about what you see later."

Isaac smiled. "Well, as much as I like to have you with me all of the time, I suppose I can let you go for a short while." He kissed her, she waved good-bye to the others, and headed toward her car.

Isaac looked at those who remained. "So, where do we start?"

"I'm really eager to show you some of the coffee farms which have been sprouting up around here," said Isaac's father. "My company has been working with the Haitian Coffee Academy at *Tè Lonj* to get these farms going. We haven't harvested coffee from any of them yet, of course, but when we do, our ability to market fair trade coffee to the world will explode. Thousands of Haitians will get jobs both harvesting and helping in our warehouses."

"We could have talked about the Port-au-Prince projects in Cap-Haitien," said Manuel impatiently. "Let's see the projects!"

"While we are at it," said Crista, "we are planting trees not far from those coffee farms. With the help of *The Eden Projects,* we are planting whole forests up in those hills, and the poor people are not cutting them down. That's another miracle!"

Manuel's sigh was more like a hiss. "Let's SEE THE PROJECTS!"

"I suppose if I mentioned the earthquake-resistant housing or the solar cookers we are subsidizing," said Isaac, "you would probably say—"

"Let's SEE THE DAMN PROJECTS!"

"Hey, I have an idea!" said Isaac. "Why don't we load up in the SUV we rented and actually go see the projects?"

Manuel was not amused.

Even though he had not felt Manuel Patrice's impatience, Isaac had to admit there could be no better lift for his spirits than actually seeing the projects around Port-au-Prince. Work that had previously been only abstract ideas in his mind or the minds of his associates now came to life. It was better than he imagined it could be. Ravaged, lifeless hills were being transformed before his eyes, and the poor people planting the trees responsible for this transformation, treated the plantings gently, as their own children. They would never burn these trees for charcoal.

Isaac knew reforestation projects had been tried in Haiti before. USAID had planted more than 25 million trees in the 1980s, but, needing charcoal to cook what little food they could eat, poor people burned those trees, as well as many more. Estimates were that seven trees were destroyed for every tree planted. Isaac believed this failure was due to two factors: (1) the poor people never thought of the trees as "theirs". It was a US project. And (2) nothing was done to provide for an alternative way for the poor to cook their food. The Sons and Daughters of Toussaint, on the other hand, were subsidizing simple solar cookers for the poor.

As Isaac watched the workers plant the trees, his mind went back to the time of Toussaint. Then former Haitian slaves fought trained French troops, knowing they would probably die in the battle, because they wanted a better life for their children. Now the ancestors of those slaves were working on minimal nourishment, risking their lives, to lay down a line of defense against the poverty which surrounded them, once again to provide a better life for their children. It was a testament to parenthood.

At first Isaac had considered driving the SUV himself on this tour, but he quickly became glad he had hired a driver instead. Not only was some of the terrain rough, but driving would have impeded his ability to see what was happening around him. He wanted to see every tree planted, and the sweaty but smiling face of every worker.

The driver followed two police escort vehicles, while two other SUVs full of press and camera crews followed behind them. Both were an important part of security in these more isolated areas, the camera crews perhaps even more than the police escort. The *Tonton Makout* would not hesitate to attack police vehicles, but Isaac doubted they wanted to risk anyone filming it and sending it out to the world.

He saw visiting some newly developed coffee farms as a lesson in the nature of hope. Coffee trees would not produce product for three to four years, even with the expert advice and support of the Haitian Coffee Academy. And yet, there were the farmers and their crews out working, carefully and meticulously attending the trees.

"How can they afford to do all this without money coming in yet from sales?" Christa asked Isaac's father.

"We are subsidizing them, of course," said Pierre Breda. "We provide food for the workers, and help them to build earthquake resistant housing. Without our help, this would not be able to happen."

"Still, you gain an appreciation for farmers all over the world," said Isaac. "They work their tails off for a crop they hope to one day see, but there is no assurance. Will weather cooperate? Will insects or disease destroy all their hard work? That's why farmers are often the most religious of people. They realize their future lies in part in a power beyond their own."

Pierre nodded reflectively. "'See how the farmer waits for the precious fruit of the earth, waiting patiently for it until it receives the early and latter rain.'" He looked at his son, sitting next to him. "That's from the Bible. Your grandfather who, as you know was a farmer, always quoted that verse to me when I was young."

Isaac smiled. "Worthy of a descendent of Toussaint." He gazed out the window again at the work they passed on the rough road. "We also are planting seeds. We will need that patience."

As their SUV crested a hill, the driver suddenly slammed on the breaks, and Isaac saw in the road ahead the reason why. An old army troop truck had stopped in the middle of the rock-paved thoroughfare, and hooded characters with semi-automatic rifles poured out. The two Haitian police vehicles had also stopped abruptly. Police exited their doors, and rolled into ditches to either side, while being peppered with gunfire. One officer already appeared to be dead.

The semi-automatic fire quickly progressed to hitting the SUV. Glass shattered all around them.

"Get out and roll into the ditch!" shouted Isaac, but even as he did, the driver was shot in the neck, and blood spurted onto the dash and steering wheel. The others all exited the vehicle, but Isaac ripped off his t-shirt, held it firmly over the driver's wound, and slid down below the level of the dash. The driver's eyes opened wide in terror, and his whole body shivered. Isaac peeked above the dash. Those planting coffee trees were also being shot at. They scattered behind what little cover they could find. The Haitian police returned fire. A couple of assailants lay motionless beside the road. Another round of fire hit off the hood of the SUV, and Isaac ducked all the way down again.

Isaac could not remember a time when he had felt more impotent. A man's life was leaking through the bandage of Isaac's shirt, slithering down his arm, dripping off his elbow and pooling on the floor. The pungent odor of the blood invaded Isaac's nostrils, swirled down to his gut, and sought to expel what little content remained in his stomach. But Isaac resisted that compelling urge. At least that much he could control. At first the man's muscles had tensed up, as if death could be pushed away by powerful enough contraction. But already the fight had begun leaving his body. His eyes had lost focus. The driver was dying in Isaac's arms.

Still, the sound of gunfire rang out all around them. He heard an occasional shout, and the sound of people running. Isaac wanted desperately to lift his head above the dash in order to look out and observe the chaos, as if observing it could control it, at least a little. He resisted that urge also.

It was about five very long minutes before the shooting subsided. He heard the engine of the troop truck roar back to life. And then it was gone.

Slowly Isaac lifted his eyes above the dashboard. Police scurried around, checking victims and survivors. Camera crews ran past the SUV toward the carnage ahead.

One photographer stopped by his door, and took a picture through the shattered window. Then he opened the door. His eyes were wide and his voice shook. "Are you o… wait, of course you are not okay. It looks like I'm too late for the other guy, but let me help you."

Isaac looked at the figure of the man in his lap. His eyes were fixed and dilated. The flow of blood from his neck had slowed to a trickle. His body felt cold against Isaac's arms. "I…uh…"

The photographer grabbed hold of one of Isaac's arms, and pulled him out from under the dead body. "Is all the blood on you from him, or are you bleeding also?"

"I don't know."

Isaac's father ran up beside him, along with Manuel, Crista, and Arturo. "Oh, my God, did you get hit?" said Pierre. "I thought you got out with the rest of us! Why didn't I check? Why didn't I check?" He touched all the bloody places on his son's shirt and pants, but Isaac did not react.

"I can't remember his name," said Isaac.

"Whose name?" asked Arturo.

"The driver. The driver's name. He's dead, and I don't know his name."

Everyone shook their heads.

"Did we lose anyone else?" asked Manuel.

"Isaac was not hit," said Pierre. "The blood is all from the driver. My son is okay. We didn't lose anyone else from our car."

"We didn't lose any of our crew," said a reporter coming back from where the police escort vehicles were. "But three out of the eight police officers died. There are also two dead field workers, and three more injured."

Isaac pulled away from his father's still trembling grasp, and crawled back into the front seat of the SUV. He searched the man's pockets for identification and found a National ID card. He slid back out of the vehicle.

"Josué. His name was Josué." Isaac looked at the reporters. "Could you find the names of the other dead and injured?" Just saying that much made him feel out of breath. Still, more needed to be said. "We can't let people die without knowing their names."

"Our crew is getting names," said the reporter. "You don't need to worry about that."

"Did you get any footage to identify these cowards as *Tonton Makout*?" asked Crista.

"I can't say without a close look at it," said the reporter. "But one thing I am sure it will show is that this is not just a dispute between 'street thugs,' as Cambronne claims. This was obviously an unprovoked attack on peaceful people."

"We should get out of here in case they come back," said Manuel.

Isaac shook his head vigorously. "The workers can't leave. Why should we? I want to talk to them. I want to reassure them that…that…"

Tears streamed down his face, and his whole body went into spasms. Crista was the first to rush to his side, followed quickly by Isaac's father, Manuel Patrice, Arturo and even the news crew. All wrapped their arms around each other.

Isaac didn't know how long he had been cocooned in the group embrace, but the next moment of which he was aware, Arturo had positioned himself right in front of Isaac's face. "Hey, man. There's something here you just got to see."

Isaac shook his head to get the cobwebs out of his brain, and blinked his eyes to regain focus. Then he looked in the direction Arturo was pointing. The first thing he noticed was that there were no bodies on the ground and one of the police cars had left. "The police…where…? what…?"

"No, that's not it," said Arturo, somewhat impatiently. "One of the police cars took the wounded to the hospital. The dead were covered up and will be picked up later. But I'm pointing beyond that. Come on! Look and you will see it!"

Isaac lifted his eyes just a little higher and slightly to the right. As he saw what Arturo had been talking about, it was like an anesthetic ointment had been applied to his soul. His breathing relaxed. His heart slowed. He could have sworn a smile even came to his face. There among the hills, the workers were back planting coffee once again. He brushed aside the hands still on him, and ran toward the workers, and his friends all followed.

Isaac looked incredulously at one old worker he estimated to be in his 70's. "Shouldn't you – I don't know – be mourning your dead? Protecting your families?"

The man's eyes were gentle as he returned Isaac's gaze. "There will be time for the mourning, my son. For now, 'Let the dead bury their dead'. Is that not what Jesus said? I heard it was so. The revolution does not wait." He raised his right fist in the air. *"Nou pa pè!"* Then he went back to work.

Isaac turned toward his gathered friends and family. "We can't idly watch as the kingdom comes." He got down on his knees in the dirt. "Let's do it!"

No one had to be asked twice.

Mare's heart raced as she ended the phone call. She dropped her cell phone absent-mindedly to the floor. "I should have stayed."

"Why? What happened?" asked Karissa, as she leaned over a drawing of a dress design.

"The *Tonton Makout* attacked Isaac and the rest of the executive committee when they were touring our Port-au-Prince projects." Mare sat down, dejected, on an old chair in the fashion company's new space in the Caracol Industrial Park. "They killed several police officers, a driver and some field workers at a coffee farm."

Karissa was silent so long, Mare wondered if she really heard her. But finally Karissa spoke. "Isaac and the others are okay?"

Mare nodded. "At least physically..."

"I'm sure he was shaken emotionally."

"Yes, especially at first. But when I talked to him, it seemed like he had recovered a little. He talked to me about how the workers went right back to work. That seemed to lift him. They believe in what they are doing. They believe in the revolution." Mare shook her head. "So, what are we doing working on something so trivial as fashion, while people are risking their lives?"

Karissa looked at Mare and raised an eyebrow. "Hey, if those coffee farmers believe so much in what they are doing for the revolution, why can't we do the same?"

Mare shook her head again. "What?"

Karissa got up, walked over and sat down beside her friend. "True fashion isn't just about narcissism and ego, Mare. I know some people think that, and, yeah, a lot of people use it that way. But I have a different view. True fashion is an expression of the human spirit. How you dress and how you walk in your clothes says something about whether you believe in yourself, as well as whether you have a *Joie de vivre* – whether you believe in the goodness of life. Don't Haitians deserve to have that? Life isn't just about survival, you know!"

Mare sat up straighter. "I never really thought about it that way." She stood up, and walked over to a sewing machine that had already been delivered for their company. "So we want to make clothes that help Haitian people and others really live. Be courageous in the midst of fear. Stand tall in a world that sometimes wants to look past them…"

"You've got it!" said Karissa. "That's our company. That's the 'New Haitian Revolution.'"

"Sounds like an idea I could sell!" The words came from Henri, who had entered the warehouse with Yvette by his side.

"Sell to ex-patriot Haitians in New York as well?" asked Mare.

"Damn straight!" said Henri. "In fact, I don't know why we can't market this to U.S. citizens of every national background."

"Great!" said Mare. "'Think Big; Act Big!' That's the company motto."

"A little fashion history," said Karissa. "Ever hear of the 'Nehru jacket'? It was popular in the U.S. back in the 1960s. It was not worn just by Indian ex-patriots."

"The key will be to get people to identify with what is happening in Haiti," said Henri. "It's not only Haitians who have to be courageous in the midst of fear. U.S. blacks facing racial profiling—"

"Victims of terrorism by radicals of every stripe!" added Mare.

Then everyone was chiming in:

"Muslims facing the backlash!"

"Cancer victims."

"What about Hispanic immigrants?"

"Syrian refugees!"

"Of course, many of those cannot afford much in the way of fashion," said Yvette. "And that is true of most Haitians as well."

"Yes, I've thought about that," said Mare. "We most certainly need levels. At the lower end, we have our '*Nou pa pè*' t-shirts. Hey, with a lot of people here in Haiti, we will have to get people to subsidize even those. Maybe some people in the U.S. will buy our t-shirts for the poorer Haitians, instead of sending their used t-shirts with stains and meaningless English phrases on them."

"Man, I sure hope so," said Yvette. "Talk about a self-image buster – walking around in someone's used t-shirt with something written on it you don't even understand. Makes Haitians feel like the world's leftovers."

"But we also need a middle level and a higher level of fashion," said Mare. "That's what will change the image of Haiti. Nice clothes with style and swagger."

"We'll start with a karabela dress," added Karissa, "with colors that say, 'Notice me!' Then we will add some contemporary flair."

"You guys remember growing up and going to school?" said Yvette. "We had bright, clean uniforms we wore with pride. My mom would tie my hair up in ribbons, and everyone talked about how cute we were. That's how Haitian kids start out. Then we become adults, most of whom wear that leftover crap. That's what happens to our joy and pride."

"Man, all these great ideas," said Henri. "Now, if one of you just had a boyfriend who could help to market them. Let's see, who could do that? Of course, if I could see Yvette squeeze into a little school girl's uniform…"

Yvette elbowed Henri in the ribs. "Remember, as far as this 'boyfriend' business goes, you're still on probation!"

Henri did his best to appear innocent. "What did I say wrong?"

Mare shook her head and looked at Yvette. "Hey, I got to put up with him because he's my brother. You, however, have a choice!"

Yvette shrugged. "But he looks so cute when he's trying to get his foot out of his mouth. Like a puppy who has knocked over his water dish. Who made this mess?" Yvette leaned over and kissed Henri on the cheek, and Henri smiled.

Mare's thoughts were drawn away to the heavier subject of the call from Isaac. "Did I tell you that Isaac and the others were staying to help the coffee farmers with their work?"

The others shook their heads.

"They did. They disregarded the possibility the *Tonton Makout* could come back, and they got down in the dirt to plant coffee trees. I would have told him to come home, but then I thought of those farmers. They didn't flee to safety."

"We are working in a dangerous place at a dangerous time," said Karissa.

"None of us are safe here," said Yvette. "Henri, maybe you should get back to the U.S. this week rather than next."

Henri shook his head. "You think I should go back to the 'safety' of New Jersey? You've obviously never been there."

Mare swatted him on the arm. "New Jersey is not that bad, and you know it."

"Yeah, well, I know some of you think I am the *Prima Dona* of this group, and maybe I am. But I know I have a job to do here, and at least I have enough guts to stay here and do it."

"Wait a minute…that almost seems like a brave thing to say…" Mare felt her brother's forehead with her wrist. "He doesn't seem to have a fever."

Henri pushed his sister's hand away. "Well, if I would have been that husband of yours, I at least would have had sense to come home to my wife. He's pushing it, even for him."

Mare nodded. "That's just who he is. Maybe I could get an order for protective custody…"

"This is getting depressing," said Karissa. "Let's get back to fashion."

"I agree," said Mare. "And as we were saying before, 'True fashion is an expression of the human spirit.' So we're here to express the courageous spirit of coffee farmers and crazy, idealistic college students. Let's get going. Fashion is short-lived."

And with that Mare put all else out of her mind.

Chapter Twenty-One

Cap-Haitien, Haiti, October 5th 2017

Isaac leaned over the work table in the office at the Caracol Industrial Park. Mare showed him the sketches which she and Karissa had been working on all night. He lingered over some new t-shirt designs they were dedicating to workers who had died. These included silhouette images of Toussaint, some field workers and one that resembled Ricardo Sante.

"I know we will probably get more money from your high fashion designs," said Isaac, "but these are the ones I like best. We need to get them out as soon as possible."

"We have hired the workers, and we can start production early next week," said Mare. "We have also arranged to be part of a fashion show in New York next month for the higher end dresses and outfits. I'm really excited! A friend of Karissa's set it up. We're going to train Yvette and Crista to help us model the designs. It will help us get our foot in the door of U.S. fashion."

Isaac put his arm around his wife and kissed her. "I'm really proud of all you're doing. We are going to flip the world's image of Haiti on its head!"

Suddenly there came a banging and rumbling centered on the sheet metal door. The sound and vibration shook the whole building.

Karissa grabbed hold of the table. "Earthquake?"

The ground, however, did not move. "I don't think so…" said Isaac.

The banging came again, even louder, but this time with voices. "Isaac! Isaac! Let us in!"

Isaac ran to the door and unlocked it. Arturo and Manuel Patrice rushed in. "Lock it again!" shouted Manuel.

Isaac's heart raced. "What the hell?"

"My daughter!" said Manuel. "They've taken my daughter!"

Arturo's face was red, and he paced the room, banging his fist on anything he could find. "I KNEW they would do something like this. The bastards! They didn't have the balls to kidnap me or one of the men, NO! They had to go against a girl! When I find them and get her free, I am going to rip their arms from their sockets, and use the bloody limbs to beat their faces in!"

Mare took Manuel by the arm. "How did it happen? Do we know if she is okay?"

Manuel was shaking. "They came this morning, dressed like furnace repair men.We had been having some trouble… I…I should have known!"

"Go on," said Mare, with a calm and gentle voice.

"When they got in, they threw me to the floor and tied my hands. I thought maybe it was the Galil Gang, wanting to kidnap *me*—"

"Yeah, well, they've captured many businessmen before," said Isaac. "I can see why you would think that. There are suspected ties to people high up in this administration."

"If I thought they were after my Crista, I would have fought harder. I would have!"

"I don't think it's the Galil Gang," said Arturo, still pacing. "If it were them, they would have taken Manuel. It's the *Tonton Makout*. They know about all the money we are taking in, and they want a cut. That's why they didn't just kill them both outright."

"Did you report this to the police?" asked Mare.

"Yes, but they never seem to get much done on these kidnappings," said Manuel.

"Have you received any ransom demand?" asked Isaac.

Manuel buried his face in his hands, and didn't respond at first. Then he threw his hands up in the air in frustration. "Not yet, but it will come. If it's money, I will pay it, whatever it is. She's my little girl!"

Arturo walked awkwardly over to the grieving father and put his hand tentatively on the man's shoulder. "Yeah, hey! She's...she's going to be okay. We'll get her back. We will."

"How come you guys didn't call, instead of coming over here?" Isaac said to Arturo.

"We knew you have a lot of security around this complex, and to tell the truth, we weren't feeling too secure where we were. Crista's mom had gone to the States, visiting family, so we knew she was okay. So we came here."

Manuel's phone rang.

Isaac looked his way. "That could be it."

Manuel stood frozen, looking at his front left pants pocket. "I don't know if I can handle this."

"We're right here for you," said Mare, and the others echoed her words of reassurance.

Manuel reached into his pants pocket, pulled out the phone, and touched the screen. "Hello." His face blanched as the voice on the phone began to speak. He put his left hand to the back of his head, and rubbed his neck and scalp. "Okay," he said. Then "Okay" again. "I'll be there." He ended the call.

Manuel's eyes glazed over as he looked at the others. "That was the call, all right. They want a half million dollars, U.S., and they want me to take it to the gate of the *Citadelle Laferriere* tomorrow at midnight. No police, or she dies."

"Did the chicken-shit cowards identify themselves?" asked Arturo.

"They said they were the Galil Gang."

Isaac and the others looked back and forth at each other. "I don't think the Galil Gang would identify themselves as such," said Mare.

"If the *Tonton Makout* is responsible, they would be delighted to have it blamed on the Galil Gang," said Isaac. "That would bolster their argument that they are needed."

"Whoever it is, I'm taking them the ransom," said Manuel. "My company is good for it."

"Manuel, Arturo and I should go," said Isaac.

"No way you are going without me!" protested Mare.

"And the police!" added Karissa. "I really think we need the police."

"What? Are you kidding?" protested Manuel. "I'm not risking my daughter's life by bringing in the police!"

"We risk everybody's life by not bringing in the police!" retorted Karissa.

Isaac shook his head. "I say, it depends on who it really is we are dealing with. If it truly is the Galil Gang, they're just after money, and they aren't going to kill anyone, so at least there is an argument for not bringing in the police. If it's the *Tonton Makout*, it's a different matter. Not bringing the police would mean slaughter for anyone delivering that money. At best, anyone who goes will be kidnapped themselves. They want more than money. They want us."

"They said they were the Galil Gang," said Manuel, "That's what they said."

"Why do you think they set up the drop at the *Citadelle Laferriere*?" asked Mare, directing her question to the group at large.

"Probably so they could have a view of who was coming up the mountain," said Arturo. "I don't know about the Galil Gang, but if it's the *Tonton Makout* – and I think it is – those thugs are really well equipped and probably have night vision glasses. They could easily spot if there were cops with us."

"Yeah, and there could be another reason, if it is the Tonton Makout," said Mare. "It could be their way of thumbing their nose at us, and showing a sick sense of irony. Think of it. The Citadelle Laferriere was built as a place of protection. They know we had our wedding there for that reason. If they are the kidnappers, it could be their way of saying, 'You can't hide from us!'"

Isaac was impatient with the talk, and he suspected that Manuel and Arturo were as well. "We've got about 36 hours to act. What do we do?"

Arturo jumped in. "I know François Cambronne is having a political rally this afternoon at Labadie. I say we all get down there and look that piece of shit in the eye. At very least it will let him know he's not scaring us, and at best it might help us read what he is up to."

"I'm with you on that," said Mare. "But I think there is something else we should also do. What if some police would be willing to go up to the Citadelle today in plain clothes. They could stake out the place. Hide there until tomorrow night. Then when the drop comes, they'll already be there."

Manuel shook his head. "I don't know…"

"There are a lot of places to hide up there," said Isaac, "and if they are already in the Citadelle, that eliminates the problem of being seen on the way up."

Karissa put her hand gently on Manuel's shoulder. "In the United States, I know, studies have shown that getting the police involved is the best way to protect kidnapping victims, no matter what the kidnapper says."

Manuel covered his eyes and shook his head. "Would all of you be advising such a risk if it were your own family member?"

The others looked back and forth at each other, and Arturo spoke for the group. "She is, Monsieur Patrice. She is."

Labadie, Haiti, October 5th 2017

François Cambronne strutted across the stage like a general reviewing his troops. Mare couldn't help but contrast his speaking style to that of her husband. Isaac always made eye contact with people all across the gathering, talking to each as if they were friends having a private conversation. The words he spoke did not seek to call attention to Isaac or his eloquence, but rather Haiti and the needs of his listeners. He won people's hearts because the genuineness of his love and sincerity showed through his eyes and flowed gently from his lips.

In contrast, every word Cambronne said seemed like another way to say, "Look at me! Look at me! Aren't I great?" He looked over people's heads, as if there was something more important beyond them. He squinted his eyes, as if in fear people might gaze into them and see his soul. Mare wanted to leave, but she knew she was here with the other *Sons and Daughters of Toussaint* to look into those very eyes.

"I am the law-and-order candidate!" said Cambronne, standing with his feet apart and his hands clasped behind his back. "Haiti needs me! Our country is wracked with violence. People with means from the United States and elsewhere would come here and spend their money, but they are afraid. I hear it all the time from my many friends abroad. 'Monsieur Cambronne,' they say, 'Why don't you do something about this? Surely, you are the only one who can! Your grandfather helped the Duvaliers maintain law and order in his day. You can do it now! Make Haiti safe again!' And I am here to tell you, I have heard their cries!"

On cue, there was applause throughout the crowd. Arturo appeared as if he were ready to storm the stage, but Isaac and Manuel held him back. Isaac held a hand over Arturo's mouth, but Arturo brushed it away.

Still, Arturo had the presence of mind to speak in a whisper. "That lying, egotistical son-of-a-bitch! This country was never safe under the Duvaliers! Do you expect me to just stand here and listen to that crap?"

"For now? Yes, I do!" whispered Isaac. "We're here to learn what Cambronne is up to, not shut him up. If all goes well, we can do that later."

With Arturo silenced for now, Mare returned her eyes to the platform. As she did, she saw something that sent shivers down her spine. Cambronne was looking right at them.

"Especially bad for our country are all the kidnappings you hear about," continued Cambronne, with his gaze still focused in their direction. "There are kidnappings happening seemingly every day…"

Mare and Isaac exchanged glances.

Cambronne motioned toward the city around him. "Businessmen and even aid workers are hesitant to come here, out of fear of being kidnapped. The United States issues travel warnings against coming here. But we need those businessmen. We need those aid workers. Would all of this be happening if we had our army back? Would it be happening if we had the protection of a revived *Tonton Makout?*" He looked back in Isaac's direction. "The work of groups like the one that calls themselves *The Sons and Daughters of Toussaint* is laudable, it truly is. But that work is floundering because they don't get enough protection from all of the violence. I saw in the news just days ago some of their farm workers were attacked by lawless bandits. Such a tragedy! And today I am hearing that one of their leaders was kidnapped by the Galil Gang."

A collective gasp was heard throughout the crowd. Isaac gathered the others in a huddle. "We have heard all we need to hear."

"Damn straight!" hissed Arturo. "Cambronne wouldn't know about Crista if he weren't the one behind it all!"

"The police agreed to send a couple of units in plain clothes to stake it out," whispered Isaac. "That's the good news."

"Do you think that will be enough?" asked Arturo.

"It will have to be," said Isaac. "It's what we've got. Let's get out of here."

As they pressed through the crowd to their car, Mare grabbed Isaac's hand and held on.

Milot, Haiti, October 6th 2017

Mare couldn't help but compare this ascent of the mountain to the others she had taken. When she had gone up with Isaac when they were first falling in love, it was like ascending to the sky to play among the clouds. Isaac had smiled all the way up, and she couldn't wait to see what surprises awaited at the top.

When she had gone up for their wedding, she had ridden on a horse, a white horse. It had been the entry she had always dreamed of as long as she could remember. She learned later that her father had seen her on her way up, and had joked, 'There goes Mare on her mare! Can you tell where one ends and the other begins?' She had felt at one, not just with a horse, but with the world on that day. The horse's mane had tickled her arm as it blew in the wind. The horse's name was Mariah. The wind. She trotted with her head held high, toward that castle in the sky, where her rider Marie-Noëlle was to marry her prince.

The wind had been at their back that day.

This time the wind was still. Afraid to move. The sky was black. Faint lights gave a shadowy form to the *Citadelle Laferriere* on the mountain high above them, but today the darkened form was no magic castle, and it held no prince.

Isaac strode steadily up the path, holding a lantern before him. Manuel, Arturo, Pierre, Karissa and Mare followed behind, struggling to keep up. All were somber. No one talked. Always before the ascent seemed annoyingly long, probably because she was so eager to reach the top. This night, when she dreaded what would meet them at the end, the destination was reached all too soon. As they rounded the final bend before reaching the outer courtyard by the Citadelle gate, Mare trotted forward to walk by her husband's side. Still his eyes focused forward. At first she thought she heard his labored breath coming from his lips, but then she realized her error. It was a whisper, a whisper that energized him, propelled him forward: *The Lord is my shepherd, I shall not want…*

Isaac walked with his head held high. He didn't pause. He didn't stumble.

Mare joined her husband in his whispered affirmation:
He makes me to lie down in green pastures;
He leads me beside the still waters.
He restores my soul…

Up ahead, Mare could see shadowy forms, holding weapons.

He leads me in the paths of righteousness
For His name's sake…

Mare thought she saw Crista off to the side, bound and struggling against two captors.

Yea, though I walk through the valley of the shadow of death,

I will fear no evil;

For You are with me...

Crista managed somehow to push a gag out of her mouth. "Stay away!" she shouted. "It's a trap!"

Still, Mare stayed with Isaac as he strode steadily forward. They stopped about five meters from where the captors stood. Manuel and Arturo ran to catch up. Manuel held out a briefcase. "Here is the money! It's all here. Now you must release her. Now you must free my daughter!"

Mare heard a man's laughter come from behind the gate. Out came François Cambronne. "Whoa! I MUST free your daughter! You are too used to being places where you are in charge, Monsieur Patrice. But I have news for you: I am in charge here! I will do what I want. See all of the *Tonton Makout* around you?"

Mare had counted twenty-five fighting men when they first arrived, and ten more had followed Cambronne out the gate.

"These men take orders from me, not you, Monsieur Patrice. And they certainly don't take orders from that college boy you follow around. And...what's that you say? You think the incompetent Haitian police you so foolishly sent up here yesterday are going to save you? Well, I'm sure they would like to, but unfortunately they are all dead. You see, just as you didn't invite me to your party here, we didn't invite them to ours. I simply HATE gate-crashers, don't you?"

285

Manuel was quivering, and tears flowed down his cheeks. Next to him, Arturo stood like a stone idol, with fire blazing from his eyes, as he looked at François Cambronne.

"I love you, Papa!" said Crista. "And I love the man next to you, my...my man!"

Isaac shifted his gaze from Cambronne to the fighters all around him. "You men of Haiti – do you not have daughters? Do you not want them to live in a safe and prosperous country? Look at this hurting father! Turn around and in the next moment he could be you! Wake up! For the love of God, stop destroying and help us build!"

Cambronne let loose with a deep belly laugh. "Oh, thank you, indeed, for bringing such humor to my day. You actually think your little sermon will move my men and save your life!" His visage transformed to a scowl. "Well, I have lost my patience. I have allowed you to be a thorn in my side for too long." He motioned toward his men. "Shoot them! Shoot them all!"

Mare's heart skipped a beat, and she stepped back. But then she noticed the reaction of Cambronne's men. A few of them had lifted and aimed their weapons, but even they hesitated as they noticed most of the men holding back. They glanced back and forth at each other. One spoke: "All...all of them, Monsieur? The old men...the young... daughters?"

Cambronne's nostrils flared, and his eyes opened wide. "Are you hard of hearing? Yes! I said 'Shoot them all!'"

The men still hesitated.

François Cambronne stormed over to one of his men. He got right in the man's face. "Have you ALL lost your nerve? Shoot them! Shoot them now!"

The cowering man straightened up, raised his rifle. He fired. Isaac fell backward. Mare screamed. In a split second the whole mountain seemed to erupt in gunfire. The *Tonton Makout* were firing at each other, but even in her panic, Mare was sure that gunfire was also coming from behind them. In the confusion, Arturo and Manuel managed to wrest Crista from the control of her captors. They scurried, low to the ground, back down the trail.

Mare looked over at Isaac. He lay on the ground, motionless and glassy-eyed. His father knelt over him. Mare rushed to his side.

"Isaac, Isaac, my boy!" said Pierre. "Wake up! Wake up! We can get away now!"

Mare's heart pounded so loudly she thought the whole mountain was trembling. She reached down and wiped splattered blood from Isaac's face. Then she slowly, hesitantly, moved her hand down to the side of his neck to check his carotid artery. No pulse. The only blood seeming to flow was still oozing from a large wound in his chest.

Karissa grabbed her by the arm. "Mare! Let's go! He's gone, Mare! He's gone! We have to run now!"

"I'm not leaving him," whispered Mare. "I will never leave him!"

A hand grabbed Mare by the hair and pulled her face upward. François Cambronne stood there, with a large knife raised over his head. Karissa grabbed his arm, but Cambronne easily brushed her away. Before Mare fully realized what was happening, the blade of the knife swung down across her face. At first she did not feel the pain, and thought it had been a mere intimidation, but then came an intense stinging, and the sense of warm blood streaming over her mouth and down her neck. Cambronne laughed as he raised the knife and brought it down again, slashing across her breasts. Her body shivered. She flailed against the air, seeking futilely to hold back further assault. Cambronne raised the knife again. This time a shot rang out, Cambronne's body stiffened, his eyes bulged and then went blank. As he fell to the side, Mare saw the fountain of blood spurting from the back of her assailant's head.

The world swirled around Mare as she looked at her motionless husband. She could no longer differentiate his blood from hers, dripping down upon him. A fog of voices made their way into her consciousness. Karissa's voice. Pierre's voice. She was being lifted off Isaac's body, and was too weak to resist. But then she saw Isaac's body being lifted also. His father was gently cradling him in his arms. He was doing what she could not do, but she knew he was doing it in part for her. She turned her head to try to see who was carrying her, but could not. Her world faded to black.

Part III
THE QUEEN'S ATTACK

Chapter Twenty-Two

Cap-Haitien, Haiti, October 8th 2017

Marie-Noëlle opened her eyes. She blinked twice, but that did not fully transform the haze around her to solid form. Nor was it immediately evident the point where the subconscious world of nightmare and dream faded into mist, and where reality would emerge and stand firm.

Slowly she became aware she was lying in a bed, surrounded by persons or perhaps embodied spirits, some familiar and some not yet so. The first to reach her recognition were her father and mother. They stood on her right side, saying something, but their message was garbled in her mind. Then she came to understand that the forms on her left were Crista and Arturo. They weren't trying to say anything. They only smiled through their tears. Mare understood.

The figures at the foot of her bed were more difficult to discern. The one to her right was female, and as Mare's vision became more clear, her identity soothed her, if only a little. Karissa. Her friend threw her a kiss.

There was only one unknown figure remaining, a male at the foot of the bed, to her left. Her heart sank. It was not Isaac. He wore a white lab coat and was crowned by gray, thinning hair. It had not been just a bad dream.

"Do you know where you are, Marie-Noëlle?" The physician slipped past Arturo and Crista, and took hold of Mare's left hand.

She nodded, an act which caused pain to flash across her face. She reached up with her right hand and tried to touch her cheek. She felt something that was rough, but soft and spongy.

"We had to do surgery to your face, and there are quite a few bandages" the doctor said. "The laceration was very deep. Your chest also. You lost a lot of blood, but you are alive because of your friends." He checked her pulse, and then released her hand.

Mare cleared her throat. "Isaac?"

The physician glanced at the others, and then shook his head. "I'm sorry."

Mare felt someone grip her right hand tightly. Her mother's hand. "You are not alone, little girl. We're right here with you."

Mare guessed the anesthetic used on her body had penetrated into her spirit. She could cry no tears. She looked back at the doctor. "Did we lose anyone else?"

"No, not from your group. Isaac's father and Arturo here both received gunshot wounds, but they will be fine. Of course, eight police and a few U.N. officers were lost."

Mare noticed the bandages wrapped down Arturo's right arm. The rest of the physician's statement made its way to her consciousness, and she crinkled her un-bandaged brow. "U.N. officers?"

Crista spoke for the first time. "Some U.N. officers had heard rumors of the confrontation, and they came up the mountain after us. They were shooting from the brush and trees behind us. Between their support and those who rebelled against Cambronne...well, that's why we were able to escape at all."

Mare cleared her throat again. "Do we know their names?"

"Whose names?" the physician asked.

"The officer's names. My husband would want us to know their names."

The doctor shrugged. "I don't know, but I can find out."

"Please do."

Tears flowed down Crista's face. "I still can't believe you guys came up after me. I feel like this is all my fault."

Mare reached her left hand toward Crista, who took hold of it before it fell from weakness. "None of us would have even considered leaving you there. And the only one we blame for all of this, the one who gave me my wounds, is dead." She turned her face toward the doctor. "At least that is what I remember."

The doctor nodded. He shuffled his feet and looked down at the floor, before returning his gaze to his patient. "Marie-Noëlle, as the surgeon who worked on you, I must be honest with you. Your wounds were quite severe. Excuse me if this is too blunt, but the laceration to your face was to the bone. Part of your nose is missing. There was irreparable nerve damage. The attack on your chest nearly severed your right breast. A piece was missing that was not recovered. There was extensive infection in both your facial wound and your breast. I wish I had better news. We did the best we could, but there will be major scars. Perhaps a premier plastic surgeon from the States—"

Mare's mother jumped in. "Yes, yes! My beautiful little girl! Yvette says that doctor you know, the one who works with you so much…" She turned to her husband. "Oscar, what is his name – that doctor? You know!"

"Dr. Paul Hansen." The answer had come from Karissa.

"Yes, that one!" She leaned over her daughter again, and stroked the small part of Mare's face that was not bandaged. "Anyway, she says he knows the surgeon who worked on that girl from Afghanistan. You know, the one who got shot in the face by the Taliban—"

"Malala." Again, Karissa.

"Yes, Malala! Why, you can hardly tell that girl ever received such a wound!" She choked back some tears, but then straightened up, and spoke with a firm resolve. "I will not allow them to take away your beauty! I will not! From the moment you were born, all my friends spoke of how they had never seen such a pretty child. And now the whole world has learned it! You will be beautiful again. You will! I will not rest until it happens."

Karissa leaned toward Mare from the end of the bed. "I agree with your mother on this, Mare. We will all—"

"But, what if that is not important?" Mare spoke with as forceful words as she was capable. "I was beautiful for Isaac, and he is gone! Why does it still matter? Our fashion company can go on without my face. We have you, Crista and Yvette. What matters is the work we have been doing. Can that go on without Isaac?"

Silence enveloped the room. There was only the beeping of monitors and distant shuffling sounds from the hall.

Mare needed to change the subject. "Where are Yvette, Pierre and Manuel? Are they okay? How come they are not here?"

"Yvette is working at the hospital in Mirebalais," said Mare's mother. "Your brother is there with her, and they will come as soon as she is off work. They were here earlier, but left as soon as they knew you came out of surgery okay."

"Isaac's father and mother are having a very hard time with this," said Crista. "They are observing the *dernier priye*, the 7 days of praying at home to secure passage of his soul to heaven..."

"His passage to heaven was secured by his life and faith!" said Mare. "He was reciting the 23rd Psalm on his way to the Citadelle!"

Crista blushed and lowered her head. Mare heaved a big sigh. "I didn't mean to criticize their mourning practice. It's just...I don't know what I'm saying. Go on."

"Anyway, my father and mother are with them, seeking to help around the house. They wanted me to convey their thanks to all of you, for my rescue."

Mare attempted to smile. It hurt.

"We will all need to meet soon," said Mare. "The work must go on. I am not myself a descendent of Toussaint, but I believe I have status by marriage."

Mare's mother and father glanced at each other. Her father spoke. "There is actually another connection. Perhaps we never told you..."

Mare wrinkled her brow. "What?"

"What people sometimes don't realize is that Toussaint and Suzanne also had daughters. We chose your name from one of those daughters—"

"We just thought it was a pretty name," interjected her mother. "A pretty name for a pretty girl."

"Not much is known about Marie-Noëlle Louverture," continued her father. "She was dead by1802, probably not living beyond the age of five or six."

Mare felt she had been given a shot of adrenalin. Invigorated, and yet anesthetized at the same time. "Then, she lives again in me. She will live in our work."

Cap-Haitien, Haiti, October 11th

Even though she had lived in Haiti most of her life, and had experienced many funerals, this one was unlike any Marie-Noëlle had ever seen. Mourners lined the street and spread out in front of and behind her, as far as she could see. People were battling each other for a chance to touch the casket, which was being hand-carried toward the Cap Haitien Cemetery. She herself was being wheeled down the street in a wheelchair, and people she had never known rushed up to her to wish her well, to briefly grasp her hand, or in some cases, to kneel beside as she passed by.

Most of the people wore white, and all along the way brass bands played loud, joyous music.

For her part, Marie-Noëlle surveyed her surroundings almost impassively, although she did occasionally wave at those who waved to her. Henri and Yvette walked about ten meters ahead and to her right. Henri staggered as he walked, and periodically had to be held up by Yvette. Some of the mourners gave him a wide berth, probably suspecting him to be a zombie. Among those who strongly held to Voodoo, zombies were much feared at funerals.

Marie-Noëlle felt especially sorry for her brother, possibly because she was taking care not to feel sorry for herself, and this was safer. At the time of a death, people gave special attention to the spouse, the parents and some of the other family members. But what about a young man who felt he had abandoned his best friend?

Henri had elected not to go up to the mountain on that day. He made his excuses. He had to work on the marketing plan while he was still in Haiti. Yvette had to work; the hospital at Mirebalais needed her. He didn't really know Crista. Of course, he knew, and everyone else knew, the real reason. He was afraid.

Now Henri was paying the price for his understandable fear. In some respect he truly was among "the walking dead."

As they neared the cemetery, more and more of the crowd simply stood by the side of the road. And as they reached the gate, the crowd to either side of that gate was overflowing. They knew the room inside the cemetery was limited, and only the closest friends and family should go in. But they stood in reverence and watched.

Up ahead, Marie-Noëlle could see the pall bearers place the simple wooden casket near a hole dug in the ground. Pastor Ronald stood nearby, looking in her direction.

"I don't know if I can make it through this," she whispered. Karissa, who was wheeling her chair, leaned over, and whispered in her ear. "You will make it, Mare! We are with you. God is with you! He is the God of Toussaint, King and Isaac."

Karissa wheeled her up to the spot reserved for her near the casket. In the chairs nearby sat Isaac's parents, Arturo and Crista, Henri and Yvette, and Marie-Noëlle's parents. The men sat somberly, and the women wailed. Marie-Noëlle stared at the side of the casket, as if waiting for Isaac to emerge.

Pastor Ronald began with a recitation of the 23rd Psalm, and for a while Marie-Noëlle heard nothing else. The ancient words of faith and comfort echoed in her mind, and the voice reciting them to her was not Pastor Ronald's. It was Isaac's.

She leaned her head back and looked up at the sky. A few wispy clouds floated overhead. Birds soared high above. A few landed in nearby trees and sang soothing songs. A gentle breeze carried the sweet aroma of nearby gardenias to what remained of her nose.

Before Marie-Noëlle realized it, the graveside ceremony had ended and Pastor Ronald stood in front of her. He leaned over and smiled a compassionate smile. "Remember your vows, Marie-Noëlle! They were special vows."

She remembered and smiled.

Pastor Ronald went over to comfort Isaac's parents, and Marie-Noëlle was left to once again gaze at the plain wooden casket which held the earthly remains of the man who was her husband. She wheeled herself closer, and gently touched a simple cross carved into the side. Her hand trembled. She longed to run her fingers through her husband's hair. She hungered for his healing touch on her wounded breast.

"Good-bye, General Nerd," she whispered. "Good-bye, noble liberator of Haiti." A lone tear escaped her right eye, and trickled down to be absorbed in a bandage already holding too many of them. "Good-bye, companion to my soul. *Nou pa pè.* We will touch each other again."

Marie-Noëlle turned her wheelchair around and saw all those still present looking in her direction. "Friends, let's not linger. The battle is not over. Isaac's spirit is calling us to it!"

And as she saw the attentive eyes of those gathered, Marie-Noëlle knew they were ready to listen.

Chapter Twenty-Three

Cap-Haitien, Haiti, October 15th 2017

Marie-Noëlle's eyes fluttered open. She shut them again, rolled onto her side and reached out. No one was there. Only a cold, unused pillow, and empty space. She moaned.

Her cell phone rang, and she picked it up from her bedside table.

"Good morning, Mare." The voice was Karissa's. "You asked me to call and let you know which projects we recommend visiting today. We have a new school project near Milot. Then there is a recycling center we're helping to build in Caracol, and another coffee farm we are starting up, also near Milot."

"Good. And I also want to stop by our office, to make sure everything is on schedule."

"Can do, girl!" said Karissa.

"And Karissa, I also have a special request of you…"

"Anything, Mare."

"Yeah, that's just it. Karissa, you know you are my best friend ever. But I need you to stop calling me 'Mare.' That name is part of my past. I have a new identity. To everyone, I am now Marie-Noëlle."

There was silence on the other end of the phone. Karissa cleared her throat. "Whatever you say, Mare…er… Marie-Noëlle. God, I'm sorry! That just doesn't sound natural."

"Thanks. I know it's a difficult change," said Marie-Noëlle. "I love you." She ended the call.

Marie-Noëlle slid her legs off the side of the bed and sat up. She looked around her bedroom. Her eyes stopped at the mirror which stood near her closet. Her hand impulsively reached to touch her face and then her chest. The day before, the doctor had taken off the last of the bandages. The nurse had taken her to a mirror, but she hadn't really looked into it. Instead, she had found a small defect in the mirror's surface and examined it. She wondered what had caused it. Then she had surveyed the opposite side of the exam room in the mirror's reflection. The doctor and nurse probably wondered why she had shown so little emotional reaction.

Marie-Noëlle sighed deeply. You can only put off reality so long. She pulled off her pajama top, stood up and let her pajama bottoms slip to the floor. She stepped out of them and shuffled to the mirror.

Sometimes an unseen trauma is not as bad as you had imagined, and Marie-Noëlle had hoped this would be one of those times. It wasn't. As she looked at her face, she thought of some portraits by Picasso she had seen when in New York. The scar divided her face into two disparate parts. The left side of her face had lost its fullness, and her left eye seemed lower than her right. Her skin was pinched all along the scar. Her nose, formerly the petite button at the center point of her facial beauty, now sat askew on the fault-line, a portion of the left nostril gone.

Cambronne had slashed her breast in the opposite direction than her face, and so the damage was on her right.

Her left breast remained full, while her right resembled a mutated blossoming of an adolescent. The scar was bold and the nipple was missing entirely.

Marie-Noëlle closed her eyes. She felt weak and dizzy. She thought of what her mom and others had said about plastic surgery in the States. *Why was she not jumping at the chance?*

Marie-Noëlle opened her eyes again, hoping perhaps the first view was distorted by the initial shock. She shook her head. Then something caused her eyes to drop even further to another anomaly which she had started to notice even before the assault. Her lower abdomen, normally flat and taut, had become slightly swollen. There was a definite bump. The surgeon had talked to her about it in private, saying what blood tests before surgery had indicated. She had put it out of her mind, because she simply did not know how she felt about it with Isaac...gone. She should have been joyful, but there was simply no joy left in her. She walked away from the mirror.

Cap-Haitien Airport, Haiti, October 16th 2017

Marie-Noëlle was still not used to seeing her brother look so uncertain. As children, he was the one who always had an opinion on which games to play, which friends to favor and which ones to snub, as well as when to challenge their parents' rules. Now, however, as they passed through the main entry to the Cap Haitien airport departure desk, he didn't even seem to know what he was there for.

"Earth to Henri! Earth to Henri!"

Her brother looked with foggy eyes in her direction. "Uh...what?"

Marie-Noëlle glanced at Yvette. "Girl, I'm thinking you might have to hold his hand until he gets to security."

"Come on, Henri," said Yvette. "Let's get your boarding pass, and check your luggage."

"Wait!" said Henri. "Are you sure you don't need me to stay and help you out in Haiti?"

Yvette's face brightened. "Works for me!"

"Get a grip – both of you!" said Marie-Noëlle. She noticed bystanders looking at her, and she pulled the hoody she wore closer around her face. "We need you back in the States, learning about marketing, and promoting *The New Haitian Revolution*. That's your role. Stop wallowing in guilt. Suck it up, and get it done."

"I'm not wallowing—"

"Yes, you are! And you've got to stop! It doesn't help Isaac; it doesn't help me; and it doesn't help the cause. You failed once. Okay, get over it! You're forgiven. I believe you can do this."

Henri gently took his sister's hand. "I won't fail you again, sis. I won't." He started to turn away, but then paused and looked back. "Are you going to be okay?"

She smiled. Even that felt distorted and uneven. "Just go. You know I don't like long good-byes. I love you."

As she watched her brother get his boarding pass and check his luggage, her mind drifted back to a time when Henri and she were both leaving, and it was Isaac and his father, standing and watching. Her trip to become a model in New York now seemed a lifetime ago. It had actually been less than two years.

Yvette did not have Marie-Noëlle's aversion to long good-byes. She and Henri stood holding each other outside the security check for what seemed like an eternity. Even afterwards they held each other's eyes until Henri passed out of sight.

Marie-Noëlle took Yvette's arm as they turned to exit the building toward the parking lot. "I'm so glad you and my brother found each other. I actually think you are helping him to grow up."

Tears streamed down Yvette's face. The two stopped near the door and she grabbed a tissue from her purse and wiped them. "I think I've helped him find a strength inside himself he never knew was there." She looked into Marie-Noëlle's eyes. "You know, he's always envied your strength of character. He wouldn't admit it to you, but he has. Your ability to walk down a runway or up a mountain, and not look back, not wonder what people think, or what obstacles lay before you. You just walk, head up, believing. I reminded him that he's your brother, and he can do that too."

Her strength of character. *How could anyone envy what she felt was falling apart?* Still, she had to hold onto the positive. She embraced Yvette, holding her for a long time, while they both cried.

As Marie-Noëlle felt Yvette beginning to pull away, she released the embrace. They quietly left the building, and walked slowly toward the parking lot, only about fifty meters away in this small airport. But just before they reached the car, Yvette turned and looked at the runway. Marie-Noëlle also glanced that way. She smiled. Her brother was walking across the paved surface toward the stairs leading up to the small jet plane. He walked with his head held high. He walked with determination. And he didn't look back.

Cap-Haitien, Haiti, November 3rd 2017

Marie-Noëlle knew she had seen the face before; she just could not remember where or when. Yet she could see in the eyes of the man who stood before her a remorseful recognition of her. He pulled his eyes away from her own and shifted his gaze to the ground.

"I am the one," he said quietly. He fell to his knees. The grieving young man pulled a semi-automatic pistol from the inside pocket of his jacket, causing an immediate reaction by the armed police around them, but as they saw the young man present the handle of the weapon to Marie-Noëlle, they held their fire.

"I am the one," he said again.

"The one?"

With his head still bowed, he nodded. "I am the one who shot him. I shot Isaac Breda. I shot your husband. The pistol is loaded. Please use it quickly."

Marie-Noëlle knelt down in front of the man, reached out and gently lifted his chin with her hand, so she could look into his eyes. "Have you nothing better to use your life for, that you ask me to take it?"

The man trembled. "I should die. I deserve to die."

Marie-Noëlle smiled. "Well, I have decided I do not deserve to have to kill."

The young man cocked his head slightly to the right and raised his left brow.

"What is your name?" asked Marie-Noëlle.

"Henri," he said. "Henri Pétion."

"Henri. The same as my brother." Marie-Noëlle stood and motioned toward the nearest police officer. "Give your gun to this man, Henri." She shifted her gaze to a brooding figure who scowled down at the kneeling man. "And Arturo, do we have any shirts in his size?"

"Rat size, you mean?" Arturo growled. "Not so much. I might be able to fit him into something in a scurrying weasel…"

"Arturo!"

"All right, all right!" He spat on the ground, just close enough to Henri's hand that some of the spittle splattered on the man's knuckles. "Yeah, I got some shirts. Just so happens that the new ones have Isaac's picture on the front, and the names of all the brave people this rat and his friends have killed, on the back." He tossed the shirt in Henri's face. "Wear it to bed. Maybe it will bring you the kind of nightmares that keep you shivering all day." Arturo bent down and glared into the man's eyes. "Man, wouldn't that be justice!"

"That's enough, Arturo!" Marie-Noëlle's glare was every bit the match for Arturo's. "We are about the future, not the past." Her eyes softened as she returned her gaze to Henri. "Henri, I am giving you a chance, a chance to make amends for your actions in a far more satisfactory way than a bullet to your head. Put on that shirt. Wear it as proudly as we do. Help us with our work. If some people spit on you, still hold your head high and work. If you feel hunger pangs in your stomach because food comes too infrequently, work so others might eat. If those you used to fight alongside threaten you with the violence you used to be part of, work. Work so that Haiti might be truly free. This is YOUR country, Henri! Lay claim to it with your sweat, your tears and your blood. Do that, and you will be part of us. Do that, and my husband will smile on you from heaven!"

Henri tore off his shirt and replaced it with the new one. Then he prostrated himself all the way to the ground. "I am your servant."

"We must go," said Karissa. "We have much more to survey."

Marie-Noëlle smiled and nodded.

Henri Pétion lifted his head slightly off the ground. "But, one more thing, Madame Breda…"

"Marie-Noëlle," she said, correcting him.

"Certainly -- Marie-Noëlle. I know others of the Tonton Makout have already defected to you—"

"That is correct."

"But I must warn you," said Henri, "others remain. There is much fighting between them, now that François Cambronne is dead. But there is one thing all factions agree on – they must destroy the daughter of Toussaint."

Arturo grabbed her by the arm. "Then we have to keep you hidden! The rest of us can run these operations."

"I agree!" said Pierre, who stood nearby. "I have already lost my son. I will not surrender my daughter-in-law to them as well."

Karissa added her voice: "There is much security at the industrial park at Caracol. You can remain there running our business, and the rest of us can update you on our projects."

Marie-Noëlle scowled. "You want me to cower behind high fences in a building of metal, while asking the people of Haiti to risk their lives? Do you think my husband would have done that? Do you think I will, simply because I am a woman?" The others looked back and forth at each other, but with no verbal response. "I am the one who must now shepherd these people. The mantle has fallen on my shoulders. I must do whatever it takes to do the job well, and I will not tolerate anyone trying to 'protect' me from it. Do all of you understand?"

"I understand what you are saying," said Pierre, "but please understand us as well. We have all lost a lot. Your husband was my son, and a close friend to all of the rest. Surely, you can understand us trying to protect our hearts from being crushed even more."

Marie-Noëlle stood frozen in place. She shut her eyes. Of course, she was aware that everyone was hurting right now, especially Isaac's parents, but she could see no way to give ground on this. How could she? It was like Isaac was looking over her shoulder, urging her on. Still, just looking at Pierre Breda broke her heart.

She gently took hold of her father-in-law's hand, and surveyed his face. The tears in the man's eyes brought instant moisture to her own.

"Might I suggest a little compromise here?" said Karissa. "As you know, I was planning to take Crista and Yvette to that international fashion show in New York next week. It's part of their Fashion Week. Why don't you come along? We can have some girl time together, the four of us, all the while promoting our fashion. We can even see your brother. And for the five days we are there, we can all know you will be safe. How about it?"

Marie-Noëlle suddenly became more aware of her scarred face, and closed the hoody she wore more tightly around her face. She hadn't yet decided about the idea of further plastic surgery, but the thought of seeing former associates in the fashion industry as she presently was, made her shiver, even in the warm Haitian sun.

Karissa blushed and shifted her gaze to the ground. "Of course, you wouldn't have to actually go out in public if you didn't want to." She looked up again and attempted a smile. "And I suppose if you wanted to stop in and see that plastic surgeon Dr. Hansen spoke about, we could probably arrange that."

"Yeah, Mom would love that. But I don't know…"

"Okay, *Tonton Makout* guy!" Henri Pétion looked up at Arturo, who was speaking. "You don't need to be hearing all of this. Get your lazy ass off the ground, and come with me. We'll see if you really can do some damn good around here."

Henri stood up, bowed contritely toward Marie-Noëlle, and followed Arturo toward a large pile of concrete blocks.

Karissa eased over next to Marie-Noëlle, and embraced her. She whispered in her friend's ear: "Look, I know that in some ways going to New York might even be scarier for you than staying in Haiti. But it will be giving us at least a few days of knowing you are safe. You can give us that, can't you?"

Marie-Noëlle heaved a big sigh. "Okay. It's what, five days?"

Karissa pulled away and nodded.

"I can handle that." Marie-Noëlle glanced at each person still gathered there: Karissa, Pierre, Crista and Manuel. "But, when I get back I am NOT hiding!"

"Fine!" said Pierre. "But I'm sticking right beside you, and if the bullets start flying, I'm personally going to throw you to the ground!"

Marie-Noëlle saw the love in her father-in-law's eyes, and she couldn't help but smile.

New York, November 10th 2017

Marie-Noëlle's heart raced as she stepped out of the cab on Fifth Avenue. Since she was once again wearing her hoody, and with her disfiguring injuries, she was pretty sure no one she had once known would recognize her. Still, after paying the cab driver, she rushed through the door of the building, keeping her head down and avoiding eye contact. The tactic worked until she reached backstage.

A voice came from behind. It was an all-too-familiar voice. "Hey, you can't be back here. You need a..."

Marie-Noëlle turned around and saw Eric standing there, with his hands on his hips. "I need a what, Eric? A backstage pass? It's in my pocket. I just haven't taken it out yet."

Eric's eyes opened wide in recognition. "Oh...my God!"

"Hmph! Last I knew, you didn't have a God, but yourself."

Eric's nostrils flared and he narrowed his eyes to slits. "Yeah, well, I warned you, didn't I? I warned you what would happen if you stayed in that God-forsaken country down there. Haiti – the poorest country in the Western Hemisphere."

"You need to update yourself on that, Eric. Haiti is no longer the poorest. We're on the move. We've risen above Honduras, Nicaragua and Guatemala."

Eric opened his eyes wide, and put his hands to his cheeks in mock surprise. "O-o-o-h! Past Honduras, Nicaragua and Guatemala! Really? Watch out, USA!"

Marie-Noëlle scowled. "Yeah, well your new administration could certainly learn from us – as the U.S. did with our first Haitian Revolution."

Eric laughed and shook his head. "Said the pauper to the king! Give it up, Marie-Noëlle. You made a mistake, and now you've paid for it. You were a world-class beauty, and now look at you! You've let them take it from you. Just be glad you don't have to show your pathetic self on the catwalk."

He turned and walked through the door toward the gallery.

★

Marie-Noëlle peeked out from behind the backstage curtain, as Karissa pranced down the catwalk. She was wearing a little black and white summer dress with a short skirt, showing off her gorgeous legs and flashing her shapely bottom as she twirled. The little dress was accented with a few bold flashes of red and blue, the colors of the Haitian flag. Karissa was obviously glad to be back on the catwalk. It was her element. She moved with grace and energy, and winked sassily at those who sat closest to that long, narrow stage. It had obviously been the right choice to have this beautiful professional go out as the first representative of their company.

Marie-Noëlle was bursting with pride.

Crista and Yvette were not nearly as professional or confident as Karissa of course. But each came to the stage without hesitation to do their part in displaying the fashion designs of *The New Haitian Revolution*. Yvette was particularly shy at first, but her demure smile won over the merchants and fashion critics. Crista, being the child of wealth in a poor country, walked like she belonged anywhere she was – a plus. And, like Yvette, she was a fresh and pretty face, so that also drew attention to her presentation. Although she walked too fast and smiled too little, Marie-Noëlle felt she had become a definite asset to the company.

As Crista neared the exit from the catwalk to backstage, Marie-Noëlle became more aware of her own racing heart. Karissa eased next to her, put her arm around Marie-Noëlle, and whispered into her ear. "Are you sure this is how you want to do it?"

Marie-Noëlle nodded, took two deep breaths, and then ascended quickly onto the catwalk. Before she had a chance to give it another thought, she was herself striding down the elevated runway with her head held high. When she heard the gasps come from those gathered, she was prepared for it, and smiled, twirled and waved to the stunned gallery. Her smile pulled at her fully-exposed facial scars, but it did not matter. Bold moves required more bold moves. She wore their contemporary adaptation of a traditional karabela dress, itself a bold move. A traditional dress of what was called 'a third world' culture, on a fashion runway in one of the world's most sophisticated cities? But Marie-Noëlle knew the key would be how she wore it. Pride was in her walk, and she did not hide her scars. Though decidedly feminine, the dress more flowed from her curves than sheltered them. A sash exposed a generous portion of her intact left breast, while shielding all but a few centimeters of the scar on her right.

Marie-Noëlle focused on projecting attitude. Taking the traditional and transforming it into defiant. And when she came to the end of the runway, she planted both feet firmly, put her hands on her hips, and held her head high. The audience instantaneously leapt to their feet and applauded.

A chant swelled from the crowd. "Marie-Noëlle! Marie-Noëlle! Marie-Noëlle!"

She breathed in the adulation for a moment, turned, and even as the chant continued, strode assertively down the catwalk to the backstage entry.

Karissa was the first one to meet her. "Oh, my God! They loved you!" She threw her arms around Marie-Noëlle, embracing her. Crista, Yvette, and seemingly everyone else backstage quickly joined them in a jubilant mob, as the chant of 'Marie-Noëlle!' continued in the gallery. She had to push people away just to get a breath. Everyone wanted to congratulate her, and several models she had never seen before wanted to order the dress themselves.

At first, faces were entering and passing in a blur until a face came into view that jolted her. The face was familiar, although it had lost the harshness it had displayed only minutes before. Eric. He took her hand, more gently than Marie-Noëlle had ever seen him take anything. He shook his head in wonderment.

"You…you…" He let out a deep sigh. "I do believe you are the most courageous person I know!"

A smile came back to her face. "Of course!" she said proudly. "I am Haiti."

Chapter Twenty-Four

Port-au-Prince, Haiti, December 5th 2017

Marie-Noëlle had recently been told by a reporter that she strode through a worksite like a beneficent queen. That was a little hard for her to believe. She surveyed what she was wearing: dirty work jeans, old tennis shoes with holes in them, and one of their *Nou pa pè* t-shirts. She was wearing neither a bra nor a breast prosthesis, so the right side of her shirt sagged.

She smiled and whispered to herself, "Some queen!"

Pierre stood on her right side, nervously surveying the workers who were putting the finishing touches to the school building, as well as those who were observing from a distance.

He glanced at his daughter-in-law. "I hope you realize that trying to protect you is giving me an ulcer."

"There are police around, you know."

He shook his head. "Not enough. Not enough." He did another visual scan of their surroundings, before returning his gaze to Marie-Noëlle. "And you realize also that your mother is harassing me to use whatever influence I have to encourage you to get more surgery."

"And what do you tell her?"

He laughed. "That nobody can get Marie-Noëlle Breda to do anything she doesn't already want to do!"

"Good answer."

Henri Pétion walked up next to Pierre. "I've looked over the whole worksite, and haven't seen any *Tonton Makout* – at least not any I am familiar with. They have been doing a lot of recruiting recently, however."

"So, you are saying there still might be threats in the crowd you don't know about?" asked Pierre.

"Possibly. But I didn't just look for familiar faces. I also searched for those doing the things we were taught to do, those with a certain look in their eyes, and moving according to a standard pattern. I didn't see anything like that."

"Well, keep your eyes open for us, okay?"

Henri nodded.

Marie-Noëlle turned toward her father-in-law. "I thought we decided this man was to help with the building. How did that decision get changed?"

"I changed it," said Pierre. "He has knowledge about our enemy that nobody else has. We need him here more than we do anywhere else."

"I assigned him to the work for a reason! Workers need to see we are winning over the enemy by recruiting their fighters. We must—"

"Do you want to die?"

Marie-Noëlle stood speechless for a moment, as she looked at Pierre. "What?"

"Do you want to die? That's my question. You fight everything we try to do to protect you, so I'm asking you the question, 'Do you want to die?' Because you've got to know, we DON'T want you to die. You are important to us, not only personally, but because of what your presence means to this movement. Isaac died, and it tore me apart, but this movement is going on, and it's going on because of your presence. If you die, then it will fizzle out, and my son's death will have been in vain. Is that what you want?"

Now Marie-Noëlle actually considered the question. *Did she want to die?* Yes, it was true that when Isaac died, something in her died as well. They had been so beautiful together. As she thought of him even now, tears came to her eyes. And yes, it was also true that when Pastor Ronald spoke at the funeral and at his church, of a life beyond this one, it made her long to be with her husband again, in whatever existence there was when beating hearts stopped and brain waves slept. Would she be able to touch him again? Beyond their physicality, would their spirits be able to merge as she felt they had when he entered her, and they had caressed each other's naked flesh? Can naked spirits merge? She hungered for the possibility.

Still, the question came to her again in her mind. Did she want to die? Her right hand slipped down to feel her slightly-swollen abdomen. "No," she said quietly. "I can't die now."

Pierre's eyes were diverted to the man on her other side. "What is it? What do you see?"

Marie-Noëlle's gaze shifted first to the alert, wary eyes of Henri Pétion, and then to where he was focusing in front of them. A lone gunman emerged from a small crowd with a hunting rifle, and raised the barrel toward her.

She screamed. "NO-O-O!"

Just as the report of a gunshot reached her ears, she saw a body flash in front of her from her left side, even as a powerful shove from her right threw her to the ground.

Pierre's body quickly covered her like a blanket. Screams echoed throughout the worksite. A breathy groan came from less than a meter in front of them.

Marie-Noëlle pushed her father-in-law off her, raised up on her elbows and looked where the gunshot had come from. Two police officers had wrestled the man to the ground and had stripped him of his weapon. One of them seemed to nearly wrench the man's arms from their sockets, as he put his hands together to cuff him.

Nearer by, the bloody body of Henri Pétion lay. The body went into spasms for a moment, and then relaxed, motionless.

Marie-Noëlle crawled to where the man lay. His eyes were open, the pupils fixed and dilated. She gently closed the lids with her hand. Then she caressed his still-warm cheek. "You took a bullet for me! You didn't have to!"

Pierre knelt beside her. "You know, there are hundreds who would do the same thing we did, to preserve your life."

She threw her arms around her father-in-law's neck and pulled him close. "Thank you!" she whispered. "Thank you for the son you raised. Thank you for all you do for this movement. And thank you for my life! I will treasure it." She allowed herself the luxury of crying on a man's shoulder.

Pierre kissed her teary cheek, and pulled away far enough to look into her eyes. "Then you will let us protect you?"

Marie-Noëlle thought for a moment, and then shook her head. Pierre's countenance sank. "But what I will do is help us build a national family that protects each other. Yes, I want to live! But I also want you and your wife, as well as

Karissa, Yvette, Crista and Arturo, and all the others to live as well. I wish I could have done something to keep Henri Pétion alive. We must have each other's back here, all of us. That is the only way this revolution will truly succeed."

Three police officers approached from the direction of the shooter. One of them bent down and checked Henri's pulse. He looked toward the other two and shook his head.

"Are you two okay?" said an older officer.

Marie-Noëlle didn't respond to that question. Instead she glanced at the still form of Henri Pétion. Tears welled up in her eyes. "Treat that body gently...respectfully. He earned it."

The officer nodded.

"How did that gunman get past you?" Pierre asked the officer angrily.

"We don't know. One of our men said he saw the man earlier, and he swore that at the time he was unarmed. Perhaps he had hidden a weapon somewhere on the grounds."

"Which is something you should definitely check for in the future!"

There was a look of exasperation on the officer's face. "I agree. But I need to say in our defense, there were four other would-be assailants we did catch. In questioning one of them, we found this was set up as an initiation exercise for new Tonton Makout recruits."

Marie-Noëlle laughed. She wasn't sure why. She just did. And it wasn't a little chuckle; it was a hearty, full-bellied laugh. When she stopped, she noticed Pierre and the police officers looking at her, perplexed. She shrugged. "I don't know. It just seemed funny – I pictured myself as one of those little ducks in an arcade, bouncing around. The barker saying, 'Shoot the duck! Win a prize!'"

Pierre scowled. "How is that funny?"

She shrugged. "Because they don't realize their only prize is, they get to keep on shooting at little ducks."

Cap-Haitien, Haiti, December 12th 2017

Marie-Noëlle smiled as she heard the ringtone. Ever since her brother had moved to the United States, she had looked forward to calls from him, but that was even more true now. Now they were working for the same cause.

She touched the green button on her phone screen. "Hey, Big Jerk. How's it going in the Big Apple?"

"Yeah, well, I remember a chess player who always said the queen needed her pawns, and should respect them. And I've got to tell ya, I'm not feeling the love."

"I'm not a queen."

"Oh, but you are in Manhattan. Don't you realize what a splash you made when you were here?"

"Well, I know we've filled a lot of orders—"

"I should say so! Everywhere I go, I see our clothing. Oprah, Jennifer Hudson, Jennifer Lawrence, Michelle Obama, Angelina Jolie – all have been seen in one of our contemporary karabella dresses. I went to a Black Lives Matter rally the other day and saw as many of our 'Nou pa pè' shirts as I did Black Lives Matter shirts. And the sportswear that Yvette and Crista modeled is showing up everywhere on the Rutgers campus. Our stuff is really hot!"

"Then you're doing a good job."

"Sorry, not me. Just a pawn! It was the fashion show and your courage in it. You're quite an international heroine right now. Oh!....and a professional player of American football, Cliff Avril, is ordering some of our shirts. Of course, they need to be in extra, extra, extra large. He has Haitian ancestry, and every time he sacks the quarterback, he has vowed to build a house in Haiti."

"Yeah, I've seen some of his houses by a school we are building in Port-au-Prince. Good quality. But he's been doing that for some time. That wasn't because of our influence."

"No, but having him wear our stuff will be good advertising."

"That's true."

"Oh, and Mare – and don't give me any crap about the name, because that's what I am calling you forever – have you talked to Mom recently?"

Marie-Noëlle decided to let the issue of her name pass for the moment. "Yes, I have. But as little as possible. She keeps harping on me about more plastic surgery."

"Yeah, I know. She keeps calling me, trying to get me to convince you. But you know what? I've decided I don't think you should have it done."

Marie-Noëlle wasn't sure she had heard correctly. "What?"

"I don't think you should have it done."

"Really? I thought I was the only one."

There was a brief pause on the other end of the line. "I don't know. Maybe it was seeing you on that catwalk. Sis,

I've never been more proud, and I've never seen you more beautiful. I mean, I know how Mom feels. When I first saw you after the attack, I felt like that jerk had vandalized the Mona Lisa. But then when I saw you on the catwalk, I thought, God, this girl is my sister, and she has a beauty that can't be destroyed! Anyway, that's why I don't think you should do it. You've got to show the world how they gave you their worst, and it didn't destroy the most beautiful girl in the world."

Marie-Noëlle opened her mouth, but she couldn't speak.

"Mare?...Mare?"

She swallowed and the lump in her throat disappeared. "I heard you. Thanks, brother. It sounded like something Isaac would have said."

Now there was silence on both ends of the phone. Marie-Noëlle remembered how before she had walked on the catwalk on that occasion, she had avoided looking in a mirror before her entry. She had avoided it because she knew the most important issue was not what was revealed by a mirror, but what was revealed by her heart. She was beautiful once again. Her heart had told her so, and apparently others had listened in.

The voice on the other end of the call broke the silence. "Hey, Sis. Are you going to be okay?"

"Yes, I am." She said it, not as one who wants to hide the shadows within her soul or the fear of the darkness around the corner on her future path, but as one at peace within that moment. She said it as a peaceable truth.

Cap-Haitien, Haiti, December 28th 2017

Marie-Noëlle had agreed to withdraw to safety for a while, and she had done so – inside their Caracol office, perusing fashion designs, examining project reports, and working with Karissa on planning future fashion shows. It was all important work, but she hungered to be outside, interacting directly with workers and encouraging them. They needed her, she was sure of that. She received letters, notes and emails every day, from people expressing their love, but subtly also asking when they would be able to see her more. Some were even discouraged. News reports had surfaced that she had died.

Even Pierre, Manuel and Arturo, protective males though they were, now agreed she needed to show herself a little more publicly. Workers wanted to hear from her face-to-face. "Just a little public speech should do it," said Arturo. "Like Isaac used to do. It's like giving them a shot of adrenaline."

"Yes, but we will need security around her as if she were a foreign dignitary," said Pierre. "No more excuses from the police. And I want to stand right up there with her on stage, keeping my eyes open as well—"

"Me, too," said Arturo. "I've dealt with the Tonton Makout enough now to recognize them."

"We all have," said Manuel. "You couldn't keep me off that stage."

"What? You all think that women can't see as well as men?" said Karissa. "I've got two good eyes, and I've been trained in martial arts. Models are used to dealing with jerks!"

"I'm with her," said Yvette.

"Me, too" added Crista. "I still need to pay back my debt from when all of you rescued me at the *Citadelle Laferriere.*"

"Okay, okay!" said Pierre. "I wasn't meaning to neglect the women—" He paused and looked more intently at his daughter-in-law. His head cocked to the right. "You have been touching your abdomen a lot recently. Is something wrong? The stress getting to you?"

Karissa's eyes lit up, and she walked up closer to her friend. "Or…is something RIGHT? Something you haven't been telling us, Madame Breda?"

Crista and Yvette caught on quickly. "Oh, my God! We should have known!"

Pierre and Manuel looked at each other with wrinkled brows. "Known what?"

Karissa chuckled. "Well, it seems there are definitely things *men* can't see as well as women." She smiled at Pierre. "It would seem that one member of our group is about to become a grandfather."

Pierre's face was blank for a moment, but then his eyes opened wide. "Oh, my God! I'm going to need to protect TWO lives up there?" His black face turned ashen gray. "I am going to have a heart attack and die!" He looked at Marie-Noëlle. "Why didn't you tell us?" Then he crossed his arms in front of himself and turned in circles. "No, wait. Why did anyone have to tell me at all? What do I do? What do I do?"

"Hey, Papa!" Pierre responded to his daughter-in-law's call by turning in her direction. She opened her arms to him, he quickly ran to her embrace, and they wept.

Manuel, man of action that he was, took over. "Okay, our job just got a little more urgent. Karissa, maybe you could help the police patrol the front of the crowd. Training in martial arts might be helpful if someone gets that close. And Crista and Yvette – if you could get hold of some field glasses, you could use them to help the police survey the periphery of the crowd, as well as checking windows of elevated buildings that might house a shooter."

Marie-Noëlle wiped her tears with a Kleenex, kissed her father-in-law on the cheek, and turned to the others. "Let's do it, then. Saturday at 9 a.m. Get out the word to the people and the press. Tell them I'm done hiding. And tell them one more thing…" She glanced at each set of eyes in the group. "Tell them, this revolution has only just begun!"

Mirebalais, Haiti, January 1st 2018, Present day

Marie-Noëlle was stunned. They had planned for between 5 and 10 thousand people. Looking over the crowd scattered before her, she saw a gathering that easily numbered 25,000. And people were still coming. Technicians were putting the finishing touches on a large video screen and projection system whereby she could be seen at a much greater distance.

"God, I've never known success to be so scary," said Karissa. "I mean, it's great seeing this response, but I don't know if we have enough security to do adequate surveillance."

Marie-Noëlle shrugged. "What choice do we have? Turn the success away? That's not going to happen. We trust that through our preparation and the strength of God we will get through it. *Nou pa pè*!"

"'We will not fear!' Okay. But somebody better tell my heart that. It's thumping like a Geiger counter!"

"Sounds like what my heart was doing the first time I walked the catwalk," said Marie-Noëlle.

Karissa nodded. "So, you're saying…"

"We both have been there. You do your job, and you get over it."

Karissa gave her a look that was half smile, and half snarl. "I really hate you when you are right." She ran toward the crowd to help with surveillance.

Marie-Noëlle saw Pastor Ronald near the speaker's stage they had constructed, looking out at the crowd. She walked over and joined him. "Quite a crowd, huh?"

Pastor Ronald nodded. "Even Jesus only fed 5,000. Of course, in that day they only counted the men, but still…"

"I'm certainly not Jesus."

"Yes, but you have his heart." The minister looked into her eyes. He didn't seem to see the scars. "You know, once when Jesus was looking out over a crowd like this, the Bible tells us he 'had compassion on them, for they were like sheep without a shepherd.' That's this crowd, too, Marie-Noëlle. They miss their shepherd. Feed their hearts. Show your compassion and they will follow."

She looked up at the sky, where a few wispy clouds drifted toward the sea. Then she returned her gaze to the minister. "Do you believe what we are doing is of God?"

Pastor Ronald nodded. "With all my heart, my sister." He looked out at the crowd again, and then to the mountains beyond them. "There was a time in Israel's history when they had gone through a long period of suffering, much like the people of Haiti have. They were held captive in a foreign land, and their homeland had been laid waste. God sent them a prophet to call them home and give them a new start, the prophet Isaiah. God spoke through that prophet to give them a word of hope. He said:

> *'For you shall go out in joy,*
> *And be led back in peace;*
> *The mountains and the hills before you*
> *Shall burst forth into song,*
> *And all the trees of the field shall clap their hands.'"*

Pastor Ronald smiled at Marie-Noëlle again. "I believe Haiti, our 'land of mountains' is more than ready for such a celebration, don't you?" Without waiting for a response he added, "And on January 1st, Haitian Independence Day. How appropriate!" Then he brushed away her hoody enough to kiss her on her scarred cheek.

The pastor's words still echoed in Marie-Noëlle's mind as the time came, and she ascended to the stage. To her left and about thirty meters from the stage, she noticed Karissa, with the assistance of two police officers had corralled a young man with an automatic pistol. Karissa disarmed him, and the officers cuffed him. Marie-Noëlle shook her head. She began to approach the microphone, but paused short of that goal. Still, the crowd noise faded to a near whisper as people saw her approach. They moved closer to the stage. In the eyes and lifted countenances of those nearest by she saw hope ready to arise. And yet she still did not move all the way to the microphone. *What was holding her back?* Then it came to mind. Her hoody. The people of Haiti should not need to brush it back. In one quick movement, she pulled it up over her head and cast it aside. Then she strode confidently to the microphone, and looked out over the crowd. Their silence of anticipation had transitioned to the silence of shock. Mouths hung open. Many who had not seen the facial scars before, looked away.

"People of Haiti, it's time to come out of hiding!"

She let that simple statement set in the minds of her audience. Many looked at each other in confusion. The officers and the man they were arresting all paused to look up at her. "It's time to come out of HIDING!" she reaffirmed. "It's time for me, and it's time for our nation. The mountains around us still bear the scars of the struggle of Toussaint. Our poverty is a festering wound from our years of slavery. You see the scars on my face? From this moment forward, I will not hide them, for they are your scars too. I have seen yours so many times before. Scars from trying to work land that has been raped and plundered for so long that it has nothing left to give. Scars on your souls from burying your children." Marie-Noëlle grabbed her shirt and ripped it open, laying bare her wounded breast along with the one that remained whole. People throughout the crowd gasped. "I who bear these scars on my womanhood, have no idea how you bear yours! Where do Haitian women get the courage to look at breasts that once suckled children, now dead from disease and malnutrition?"

A woman's voice called from the crowd: "We love you, Marie-Noëlle!" Other voices now came forth with the same message: "We love you, Marie-Noëlle! We love you, Marie-Noëlle!" She even saw tears in the eyes of the arrested man.

"Yes, love!" cried Marie-Noëlle. "Loving each other. Loving our land. That is what will heal our wounds! Hating and striking back destroys. We are still paying the price for the violence of Jean-Jacques Dessalines, Henri Christophe, and the Duvaliers. But love plus courage wins! That's how we beat François Cambronne. It wasn't because we were armed, because we weren't. Nor was it merely because we were lucky. It was because we had love for each other, and the courage to face fear. Love plus courage wins! *Nou pa pè!*"

The crowd, silent at first, began to rumble, like a powerful energy barely restrained. But with these words, which had become the heart and soul of their hope, that energy burst forth in eruption toward the sky.

"Nou pa pè! Nou pa pè! Nou pa pè!"

Marie-Noëlle did not wait for the crowd noise to subside, for there was a power inside of her that could rise above any clamor and could not be restrained. It shot through her voice like a cannon, and ionized the very air around her. "Yes, I have come back from vicious assault! How could I do any other? I am Haiti! We are the sons and daughters of Toussaint. We break through rocky ground to lift our spirits to the sky. We rise from the rubble of earthquakes; we ascend from the murky waters left by hurricanes! There is no ill wind, no boogeyman's sack, no fury from the depths, from which we cannot break free and stand tall. Take courage and arise, brave people!"

As far as Marie-Noëlle could see, people now danced in jubilation. She thrust her fists high into the air, and jumped up and down, her naked breasts bouncing in the joy of their separate freedom.

The mountains on the horizon seemed to lift their heads a little higher, and were those trees swaying nearby in the wind merely rustling, or were they clapping their hands? Her heart burst with joy and love because she knew. She knew the land was with her. She knew God was with her. And she knew the wind that day carried with it voices of the near and distant past, voices of Isaac Breda, Martin Luther King and Toussaint Breda Louverture, voices of love and courage, voices that echoed through the hills and across the valleys a blessing that brought Marie-Noëlle to her knees:

"Free at last! Free at last! Thank God Almighty, free at last!"

And for the first time in her life there came a little quiver, a life leaping in her womb for joy.

About the Author

Keith Madsen is a retired minister who is using his retirement to pursue a lifelong interest in writing fiction. In addition to writing, he has also acted in community theater, having particularly enjoyed playing the roles of Jack (C.S.) Lewis in Shadowlands, Atticus Finch in To Kill a Mocking-bird, and Porfiry in Crime and Punishment. This back-ground in drama has helped him both with character development and his dramatic touch in writing. Keith finds that being part of helping characters come alive is one of his greatest life pleasures. He has visited Haiti four times, while helping to build a grade school there. In the process he has become fascinated by Haitian culture and history, a fascination which inspired the writing of this novel. Keith has published short stories in Mobius: The Journal of Social Change, Talking River, Short Story America and Adelaide. He is a member of the Pacific Northwest Writers' Association. Keith lives in East Wenatchee, Washington with his wife Cathy, where he enjoys teaching chess to grade school children.

Made in the USA
Middletown, DE
21 September 2022

10399413R00201